THE DEATH
OF
THE WICKED

ANNE BARTON

The Death of the Wicked
Anne Barton

Carrick Publishing
Print Edition 2014
ISBN 13: 978-1-77742-000-5
Cover Design by Sara Carrick

The people, places and events in this story are entirely fictional.

To the staff, past and present, of Sorrento Centre.

Author's Note

Some readers will recognize the similarity between the fictional Idylwyld and the real Sorrento Centre in Sorrento, British Columbia. I can assure them that none of these events ever took place there, nor is the staff of Sorrento as inefficient as that of "Idylwyld."

All the people, places and events in this story are figments of my imagination.

I have taken liberties with the geography of this most beautiful province, but without, I hope, destroying the sense of its wild beauty. It is a country of deep canyons, each with its own character, separated from each other by spectacular mountain ranges; of Technicolor lakes and primitive forests; where free ferries are part of the highway system, and flying is a way of life.

"As I live, says the Lord God, I have no pleasure in the death of the wicked, but that the wicked turn from their ways and live;..."

Ezekiel 33: 11
Holy Bible, NRSV

PROLOGUE

Swirling gusts sketched shifting designs in the dust blowing across the tarmac as two men hurried toward the waiting plane. Invisible frigid fingers searched under turned-up collars, crept into sleeves, and rocked the wings of the Cessna 182.

The younger man's dark hair stood on end in the wind. He shoved his hands deep into the pockets of his blue anorak, staying a half pace behind the other. The older man was fortyish, sleek blond hair showing above the collar of his belted London Fog raincoat. He exuded authority in his walk, his speech and his direct, unwavering gaze. The two conversed in loud tones, their words picked up and flung away by the wind. They stopped briefly. The older one seemed to be giving last minute instructions to the dark-haired young man, who nodded — it appeared doubtfully — in acquiescence.

The blond man renewed his progress toward the plane, which sat with its engine ticking over, almost inaudible above the gale. The other watched him, a frown on his wind-reddened face. He called out, "Alec!"

The man called Alec stopped mid-stride and pivoted on his heel, his mouth thin and straight as if his angular face had been sliced with a knife.

"What do you want?"

"I think you'd better look out."

Alec gave him a cold stare from ice-grey eyes. The other dropped his gaze and shifted uncomfortably, then shrugged and walked away. Alec watched his retreat, gave a contemptuous snort and turned back toward the airplane.

Seconds later he was dead.

CHAPTER 1

"They aren't going to fly anywhere in this weather, are they?" I asked in amazement. Three men had decamped from the airport limo outside the office of Red Robin Flying School. One headed across the ramp toward a parked Cessna 182 while the other two gathered up suitcases and other gear and made for the office.

Gayla, the dispatcher, looked up from the employees' work schedule she had been typing into the computer. "It looks like it."

"I'd better go out and talk to him," I said. The man was unlocking the parked plane.

Large ugly clouds were boiling up behind the peaks of the rugged, white-capped mountains to the west, part of the vast MacDonald Range stretching for hundreds of kilometres from the US border northward through British Columbia. The clouds were pushing their way toward our valley in which sits the small city of Exeter. Overhead, less ominous sky cover, slate grey and restless, pushed eastward, leaving only a thin line above the horizon where the last of the bright afternoon light was rapidly disappearing. I had been listening for over an hour to radio conversations between the control tower and aircraft in the air. Every time the tower gave the altimeter setting, it was significantly lower than the last report. The barometric pressure was plummeting. I'd called the tower during one lull and asked whether the pressure was really falling as fast as their reports seemed to indicate.

"It sure is, Robin," the controller had responded. "I think we're headed for a record. There's a Sigmet out for a fast moving, very intense cold front stretched all the way across British Columbia from northeast to southwest." He had given me the latest position of the front, only about fifty miles to the west. By now it would be much closer. And a Sigmet was something of concern to the pilot of any airplane, large or small, warning of extremely severe weather.

The controller's voice, when he talked to pilots, was tight with anxiety. High-pitched excitement rang in theirs. His advice — get on the ground and stay there! Two commuter airliners, which normally stopped only a few minutes, had unloaded their passengers, taxied to secure tiedown areas and let the ground crews chock and tie the planes. Normally, even when staying overnight, these heavy planes were only chocked, left sitting in front of the terminal, ready to be boarded in the morning.

Yet here was an idiot getting ready to take off with two passengers in a small four-place Cessna 182 into vicious weather. Hadn't he an ounce of sense?

I snatched open the door and stalked across the tarmac. By the time I reached the plane, the pilot was climbing into the cockpit, ready to fire it up. He hadn't bothered doing a pre-flight inspection. I approached the open cabin door from behind the wing strut so that if the plane lurched forward on being started, I wouldn't get myself bowled over into the prop.

"Hello, there!" I called out, forcing a civil tone. It's best to sound calm and non-judgmental when dealing with reckless people so they don't become aggressive and shut their minds to well-meant advice. I needn't have worried. He became aggressive on merely looking at me.

He scowled. He was middle-aged, of medium height, medium colouring, receding hairline, slightly overweight. Sort of medium everything; completely unmemorable.

"I'm Robin Carruthers. I run this outfit." I jerked my head toward the flight school buildings to indicate which outfit I ran. Most men think I'm the receptionist, not being willing to accept that women can really fly.

The man's look said more clearly than words, so what?

"If you're planning on flying anywhere, I wouldn't suggest it. There's a very severe, fast-moving cold front approaching. It's due to hit any time." I pointed toward the thickening clouds in the west, which had become darker and more menacing even while I had crossed the ramp. "The tower and Flight Service are advising everyone in the air to get on the ground and everyone on the ground to stay there."

"I don't need your advice."

I felt my face flush and the muscles in the back of my neck tighten. I'd better keep my cool, I thought. That can be difficult for a redhead when confronted by an obvious ass. I asked in a smooth, conversational voice, "Have you checked with Flight Service?"

"That's none of your business."

I felt another surge of anger, like an electric current running through my body. "Actually, it is my business. I'm the safety officer for the airport." Well, not exactly, but under the circumstances I felt no guilt for the fib. Lives were at stake. I had been the safety officer at one time, based on my years of flight training experience. During a cost-cutting campaign a few years ago, the city had axed my voluntary job first, then let part-time and low-paid workers go next. The manager was still raking in his hefty salary.

"Look, get out of my hair!" His voice grated with anger. "What I do is my own damn business. I don't need you to tell me whether I can fly or not." There had been a very slight rising inflection on the word "you" accompanied by a flick of the eyes over my feminine frame. Even my corduroy slacks and heavy wool sweater couldn't hide my curves.

He pulled the door shut with a bang and reached for the starter. As soon as the engine caught, he gave it a shot of power and stomped on the right rudder pedal. I scrambled out of range of the tail as it swung around in my direction.

"Bastard," I shouted after him, the word lost over the roar of the engine. He didn't taxi across the ramp, but sat there warming up, giving me the full blast of the slipstream.

Enough of him! What about the passengers? Two men were waiting in my office. Should I tell them their pilot was out of his mind to go up in this weather? Would they understand? Actually, it did not seem bad right now, right here. The wind was calm, and visibility was good in spite of a humid haze. There was an airless feeling that goes along with low pressure just before a storm. To anyone but an expert, it wouldn't appear menacing. It was the pilot, trained in weather analysis, who should know that this was deceptive, the calm before the immense storm that was rolling across the province.

This dilemma occurs from time to time with flying. If the pilot cannot be talked out of a risky flight, should you tell the passengers of the danger? There are serious drawbacks to that course of action. You lose the pilot's business; he'll probably bad-mouth you to all his flying acquaintances; you can get a reputation as a sissy; and worst of all, you can be sued for slander. It's even worse for pilots who are employed by others. They may face the wrath of the boss who has to deal with the angry customer, and can lose their jobs.

I've given this a lot of thought over the years and these concerns tumbled through my mind as I hurried back to the office. I remembered one time I'd thought of warning the passengers of a pilot as stupid as this one, but had backed down. Perhaps because he wanted to show up that prissy dame (me) who'd told him not to fly on a very windy day, he'd taxied out too fast, lost control in the gusty wind, ground-looped and ended up on his back. Everyone got out of that one without injury, and the pilot had never been willing to face me again. But today was different. Today, they would get off the ground in calm clear air, then get hit by the storm somewhere over the mountains. They wouldn't be able to outrun it to an airport. This kind of storm would break apart a light plane.

I rubbed the back of my neck to loosen the knotted muscles. What to do about this predicament! Then I remembered that I could receive help from an unexpected source. My mind flicked back to one Sunday morning in church. I'd been half-dozing during the scripture readings, which at that time, I didn't listen to very intently. On that occasion, however, I'd sat bolt upright and listened with concentration. It was from Ezekiel, the passage about the watchman, or as it says in the version we use in the Anglican Church, the sentinel.

7

"...I have made you a sentinel for the house of Israel; whenever you hear a word from my mouth, you shall give them warning from me. If I say to the wicked, 'You shall surely die,' and you give them no warning, or speak to warn the wicked from their wicked way, in order to save their life, those wicked persons shall die for their iniquity; but their blood I will require at your hand. But if you warn the wicked, and they do not turn from their wickedness, or from their wicked way, they shall die for their iniquity; but you will have saved your life."

There it was! The vivid recollection was like a command from God, telling me that I had to give the warning. It might not be an easy course to follow on earth, but when your life was reckoned up by God, could you say you'd done the right thing?

And who other than the most experienced flight instructor and pilot examiner on the airport would more fit the role of "sentinel" when it came to aviation safety? I hadn't been required to make this decision in recent years. But here it was, staring me in the face. I snatched open the door to the office, where the two passengers stood waiting with their luggage for the pilot to bring over the plane and load them on board. They snapped their heads around and stared in my direction.

The men were both tall, but there the resemblance ended. The younger one, who I guessed was about thirty, had an unkempt air. His dark brown hair was tousled; his black trousers had lost their crease. His plumpish face was pocked with the scars of teenage acne. Though it was hard to tell because of his sweater and quilted jacket, he was probably slightly overweight. Lumpy, that's the adjective that came to mind. In another twenty years he'd be fat and jowly. He stood in the background, on the far side of the pile of luggage, wearing an expression that was one moment diffident, another apprehensive.

I turned to the other man. An air of authority stamped his lean, chiselled face. Clearly, this was the boss. He gazed at me through ice-cold grey eyes under pale yellow eyebrows. Corn-silk hair lay in sleek obedience across his head. He was slender. His movements were spare and graceful. He would have been handsome except for the mien of cold distrust. Neatly and expensively dressed, he had brought a hand-tooled leather suitcase and matching briefcase with the monogram "AC" in gold inlay.

"Where are you headed?" I asked.

"To Georgetown."

"I don't think you'd better go. Some really bad weather is about to hit."

The man's brow furrowed into deep creases, his grey eyes unwavering. He said nothing.

"I'm Robin Carruthers. I run this flight school and am a pilot examiner as well as a flight instructor. I've been flying in this area for twenty-five years. I know how hazardous it can be when there is bad weather in the mountains."

The man continued to bore holes through me with his unblinking "convince-me" eyes.

"There's a very severe and very fast-moving cold front approaching," I explained quickly. "It will hit within the next half hour. The weather may look good now, but it won't last. The front is northwest of us, so it's between here and Georgetown. You might take off all right, but when you entered the bad weather, you wouldn't have time to get back to the airport, and you couldn't outrun it to another one. A storm like this will have enough turbulence to tear apart a light airplane."

Still frowning, the man replied, "Some friends of ours left for Georgetown about an hour ago. They didn't seem concerned." His emotionless voice would have cooled a cup of scalding coffee. Behind him I could see the pilot, who had taxied to the parking area in front of the office, now standing beside the 182. He checked his watch, gestured impatiently to his passengers and, when they didn't move, started toward the door.

"I hope your friends found someplace to land before they got into the storm," I said to the boss.

I hadn't convinced him yet. I went to the phone, autodialed the tower, and turned on the speakerphone. When the controller answered, I asked, "Did a light plane leave here about an hour ago for Georgetown?"

"Yeah. I gave them the Sigmet, but they went anyway. I was kinda concerned about them, so I called Flight Service about fifteen minutes ago and asked if they'd heard anything. Georgetown Flight Service was on the lookout for them, too, and finally got them on the radio and steered them over to Raymond Bay. They landed there okay, but I guess things got a bit hairy toward the last."

Serves them right, I thought uncharitably. Raymond Bay is a dirt strip located way around on the far side of the huge Squilax Lake, about a two hour drive from anywhere (even if they could find someone foolhardy enough to drive them over the backwoods roads in a severe storm.)

"Thanks." I hung up the phone.

By now, the pilot had bustled into the office, his chest pushed out like a pouter pigeon. He jerked his head toward the door. "Come on! Let's get a move on."

The tall blond man gave me one last hard stare, swivelled his head sharply toward the pilot and said, "No."

Oho! I thought. Finally, he's convinced.

The pilot exploded. "Why the hell do you have to listen to her? I know what I'm doing. I can fly us there." He whirled toward me. "You've no business talking to my associates. I'm in charge here."

The younger passenger smirked but said nothing. The other repeated, "No. On both counts. No, we are not going, and no, you are not in charge here."

"What the hell do you mean by that?" The pilot's jaw dropped in disbelief, his voice incredulous.

"We aren't going to talk about it here. Now, where can we get a place to stay?"

Gayla, who had been following the conversation with rapt attention, spoke up. "There's a motel down at the end of the runway. It's quite nice. They'll send a van around to pick you up. Shall I call?"

The blond man nodded curtly then said to the pilot. "Put your plane away. We'll talk about it at the motel."

"Whew!" I exclaimed as the motel van pulled out of the parking lot with its three passengers. I made a mocking gesture of wiping my brow. Gayla dissolved into howls of laughter.

"Imagine," she said, "going on a trip with those guys. It'd be like sitting in a kennel with three dogs that can't stand each other."

"That's a pretty good way of putting it."

I saw the barrel-chested, muscular frame of my maintenance chief, Rod O'Donnell, start across the ramp carrying chocks, rope and a towbar, headed toward the plane. I followed him. I needed a physical outlet for my tension. The Cessna 182 was parked in a sloppy fashion, not straight on the tiedown, with only the nose wheel chocked. I helped Rod straighten the plane and park it properly, chock all three wheels and securely fasten the tiedown chains attached to rings set in concrete. There were heavy chains for the wings, with a device to adjust the length, and a lighter chain for the tail. Then Rod uncoiled an expanse of stout rope and cross-tied the wings to adjacent tiedown rings. This plane wasn't going to blow away in the coming storm and go tumbling into other parked planes! I noticed that he had already secured every plane on our ramp in the same way. The school's half-dozen planes were all crammed into the hangar: getting them in and out without touching each other, with resultant "hangar rash," was like solving a Rubik's Cube.

"There, that's the last one," Rod grinned with pride. "Just so long as nobody else taxis in and parks."

"I think that everyone who was in the air is on the ground by now," I reassured him. The health of the airplanes under his care was Rod's almost fanatic concern. He picked up the towbar and headed toward the hangar, to which the flight school office was attached. Then he dropped the towbar and stood riveted to his tracks, staring westward.

"Holy shit! What the hell is that?"

I turned to look and felt a tight constriction in the pit of my stomach. Black clouds, seething like a cauldron, obscured the mountain tops, and down the steep narrow

12

canyon of Mason Creek, a pillar of luminous white streaks like a frayed nylon rope advanced toward the city.

"It's hail. Big stuff! Let's get out of here before it hits. Lock the hangar and get going."

I dashed for the office. "Close up," I said to Gayla. "Put the phone on the answering machine and get home. We're about to get hit." I could hear the ponderous rumble of the hangar door as it descended, followed by a clang as it hit bottom. The three of us raced to our vehicles and sped out of the parking lot.

Rod lived on the other side of the airport. He would be there in only a couple of minutes to be with his wife and six children in the comfort of their sprawling ranch-style house during the storm. I wondered if the older kids, aged 7 through 12, were home from their classes. Then I remembered hearing a snatch of a radio report that the schools had closed early in anticipation of the severe weather. Gayla made the light at the junction of the airport entrance road with the highway and sped northward, but I just missed it. My fingers drummed an impatient tattoo on the steering wheel; my foot poised a hair's breadth above the gas pedal. By the time I'd reached my turn-off at the far end of the airport, a great billowing cloud of dust rose from the margin of the runway. The windsock snapped to attention and spun 180 degrees as the "first gust" of the charging storm hit. The squall buffeted my Ford Ranger pickup. When I turned onto my street, I saw a limb snapped by the wind from a nearby tree lying across it. I pulled over to the edge of the street, my tires crunching across the smaller branches as I inched my way homeward.

At my house, my big fat white cat, Cloud Nine, was alert and wide-eyed, fur bristling. A former stray, of indeterminate age, he was a nervous animal who did not take kindly to disruptions of any sort in his daily routine. He rushed to my side wanting reassurance. Lightning and thunder now flashed and rumbled above the rooftops. The air was green, and dark enough for the streetlights to turn themselves on. Then one searing streak of lightning engulfed us, bright as a million anti-collision strobes. The flickering streetlights died. There followed a deafening crescendo of thunder and the roar of walnut-sized hail smashing into the ground and bouncing off roofs and pavement. Cloud Nine made his own white streak as he shot under the bed. Dishes rattled in the cupboards. The scorched smell of ozone hung in the air. As if a giant hand had thrown a power switch, the lights dimmed, then surrendered. Blinded by the brilliant flash, I groped my way through the darkened house.

I leaned on the windowsill, watching the surrounding landscape disappear in a flurry of hail. Would the hail damage planes parked outside at the airport? At least, I thought, that jerk with the Cessna 182 will thank me for not letting him take off in this.

Fat chance!

CHAPTER 2

The next morning, I drove cautiously through downed tree branches and wind-blown trash to the airport. Rod was there ahead of me.

"Everything's okay," he reported. "Nothing of ours is damaged or missing. We collected a stray garbage can lid. I figure it must have come from the mobile home park over there, so I went around and hung it on the fence where people could see it. There's probably not a can left with a lid on it anywhere in town. I'll have to get the kids to come over after school and help clean up all that trash that ended up along the fence." He waved at an accumulation of plastic bags, candy wrappers, Styrofoam cups and tumbleweeds caught along the base of the chain link fence surrounding the property.

"How's the family? Any problems yesterday at your house?"

"Not at all. Turned out to be a good excuse for the whole family to cuddle up around the fireplace. We made popcorn and told ghost stories. The kids thought it was exciting." Rod smiled, the lines of his square, red face softening. "We had a few tree limbs blown down, and one of them damaged a fence, but nothing serious."

The children presently at home were his second family. At the time I'd taken over the school, which I'd gotten in the divorce settlement with my ex-husband, Rod had offered to stay on as maintenance chief. He had three children and seemed a well-settled married man. But a few years ago his first wife, chafing at the restraints of isolated and relatively small Exeter, a city of under 50,000 people in an interior British Columbia valley, decided that Rod should leave his "dead end" job, as she called it. The airlines were hiring maintenance people at a salary well above what I could afford to pay.

He considered his options. The higher salary meant moving to Vancouver and commuting to work, possibly doubling the family's living expenses. New strains would be put on the family, and the excitement of the big city would soon wear off when the bills began to come in. And, he figured, the boom would end, and when the bust came, the newer employees would be the first laid off.

He enjoyed his work at Red Robin Flying School. He treated the airplanes like children, knowing every part of every one of them. He wouldn't have that sort of satisfaction in an airline job. He might even have to compromise his high standards. Here, his satisfaction in his work and his life was evidenced by the fact that all three of his children from his first family chose to follow in his footsteps, going into aviation-related careers.

Rod's wife divorced him and took off with an airline pilot who was on his way up, recently promoted from Dash 8s on the commuter runs to right seat in small jets with the parent airline. His future looked good, and his new lady-love had big ideas of free flights to Hong Kong or Europe. But the inevitable downsizing had come, and he was stuck with occasional flights from Vancouver to Calgary or Prince George, still in the right seat. His time would come eventually, but it was going to take a while.

It wasn't long before Rod met Julie. She came to work for me as a fill-in while Joyce and Gayla, my two regular dispatchers, took their holidays. Vibrant, smiling, enthusiastic, Julie was an instant hit with all of us, especially Rod, who also adored her two small children. They quickly married and have had another four offspring. Both Rod and Julie seem content in their hectic household amidst children, dogs, cats, rabbits and a pet tortoise. A placid pony occupies the adjacent pasture. They raise a garden. There is always some project a child is working on with the help of a parent. When you enter their house, the first thing that hits you is that this is where Love lives.

As a reward for his loyalty, I gave Rod the option of taking his bonuses in the form of shares in the business. He jumped at the chance to become an active part owner.

"Do you know whether there was any damage elsewhere on the airport?" I asked.

"Yeah. The flying club's 152 turned a few cartwheels and self-destructed on the side of the clubhouse." Rod snickered. "Not much of a loss. At least it didn't hit any other planes."

A rather disreputable flying club had digs at the far end of the runway. Their dirty, beat-up old Cessna 152 was not a good advertisement for our airport, and I always discouraged them from parking it near Red Robin Flying School for fear someone would think it was mine. The school's Cessna 150 trainers, Cessna 172s and Beech A36 Bonanza, all painted identically in red and white, with a chirpy red bird logo on the tail, were kept immaculate. I shared Rod's disgust with the way the flying club abused their airplane.

But another thought crept into my mind. "I suppose that means Lance Brock will be back wanting to rent from us."

Rod groaned. "That little shit! I hope he's moved to somewhere back east."

"No luck. He's still here. We're on nodding acquaintance, if not speaking, and I see him in the coffee shop every now and then."

Rod made further, disparaging, references to Lance Brock then went on about his chores. Lance was a young man who arrived at Red Robin Flying School after being told very firmly by Garth Hughes, a flight school operator at neighbouring Pine Hill Airport, that he could not get away with taking "flight instruction" from his pilot buddy, who had only a private pilot license. Lance and his buddy owned an aerobatic Citabria, but Lance was forced to come to my school when his partner rolled the Citabria into an untidy ball of crumpled metal and fabric, fortunately escaping with only minor injuries.

He was a difficult student, and I employed the services of Ace Flynn, an old-time instructor, to fly with Lance. I ordinarily didn't allow the threat and fear method of flight instruction. Positive motivations work better than negative ones. Besides, I want happy pilots who will continue to rent planes from me. But I turned a blind eye toward Ace as he flew with his recalcitrant student, and eventually Ace sent me a subdued and moderately competent pilot for his flight test.

Lance continued to fly with us until I caught him in some illegal acts and kicked him out. He joined the flying club, but once again, when their plane was down for extended maintenance, he came begging. He did reasonably well for a while, working toward his commercial license. But as soon as the club's plane was back in service, he took off amidst a stream of invective, after being caught flying one of my one-fifties in reckless fashion. He hadn't ventured down to our end of the airport since. No one at Red Robin missed him.

The weather remained foul, gusts of wind flinging sheets of rain across the tarmac. My staff could take care of the school, so I drove downtown to St. Matthew's Anglican Church for morning prayer. I was the only hardy soul present, other than our priest, the Reverend Douglas Forsythe. We both knew the words of the prayers almost by heart. He led and I gave the responses. Our quiet voices were swallowed up by the vastness of the high-ceilinged nave.

I always enjoyed this quiet time in the church, and came whenever work permitted. In the summer, we started at six in the morning and flew all day, but during other seasons there were times when it was not possible to fly, and if I didn't have any other pressing work to do, I would head for the church for morning prayer.

I'd started going to church a few years ago, even though I was a non-believer. I'd reached the point in my career when everything I tried became a success, where fortune smiled on me. It was at that point, not at some time when things weren't going well, that I began to wonder if my fortunes were steered by some greater power. If there was a God, He must have read the flight training manuals on the subject of positive motivation. He got me on the upswing. I had stayed in the church, hoping for enlightenment.

Then a couple of years ago, Douglas had come. He was able to reach me in ways that no one else had done, explaining the Christian faith in terms I could accept.

Suddenly one day, I realized that I believed. It wasn't an easy struggle for me, trying to put my newly learned Christian doctrine to practical use, but I kept working at it.

I had business to do at the church too, so after prayer I walked with the priest to the office, where the secretary, Shirley Meacham, a lady of about sixty with carefully coifed grey hair and a stylish grey suit, was putting on a pot of coffee.

I'd been coerced into taking on the role of treasurer at St. Matthew's. Since I was a successful businesswoman, the church wardens, who appoint the treasurer, assumed I knew about budgets and balance sheets. I do, though I have an accountant do the school's books, but I soon found that knowledge of normal business financial affairs doesn't prepare one for those of the church. Still, I thought, income is income, expenses are expenses, and if you have more of the latter than the former, you go in the red. Which is where we were.

Douglas saw me get out the ledger and the instruction manual for the computer program, which I still needed to refer to on frequent occasions. He paused on his way to his office then, frowning, he turned toward me.

"The ladies of the Altar Guild are upset about what you're doing."

"What do you mean? I'm not doing anything to them."

"They say you're trying to take over their finances."

"What!"

"You spoke to their treasurer?"

"Ethel Fuller. Yes. Why?"

"Ethel says you told her you wanted to pay their bills for them."

I felt my forehead crease into a frown and the tension hit the back of my neck. The Altar Guild had a bank account of its own, but also a line item marked "Altar Guild" appeared in the church budget. People donated money to the Altar Guild, especially around Christmas and Easter, for flowers. This money was paid out to the Altar Guild, after the person giving it received a tax receipt. The Altar Guild then bought the flowers. At least, that's the way it was supposed to work. The trouble was that donations for flowers were never enough to pay the bills at the Plant House. So the Altar Guild would send the bills back to me to pay. I had gone to Ethel to try to straighten this out. I had suggested that, rather than passing along the funds earmarked for flowers to the Altar Guild, only to have to pay for the flowers out of our regular account, I should just keep the money and pay for all the flowers. It seemed simple to me.

But not so to the Altar Guild apparently.

"You can't keep their money. You have to pass it along to them," Douglas told me.

"Then they should pay for the flowers."

"They do. They also buy wine and wafers and candles."

"But they don't pay for the flowers. That's what the trouble is. We pay it out of the regular account because the Altar Guild says they can't afford it. What are they doing with the money I pass along to them?"

Douglas frowned. "Are you sure?"

"Yes, I'm sure! They did the same with the new red frontal."

A gift to the Altar Guild had been received, along with the request that it be used to help pay the cost of a new

21

altar frontal to replace the old red one that looked as if it had survived the Napoleonic wars. I dutifully passed the money along to the Guild, only to have them bounce it back, with instructions to pay for the frontal out of the Guild's budgeted funds, which weren't nearly adequate for the task.

"Well, don't interfere with the Altar Guild's finances without my personal consent. The work those ladies do is invaluable and I don't want them upset."

What about my work? Didn't my work have value? It was the first time I'd ever had a disagreement with Douglas.

Seething with resentment, I returned to the books, but soon hit another snag. A group of little old ladies put on funeral receptions. Not wedding receptions, just funerals. Wedding receptions were planned and were catered. But when someone died, the grieving heirs had neither time nor inclination to call in a caterer. The same group of ladies had been doing these receptions for years. They tottered around, serving tea and sandwiches, and doling out heart-felt sympathy to the mourners, many of them friends or acquaintances. I think they treated people as they hoped their heirs would be treated at their own funerals.

No one is charged a fee as such for any of the sacraments of the church, but a polite suggestion is made that if they wish to help defray the cost, a donation would be gladly received. Nearly everyone pays up. My problem arose from the fact that a line item for income from weddings and funerals appeared in the budget, but no one told me that funeral receptions did not come under that category. Instead, the money went directly to the informal and unnamed committee who did the work. They didn't have a bank account, so the church bookkeeper and treasurer had to handle their finances for them. As money in excess of the cost of food for the receptions began to accumulate, the group of women would decide on their own how to spend it, often opting for things far in excess of their means, and expecting the church to pick up the rest of the tab. This played havoc with my carefully prepared estimates.

The bill for this unofficial group's latest purchase, a new paschal candle stand, had just come in, and the amount greatly exceeded the money in the account. "What should I put it under?" I asked Shirley.

"Church service supplies, I guess."

"We've already blown two thirds of the budget for church service supplies and it's only March."

Shirley shrugged. "Maybe we should have budgeted more."

"We put in the same amount as we spent last year. How come our expenses are so much higher this year?"

"I don't think they are. They seem normal to me. Maybe we haven't gotten as many gifts."

"But gifts don't affect expenses," I explained. "That's income."

"All I know is that Rupert used to deduct the amount of the gift from the cost of the item and record the difference. So if we haven't gotten as many gifts, we have to pay more out of the budget."

I stared at her. For a moment my brain refused to sort it out, but finally I got my thoughts in order. "We can't do that! We need to record income as income and expenses as expenses."

Shirley shrugged once more. It wasn't her problem. My problem was that Rupert Tomlinson, our previous treasurer was in Arizona for the winter and I couldn't ask him questions that were constantly arising. I had my own ideas about how the books should be kept, but obviously my ideas weren't the same as his.

Douglas heard us and came over. "What's the problem?"

"The problem is the same as with the Altar Guild except that the ladies who do funeral receptions don't have their own bank account. They bought a new paschal candle stand, but there isn't enough income from funeral receptions to pay for it."

Betty Forsythe, Douglas' wife, came into the office in time to hear my complaint. "They looked up prices and said there was enough."

"Then they must have been looking at old catalogues, because we can't pay for it with the money we have. Besides, it's an extra-budgetary expense and should have been approved by the church executive committee."

"I think we'd better just get it," Douglas decided. "More money is bound to come in. They've been doing this for years and I don't want to upset them."

"But will they know that they're overdrawn and that they can't get anything else until this is paid for?"

I went round and round with Douglas about this. In fact, it was not the first time. On a couple of previous occasions, I'd complained about this group's attitude that the money was theirs, but Douglas regarded my complaint as trivial. No regular committee of the church could even send out a letter to the parishioners without having it torn apart, amended, and re-written by the church committee (which did not improve either grammar or train of thought.) Yet an informal group could confiscate funds and buy things they couldn't afford, with not a breath of a whisper from any official body of the church, merely because they had been doing it for years. No wonder it was hard to get the younger members of the church to volunteer for anything. They must have run into the same wall of resistance that I was now experiencing.

I'd never before felt so betrayed. No, on second thought, that was too strong a word. I felt that my efforts were not appreciated. I'd been named treasurer because I was supposed to know what I was doing. Then when I tried to do it, I was shot down! I'd built up a successful aviation business from scratch, starting when I was in my early twenties. Didn't that count? If they wanted my expertise, why didn't they let me use it? Even in the masculine world of flying, my knowledge was respected. I wasn't used to being told I couldn't do things the way I felt they should be done.

Betty Forsythe finally told me there was nothing I could do about it, so I might as well give up the fight. That certainly didn't help my mood.

By the end of the morning, I felt as if dealing with Lance Brock would be far easier than handling the church's financial affairs. As I sat grumbling over the books, I managed to inflict a paper cut on the tip of my index finger. At first, I didn't notice how much it was bleeding, but Penny Farnham walked into the office, stared at me and exclaimed, "Robin, you're bleeding!"

"I wouldn't be surprised," I replied. "I've just been gored by a couple of sacred cows!"

CHAPTER 3

By noon, the rain had stopped and the ceiling was beginning to lift, though damp, ragged clouds hung low over the valley. The airlines were back in operation, a Medevac flight arrived and departed again, but light aircraft still sat forlornly on the ramp. The Cessna 182 remained parked all afternoon. I kept a wary eye out for its foolhardy pilot, for fear he'd try again, this time into icing conditions that the small plane was not equipped to handle. There was no sign of the three men.

A gusty wind continued to swirl around the open spaces and shriek under the eaves, setting nerves on edge. All the school's planes were left in the hangar, even though it meant that Rod could not get on with scheduled maintenance work on one of them. When the wind blows, the sandy soil dries out rapidly, and even while puddles of rain water still stood in the low spots, mud turned to dust, insinuating itself through cracks, and billowing through opened doors.

The human inhabitants of this besieged domain huddled in pools of light and warmth, and closed off unused rooms. We grumbled and snapped at one another. Feeling sorry for ourselves, we accomplished little useful work. I was idling in the outer office, not in the best of moods when a blast of icy wind ushered Lance Brock through the door.

Right on schedule! I thought.

For a long moment, we stared at each other. Lance is in his early twenties and shorter than I am, causing him to bluster, and practically to stand on tiptoe when facing me. He has a long thin face, long nose, narrow-set brown eyes and a mouth that is too wide for his gaunt visage. His mousy hair is cut in the modern style that looks as if someone put a bowl over his head and applied electric clippers to everything that stuck out. On this day, an unruly cowlick hung down his forehead. He wore dirty grey sweat pants, a faded black sweatshirt ragged at the neckline, and a parka that had seen better days. The steel-toed work boots on his large feet declared that he had come directly from his job at Exco Modular, a plant that manufactures mobile homes. He squinted under a knotted brow, like a cat confronting another one, expecting to get hit in the face by a paw-full of claws. He had come to ask me for something he didn't expect to get.

He received no reassuring signals from me. I knew my dour countenance was not welcoming.

Rather than talking to me, Lance turned toward Gayla. "I want to rent a 150 to fly down to the coast to take my flight test."

Gayla said nothing, but turned her head toward me, tossing the problem into my lap.

"I can't rent you a plane without a check-ride. You know that," I told him.

"I just got recommended for my commercial flight test. That ought to be good enough."

"Who recommended you?"

"I've been getting instruction from Shannon down at the flying club. He's the instructor there. Our 152 just got totalled by the storm."

"Who endorsed his recommendation?" I asked again, more forcefully.

"I just told you." His voice lacked conviction.

"No you didn't. Shannon is only a Class Four instructor. He can't send you for your flight test without an endorsement from a Class One or Two instructor."

Lance shifted his weight from one foot to the other and glanced down at the floor. "Well, he got this other guy to sign me off."

"What other guy?"

"I don't know his name. But I guess he was Shannon's instructor and knows him and is willing to sign off someone Shannon has trained."

"You've never met this person or flown with him?"

Lance shook his head.

I emitted an expletive of disgust. "Then you're not properly signed off. Not in my books, anyway."

"Well, there's this guy down at the coast who knows this instructor and says he'll give me the flight test."

I let a tone of incredulity ooze into my voice. "And you want me to let you have an airplane to fly down to the coast, in bad weather, to take a flight test from someone who is willing to test you on the basis of a friend signing off another person's student, sight unseen?"

"I still have block time on the books," he blustered.

"I know you have, but that doesn't mean I have to rent you a plane without a check-ride."

The look of defiance was replaced by one of anguish. "But my block time is about to run out, and I can't afford anything more after I pay the price of the test."

Block time is a way to pay in advance for flying time, at an attractive discount. When Lance last beat it out of my establishment, he had some block time left over. My policy was that it would be good for one year from the time of purchase. Nearly a year had passed since the last time he'd used it. But why should this jerk think I'd throw all my rules out the window just because his block time was about to run out?

I could feel the hot wave as exasperation made my face flush red. I gripped the counter, willing myself not to let my emotions show.

"Why don't you take your flight test here? That way, you can use your block time and you don't have to fly down to the coast." Besides running a flying school, I was a pilot examiner. I had a pretty good idea, however, why Lance didn't want to take the test from me. He probably felt that he had no hope of passing it, and would rather pay the hefty fee to go to one of the, fortunately rare, examiners who will pass anyone arriving with an airplane that runs. I thought I knew who this examiner was. I'd never met him, but I'd dealt with a few of the pilots who had gotten their licenses from him, and would not recommend to anyone I knew that they fly with these airplane drivers.

Lance bent his head and carefully examined a small area of the vinyl floor, which he restlessly scuffed with the toe of his boot. His bunched fists were shoved into the ripped pockets of his parka. His lower lip stuck out. Without raising his head, he lifted his eyes to glance speculatively at me.

"Well, you see, I've got this appointment down there," he essayed tentatively.

"Which you can cancel, especially considering the weather."

He pulled his neck down into the hollow between his shoulders as if trying to hide. I had him boxed in and he knew it. Mine was the only place left on the airport to rent a plane now that the flying club was out of business. He examined his dilemma.

I broke the silence. Holding out my hand, I invited him, in a softer, more friendly voice, to show me his recommendation for the flight test. Reluctantly, he dug into a pocket of his parka and extracted a somewhat soiled and crumpled paper. I spread it out on the counter-top, smoothed the wrinkles and inspected it. Everything seemed in order, but I couldn't read the signature of the person who had endorsed it, and the number that followed the indecipherable scrawl was smudged (on purpose?).

I feel a great deal of frustration these days when I have to unravel what passes for the signatures of instructors who give the impression that they don't know how to write their own names. I have been known to send forms back and ask these people to please type or print their name legibly underneath their autographs. Ditto for the number they are required to append to their names. It is often just as difficult to decode.

"I'll give you a couple of choices," I suggested, trying to sound amiable. "Leave this recommendation form with me and I'll make sure it is legit. Don't worry; you'll get it back. If it's on the up and up, I'll give you your flight test. It will be a fair one. I'll rate you only on your competence. Or, you can take a check-ride, and any dual you need to upgrade your flying to our standards, then rent a plane to fly down to the coast. The instructor who gives you the dual will have to okay the weather for your flight."

I could see that it irked him to have his flying skill degraded to the status of student pilot. His face flushed with anger, his teeth clenched, he started for the door, then turned back and held out his hand for the recommendation form. I gave it to him. He marched to the door and yanked it open, admitting another frigid whirlwind.

Ten minutes later, I noticed that Lance's beat-up old Mazda pickup was still parked outside the office, and I could see the silhouette of his head in its cab. Then I watched him get out of the pickup, skulk back to the office and worm his way around the door, which he seemed reluctant to open all the way. He shuffled across to the open door of my office, where I was standing.

"I guess I'll have to take my test from you."

"Okay, give me back the form."

He handed it over.

"When would you like to schedule it?"

"Tomorrow." He sounded as if he expected me to veto this.

I reviewed in my mind the forecast I had received. The Met people said the clouds should be clearing out of the area, but the wind would still be with us. "We'll make a tentative appointment, depending on the weather."

"I don't mind a little wind!"

"Maybe you don't," I reminded him, "but your passengers may. Remember that on a commercial flight with passengers, you have to think of their comfort and safety. On this test, I want you to plan as if you have been asked to take a charter flight with passengers."

"Okay. Where to?"

"I'll tell you that when you come in tomorrow. We'll take a Cessna 172 rather than a 150. You need to demonstrate your ability to use more types of navigation equipment."

Lance frowned. "That'll cost more." Still, the hesitant way he said this made me think that the idea of using the extra avionics appealed to him. I had learned previously that Lance was a whiz at electronics.

"I know. But in a charter operation, you'd likely fly the more advanced equipment."

He reluctantly agreed and we scheduled him for eleven the next morning. I thoroughly expected to have to cancel the flight.

***

For several weeks, I'd been making excuses for missing our twice-monthly bible study sessions; a meeting, too much work to do, a bad cold. I thought of using the weather as an excuse that night. As soon as this crossed my mind, I kicked myself for letting it surface.

Why was I doing this? I enjoyed the bible study. I liked the people I shared it with. I needed it. So, why?

I stacked the supper dishes by the sink to be done later. I had a tendency to put off those hated, recurring chores. Cloud Nine, licking his lips after polishing off his own supper, saw me flop into an easy chair and levitated himself gracefully into my lap. One thing about a cat, I mused, they don't get clumsy even when they put on weight. I was getting a bit thick around the middle myself, and couldn't bend over as comfortably as I used to. My lifestyle hadn't changed. Perhaps it was my metabolism.

I'd rejected the thought that I'd reached middle age and still considered myself to be young, vigorous and healthy, though I was in my mid-forties. Yes, I agreed with myself, my health was excellent, but I had to admit that my youth and vigour were ebbing away. There were other changes as well. These last few months, my self-confidence had been eroding.

Then here was this damned cat who had weaseled his way into my house, and was now living the life of luxury and ease, displaying to me how little it had affected his physical capabilities by contorting himself into an impossible shape in order to groom his nether regions. That done, he lay on his back in the groove made by my legs and swivelled his head 180 degrees so that he could look into my face and see it right-side up.

"Show-off!" I accused.

"Mrrp!" he replied.

It had been a long time since I'd seriously taken stock of myself. I'd gone through this process when I first met Douglas Forsythe and thought I'd fallen in love with him. I'd been jolted out of my comfortable life as a self-sufficient divorcee who ran a successful and satisfying business, and appeared to have the world by the tail. I became aware of what was missing in my life. I'd started to go to church some time before, but it was only after Douglas came into my life that I'd found myself on the road toward belief in God.

For over a year, the road had been a beckoning highway, the journey easy. Then the highway ended and the road became a muddy quagmire. I felt bogged down. It had started with my becoming treasurer of the church. And it was tied up with my perception of my relationship with Douglas.

As long as he led me on, encouraged me in my spiritual search, and involved me more and more in the working of the church, life was gloriously rewarding. Occasionally, I'd wondered whether this feeling would persist if Douglas were not there. I'd never satisfactorily answered that question, and tended to shove it into the back reaches of my mind, telling myself that it would be another eight or ten years before he would retire and I would have to adjust to another priest.

Then I'd become the treasurer, and I'd come away scarred and weary. Douglas seemed always to side with the established order, and now we were having serious arguments. Was it my imagination that he no longer asked me to do things in the church?

Should I challenge him, or quit as treasurer, or just swallow my pride and continue on? So far I'd followed the latter course, which was an unusual way for me to act. I'm usually outspoken. But I didn't want to hurt Douglas' feelings. I wanted him to change. I didn't want to confront him.

I turned in on myself, and reduced my contacts with other church members who had no connection with finance. And I felt very sorry for myself.

Cloud Nine righted himself with a graceful pirouette and bumped me under the chin with his head. I stroked his sleek, fat back, and he turned on his purr motor.

That's what I need, I thought. Someone to figuratively stroke my back and set me to purring again. Perhaps I shouldn't cut myself off from the rest of the church. Christianity is a community faith, Douglas always reminded us; you can't do it alone. So where was my community? Not in the office, working on the books. The bible study then? Yeah, that's where I should be. I'd been reacting in a manner exactly opposite to what I should be doing; shutting myself off from the community of the faithful, rather than going to them for help in time of trouble.

Gently, I removed the cat from my lap and set him on the warm chair cushion, slid into my coat and picked up my keys. I just had time to get to the Meacham's house in the old Victoria Hill section of town in time for the bible study.

***

"If you had to prove that you were a Christian, could you do so?" Penny Farnham's glance swept the assembled members of the bible study group.

Paul St. Cyr rubbed his chin. "I think that the question is actually, 'If you were accused of being a Christian, could you be convicted?' It stems from the persecutions of Christians by the early Romans. Many of them didn't deny it. They had the examples of the apostles to bolster their courage, and many of the apostles had the first-hand example of Christ. They knew that they would be killed, but were willing to become martyrs because of the examples of Christ and his apostles."

"Don't you mean all the apostles had first-hand knowledge?" Harry Meacham was a stickler for exact statements and precise measurements.

"No. The apostle Paul didn't. He had an encounter with the risen Christ, after the resurrection, but wasn't an apostle when Jesus was crucified. In fact, he initially participated in killing the first Christian martyr, St. Stephen."

I wasn't very knowledgeable about theology, but for once I felt I knew enough to express an opinion. "I would never have believed in the resurrection on the basis of Paul's story; the sudden encounter and immediate conversion. He might have been a suggestible type who saw visions after hitting his head, or who had a particularly vivid dream. But the other apostles' story is much different.

35

There is no way they could have been convinced unless they had seen the risen Christ after witnessing him being killed. So, because I can believe in them, I can also believe in Paul."

"Yeah, I've hit my head and had all kinds of revelations." Penny crossed her eyes and let her head loll to one side. Everyone laughed.

"Still," Penny mused, "I'll bet there were some who were willing to deny their faith in the face of death. Fortunately. Because if all the Christians had been killed, there'd be no Christian church now."

A quiet laugh rippled through the group, but we then became serious again.

"Like Peter on the night Jesus was betrayed." This from Paul.

"Yes. Peter learned better, and he was eventually crucified, himself. But I'm sure there must have been others who took the easy way out."

"Not the ones who saw Jesus after the resurrection," I argued, feeling I had to get my point across. "And not the ones they told. It must have been such an overwhelming experience that in trying to explain it, they must have really let their excitement show."

"How could you possibly describe something like that?" Shirley Meacham glanced upward as if seeking inspiration from on high.

"How can you describe anything that relates to God?" Paul spread out his hands as if in helplessness at the impossibility of putting the biblical experiences into words. "Words are so imperfect, and as a journalist, I hate to admit that. But nearly the entire Bible is someone trying to describe the indescribable."

Sue Ambler leaned forward, thick, honey-blonde hair cascading off her shoulders. "The apostle Paul doesn't impress me as the suggestible type. He seems very practical and down-to-earth. I think if I were going to cast him in a play, I'd portray him as short, thin, ascetic, dyspeptic, opinionated and totally lacking in humour." Sue was a teacher of English and a drama coach in the senior secondary school.

"How would you cast Peter?" I asked.

"Oh, sort of big and bumbling; someone who shoots off his mouth before he puts his brain in gear. At least that's how I'd portray him before the resurrection. Afterward, he'd be remorseful and earnest."

"Still, Jesus saw in him the leader of the future church."

"Jesus had inside information!"

We adjourned to the kitchen for some of Shirley's famous brownies, tea and coffee. The suggestion had once been made that we rotate to different member's houses, but Shirley assured us that she enjoyed hosting the bible study and hoped we would continue meeting at her house. In a four block area of Exeter, the houses had been lovingly restored or renovated — large, comfortable old houses, once owned by the elite of Exeter society, their extensive lawns overhung by ancient trees. The street even made a detour around one grand old sycamore.

Harry Meacham was a retired lumber dealer. He added a solarium to his house, and installed a modern kitchen with every conceivable gadget. But in the living room, the decor was redolent of the graciousness of a bygone age. One sank into the luxurious comfort of the couches and chairs, hoping never to have to get up. Pictures, carefully hung and discreetly lighted, were of an older style not suited to my taste, but obviously of superior quality.

I was glad I'd come. I'd almost forgotten how much spiritual fulfillment I got out of discussions with these people. Penny Farnham, my best friend, was a vivacious young public health nurse. A treat to the eyes of those she worked with, I could imagine her good looks and vibrant personality livening up the day of the patients she visited. She frequently rode a ten-speed bicycle, and sometimes when I said her name, it came out "Penny Farthing" which made her laugh.

Paul St. Cyr doted on her. Penny treated him like a much-loved uncle, but I'm sure that was not Paul's perception of the relationship. He was a small man with wispy white hair and a little pot belly which he sucked in when Penny was around. He had the most thorough theological knowledge of any lay person in the parish. I sometimes wondered why he bothered to come to bible study. He said that it was because one should never stop learning. I thought that it was to be near Penny.

"I'm glad we only meet every two weeks," Sue Ambler remarked as she bit into a rich, nut-filled brownie. "That way, I can fast in between."

Sue was married to Lesley Randall-Jones, but I've never heard her use his last name. I wondered idly whether, at school, she was called Miss Ambler, Ms. Ambler or Mrs. Randall-Jones. She was on a one-woman crusade to keep Shakespeare alive in Exeter, producing one of the Bard's plays each year. She could recite lines from his works at any moment to celebrate any occasion.

I knew little about the other members present, but they were congenial company nevertheless.

We never did resolve the question of how one could prove oneself to be a Christian. It had been merely a topic of idle discussion. I'd have pursued it further if I had known that in a short time, I'd be asked that very question in a court of law.

CHAPTER 4

When I arrived at the flight school at ten the next morning, Lance Brock was already waiting. Good for him, I thought. I recognized in him a keen desire to be in the air as much as possible, and wished that his work habits matched his enthusiasm. Perhaps military training would have been the thing for him. The armed forces might have kept him on the straight and narrow long enough to instill into his mind the idea of professionalism. Oh well! It hadn't happened, so here he was.

I told him to plan a flight to Edmonton, and he trotted off to the ground school room, spread out his chart, and went to work. Half an hour later, he presented an acceptable flight plan to me, and I spent the next thirty minutes quizzing him on a variety of subjects, most of which he should have learned in the ground school he had taken at Red Robin the previous year. His answers were marginal, but I decided to hold my judgment until I had flown with him. I sincerely hoped that he would redeem himself on the flight.

There was something vaguely likable about Lance; his ardour for everything connected to aviation perhaps. I could understand that. I felt the same way myself. There are people who make excuses not to fly, and eventually give it up. There are others for whom no obstacle to getting into the air was insurmountable. Lance was one of those. Since he was of that type, he needed to be made as competent as possible, so he would not become an accident statistic at an early age.

Lance picked up the clipboard and key for his scheduled airplane, a recent model Cessna 172, with all kinds of navigation equipment. This was our instrument trainer, but I usually scheduled it for commercial flight tests because commercial pilots needed to be familiar with the latest in navigation gear. Some of Lance's previous training at my school showed through. He pulled out an old, battered copy of our pre-flight checklist and placed it on the clipboard. I'd still watch him closely while he checked out the airplane, I thought, as I prepared to follow him out to the flight line.

A man I didn't recognize was waiting in the outer office, hands thrust in pockets, rocking back on his heels, looking very casual and at ease. A salesman, I decided, since he didn't strike me as an aviation type. He'd just have to wait if he wanted to talk to me.

He had no intention of waiting, it appeared. With cat-like quickness he moved to interpose himself into my path. I eyed him with annoyance. He was slightly built, middle-aged, non-descript. His balding head shone in the light from the fluorescent fixtures. He wore a shiny blue suit and a flamboyant red-patterned tie. His overcoat lay across a chair, so he'd been waiting for a while. Well, he'd have to wait a while longer, I thought, and sidestepped around him. He cut me off. I glared at him, but he gave me a bland, self-effacing smile, took something out of a folder that had been tucked under his arm, and held it out.

"Robin Carruthers?"

"That's right."

He placed the document in my hand and was gone as quickly as he had moved to intercept me. I glanced at the papers. They were official looking, with some sort of seal or logo that appeared to be government-related. Puzzled, I paused to glance through them, forgetting my vow to watch Lance as he pre-flighted the plane.

I had to read the missive three times before the words sank in. Harris Margolin, plaintiff, was suing Robin Carruthers and Red Robin Flying School for slander.

My eyes skimmed over the ponderous wording. It seemed that I had caused grievous harm to his reputation as a pilot and to his business by telling his business associates, in the presence of other people, that they should not fly with him. He was asking for a million dollars.

So much for my vow to follow the Bible's direction and do the right thing!

Lance was well along in his pre-flight and I couldn't keep my mind on what he was doing. My stomach churned, my mind skipped, and a feeling of impending doom enveloped me. Get hold of yourself, I thought. You can sort out this mess afterward. In the meantime, there was a difficult flight test to conduct.

I could see that the perpetrator of this assault was untying his Cessna 182 and loading suitcases on board. The knowledge did not help me concentrate on what Lance was doing. At least today it was safe for this Margolin character to fly his business associates back to Georgetown. It was windy, which meant it would be rough, but a good jouncing for the hour and a half it would take them to get there would serve him right.

I climbed in beside Lance. I watched him lay out his navigation materials and fire up the Lycoming which powered the 172. As we taxied out, I had a brief glimpse of the sleek, blond head of the man I thought of as "The Boss", and the rumpled darker form of the younger

42

associate as they walked toward their plane, collars turned up against the buffeting wind. Then we rolled onto the taxiway, and my tormentors were left behind us.

I watched Lance closely while he did his run-up, but once we had accelerated down the runway for a few hundred feet into a stiff headwind, we lifted off like an elevator on its way to the penthouse, and my mind began to drift again. As we passed abeam the flight school, the left wing dipped briefly in a spot of turbulence, and looking across Lance at the ground on the far side of the plane, I had a brief glimpse of someone running across the ramp. Lance quickly picked up the wing, and I forgot the scene below so fleetingly caught. Later, as I tried to recall it, I couldn't even remember which direction the running figure had been going.

Again my mind drifted. Subconsciously, I was watching Lance's performance as he set himself on course and levelled off at altitude. My mind reviewed the entire fiasco, from the moment Margolin and his pals entered my place of business to the time they left for the motel. I had only done what I thought to be right. The storm had proven me correct. How could he possibly think I had done him an injury, when it was obvious that I had saved his life, and the lives of his two passengers?

After a while, I came to with a start. I looked out at the terrain below and realized I hadn't the faintest idea where we were. How could this have happened? Below, summits of a vast, unbroken tract of densely timbered hills, still wrapped in a blanket of snow, slid to the rear as the turbulence that occurs over mountain terrain in a strong wind bounced us around. Open areas indicated the locations of still-frozen ponds and lakes. There was not a road, a town or even a puff of smoke from a cabin. I felt a tight, tingling sensation in the back of my neck. Sweat moistened the palms of my hands.

How long had we been flying? I glanced at the clock on the instrument panel. Not long really. We couldn't be far out of Exeter. Lance sat in the left seat, relaxed and easy, unconcerned.

It had been years since I'd found myself lost in an airplane. I'd been flying in this area for a quarter of a century, and thought I knew every inch of it. That in itself made me aware of where we must be. I realized that I actually didn't know every inch of the terrain. There was one area of wilderness I never flew over, because there was no reason to do so. The mountains to the east rose so steeply from the valley that, in normal weather, it was impossible to gain enough altitude to clear them without making a detour or spiralling up. So, if you were flying in that direction, you always flew up the valley until you had gained sufficient altitude, or merely followed the valley north-eastward, which was the route Lance had planned.

We had taken off toward the northeast, and with a strong north wind, Lance must have been able to clear the nearest ridge with ease. Obviously, now we were to the south of our course, above the land we never flew over.

He was way off course and should have made a correction long ago. It was clearly enough to cause him to flunk his flight test, but I experienced a totally unreasonable feeling of guilt that I was judging him on his error when I had made the same one myself; I had not remained aware of our progress. Almost as if I thought he could read my mind, I was afraid to call off the test and send him home.

I could remember my own commercial flight test, done in mid-winter. The examiner had asked me to land at a short, narrow strip, piled high on either side with snow. His hands had hovered near the control yoke all the way down final approach. He evidently didn't expect a girl to be able to handle the gusty crosswind. I suspect that he had asked me to land at that airstrip thinking that I'd blow it, and he'd have to take over and could fail me on the test. I'd made an excellent landing, but as we turned off at the end of the runway onto a taxiway coated with ice, across which the wind drifted riffles of snow, he had insisted on taking over. It was his own airplane, not mine — one he used to make a little extra money from aircraft rental. I'd relinquished the controls and sat, hands folded in my lap, watching him manoeuvre around the corner. He was taxiing faster than I would have done, and a gust of wind caught the plane and sent us skidding across the ice into a snow bank.

We were stuck fast and had to shut down, get out and push the plane out of the drift back onto the taxiway. I'd known then, with smug satisfaction, that I had it made. He couldn't possibly flunk me after that!

But today was different. Lance didn't know that I had lost track of where we were. He undoubtedly thought I was merely giving him lots of leeway. I fought the sense of guilt. It was irrational. And I'd better start concentrating on my own job.

"Where are we?" I tried to keep my voice casual.

Lance turned toward me and frowned. "Do you mean exactly?"

"Yes."

Lance let his gaze fall onto his chart. "Well, we're somewhere in here." His finger traced a vague circle over the chart.

"I know we're somewhere in there," I replied, trying to keep emotion out of my voice, "but where in there?"

Lance studied the chart a while longer, then shifted his attention to the Global Positioning Satellite receiver. The marker that indicated our position was full scale to the right of the course line. Lance punched the "direct" button, the marker lined up in the centre and a new heading popped up on the display. He turned the plane to the left, onto the new heading.

I sighed audibly and Lance shot a quick look at me, immediately turning his head back toward the instruments on the panel. The downward turn of the corners of his mouth, and his tightly knotted brow, indicated that he knew he'd blown it.

"Get back on course and stay on it," I ordered.

He gave that some thought. Then he shrugged slightly and asked, "Why can't I just go direct from here to my next checkpoint?"

"To answer that, you might take a look ahead."

Lance looked up sharply from the instruments and surveyed the scenery ahead. The first thing that was obvious was that a bank of thick cumulus cloud was rapidly approaching. Glimpsed briefly, through ragged breaks in the cloud, was a vista of high, snow-capped peaks rising well above our altitude. A quick glance at the chart was all he needed to convince him that a straight-ahead course would spell disaster. The elevations of the mountains looming before us were reaching toward the ten thousand foot mark. To our left, where our flight-planned course would take us, a valley wound around the mountains. We were already entering the first wispy vestiges of the approaching scud. Lance turned left with alacrity and began to look for the valley. Within minutes, we slid over its rim, the clouds that had been closing in on us opened up, and familiar landmarks came into view.

I waited until he had re-established himself on our course line, watching to see whether he would make an appropriate correction for wind drift. He didn't, and soon we found ourselves again moving off into the wilderness to the right of course.

"Turn around and fly your course-line back to Exeter. And try to stay on course."

Lance's narrow forehead, under his cap, creased into a frown. He didn't say anything, but made a left one-eighty, found his proper track and flew us home.

As we entered the downwind leg, I had another brief glimpse of the flight school ramp. There seemed to be an inordinate amount of activity. I turned my attention firmly back to critiquing Lance's landing approach, momentarily squelching my curiosity. Lance flew a good approach and made a decent landing, things he could easily do if he tried. It certainly wasn't enough to make me change my mind, however, as he had clearly not met the qualifications set out for passing the test. I hoped he'd realize that I wasn't flunking him out of spite, but only because he did not perform well enough. That thought brought me back to Harris Margolin. He obviously didn't expect to take any of the blame for the scene that had occurred two days ago. I hoped he'd had a really rough ride back to Georgetown.

He hadn't, though. He'd never even gotten off the ground.

As we rolled out after landing, a brief glimpse of the school ramp showed a lot of activity. But it wasn't until we taxied back and turned off at the school that I realized that the people there were police.

They were gathered around Margolin's Cessna 182, which was still where it had been for the last two days. A man in navy blue trousers with a wide gold stripe down the side, and the gold-banded cap of the RCMP, stepped out of the crowd and motioned us to taxi around the area rather than coming through on the regular taxiway. This we did. Lance shut down the engine. I saw Rod O'Donnell hastening toward us. He came to my side of the plane and said breathlessly, "One of those guys got killed. He walked into the prop. They want you over there."

"Okay. Lance, I'll see you inside in a minute."

The youth nodded, a gloomy expression on his long face, which I deemed not to be from the news of someone else's death, but as a result of the demise of his own ambition.

I walked toward the parked 182, registering the scene. The green and white plane sat askew on its tiedown, the right main wheel up against the outside of its rear chock, which was twisted sideways. The left main rested on the edge of the paved taxiway, its chock farther back on the grass. The nose wheel strut was fully extended, and since that wheel was on the slightly rising pavement of the taxiway, the plane had an unbalanced, tail-low stance. The pilot's door was unlatched and banged fitfully in the wind. On the crest of the taxiway, a small orange tarp had been spread, its corners held down by aircraft tires. Under the centre of the tarp was a hump, and with a tight feeling in the pit of my stomach, I hoped the swirling wind would not insinuate itself under the plastic and lift it out from under the weights. I had never seen the victim of a propeller accident. I had no wish to.

I tried not to look at the plane, but the one swift view I could not escape showed the telltale signs of the destruction a spinning propeller can cause. The prop, cowling and windscreen were spattered with blood and flesh. I fought down a wave of nausea.

Had Margolin gotten out and walked into the prop of his own plane?

CHAPTER 5

No such luck, I soon found out.

The policemen at the scene sent me into the school's office where, they said, Corporal Nash had gone. The corporal, who had removed his parka in the heat of the office, was readily identified by the two chevrons on his sleeve. And talking to him was an agitated Harris Margolin. The untidy younger man of the three sat on a couch, his head in his hands, shivering though he still wore his coat. I did not see "The Boss" anywhere around.

If "The Boss" was the victim, I felt a twinge of regret. He'd been the only one of the three who had shown an intelligent regard for the advice of an expert. The other two could disappear out of my life any time they chose.

Margolin's two passengers had been named in his lawsuit as the witnesses to whom I had made my slanderous statements. One's name was Alexander Conrad. I remembered the hand-tooled gold letters, AC, on the expensive case "The Boss" had been carrying. In that event, this distraught wretch sitting huddled on the couch must be Samuel Gilley. I moved over toward the couch to speak to him, but before I got there, he jumped to his feet and scurried toward the washroom, his hand over his mouth.

I looked around for Lance. He was gone. According to Joyce, the dispatcher on duty, he'd handed in the clipboard and key for the plane and had hastily departed before I came in from the ramp.

"He failed, didn't he?" Joyce asked, concern in her voice

I nodded. "I hadn't told him so, but he must have realized it."

"Poor Lance," Joyce remarked wistfully. "I'm sure he didn't want to stick around and hear you tell him. I wonder if he'll ever be back?"

Under my breath, I said, "I hope not."

I was kept cooling my heels while Cpl. Nash, his patience wearing thin, tried to get a coherent statement out of Margolin. The pilot was refusing to accept any responsibility for the disaster. He hadn't done so two days ago, either. In a high-pitched, angry voice, his arms waving wildly, he lavished blame upon the victim, the wind, the tiedown area, the pressure of business, and a few more things I've forgotten because they didn't make sense to me.

"Alec should have known better. He's flown with me enough times. Walked right into the prop. I can't see how he could be so stupid."

A grimace of distaste passed fleetingly across Cpl. Nash's face, but was quickly replaced with a grave, neutral expression.

"Do you always start up before you load your passengers onboard?" he asked.

"Not always. But it was cold. I wanted to warm up the engine and also the cockpit. If it hadn't been so goddam cold, I wouldn't have started up ahead of time. Just my luck for Alec to forget himself on a day I had to start up that way."

"Why didn't you shut down when you saw him coming over?"

"Why should I? He should have known better."

"I've done a lot of flying on the job," Nash stated. "I would never approach an airplane with the engine running. I've always been taught to wait for the pilot to shut down. I'm surprised that Conrad would agree to board while it was running, if as you say, he was familiar with planes."

"You don't need to lecture me. I've always done things safely."

"Until this time." As Nash's shaft shot home, Margolin turned red as an over-ripe tomato and spluttered a string of invective.

"Calm down, sir." Nash made the downward motion with his hands that every motorist knows the meaning of.

Gilley returned from the john. I shifted my attention from Margolin to him. He was no longer shaking and his colour was a bit better. He sat down on the couch and stared at the floor.

"Are you called Sam?" I asked.

The young man looked up, frowned and nodded.

"Can I get you anything, Sam?"

"I could use a stiff drink," Gilley said listlessly.

"I'm afraid there's nothing like that around here. Do you think you could keep some coffee down?"

He nodded. "I could use some."

"Milk or sugar?"

"Both."

Joyce jumped to her feet. "I'll get it." She went to the canteen and soon returned with a mug filled to the brim with steaming coffee. Gilley wrapped his hand around the mug, sipped tentatively, swallowed and waited. The coffee stayed put, so he tried a bigger gulp. All was well. He began to relax. After a few moments, he set the mug down carefully on the table beside him and removed his blue anorak. Colour had returned to his face.

"What exactly happened? Or don't you want to talk about it?"

"Might as well," he sighed. "Everybody's going to be asking me that." He sat for several seconds staring at the floor. "Alec and I were walking out to the plane. I wasn't going along. There was some stuff Alec wanted me to do here in Exeter. He waited till Harris had gone out to start the plane before telling me some of it. We walked out almost to where the plane was parked and stopped for a minute, talking. Then I turned around to come back. I'd gone a little ways when I heard Harris screaming at me. I didn't quite hear him at first. The wind was making such a damned racket you couldn't hear yourself think. But I finally realized something was wrong and turned around. Harris was outside the plane, looking down at Alec. Alec was all bloody. You could hardly recognize him. The prop hit his head."

Gilley's voice ended on a rising note and he put his head in his hands. I laid my hand on his shoulder. "I'm sorry," I said inadequately. Gilley nodded.

"I liked Alec. What I knew of him anyway," I told Gilley. "He seemed to have some common sense and was willing to listen to reason."

Gilley lifted his head and stared at me, an expression of incomprehension on his haggard face. "What do you mean?"

"I mean his being willing to take the advice of an expert on whether it was safe to fly."

"You've got to be kidding."

I raised my eyebrows as Gilley continued to stare at me. Colour flooded back into his face and the expression turned to one I would have said was acute embarrassment.

"That's not why he told Harris we weren't flying to Georgetown."

"Oh?"

"Hell no." Gilley's laugh was a hoarse croak. "He made up his mind when you found out that those other guys had to land over at Raymond Bay."

"Made up his mind about what?"

"Well, see, it's like this. Those guys were our competitors, and if they could have got back to Georgetown and we couldn't, our scheme would have fallen through. That's why Harris was so anxious to go. But since they hadn't made it, then they were in the same boat as we were. So Alec wanted to get over to that motel and get on the phone as quick as possible."

Gilley laughed at a memory. "You should have seen them! Alec, he left Harris to lug the suitcases in while he took a private room, holed himself up, and hit the phone. Old Harris, he didn't like being treated like a bellboy, so he passed the buck onto me. He went and called his wife, but her line was busy. He kept getting a busy signal every time he called for at least half an hour. Finally he got through, just when Alec hung up his phone and came into Harris' room. Old Alec had been on the line to the fair Diana, Harris' wife, all that time. Boy, was Harris pissed off!"

"Are they partners in a business?"

"Yeah. Supposedly equal partners, but you saw how Alec treated Harris. Actually Harris and Diana each own a quarter of the company, Harcon Holdings. I guess Harris thinks Alec was teaming up with Diana and was going to squeeze him out." Gilley paused for a moment's thought. "He's probably right, too."

"Was there anything personal between Alec and the lady?"

"D'you mean, was Alec shacking up with her? I wouldn't put it past him."

"What does the company do?"

"Harcon Holdings?" He waited until I nodded. "Real estate speculation. They nose out things that are going to happen, and get hold of property that's going to be needed. They buy when the present owner doesn't know what's in the wind, and sell at a big mark-up."

"You don't sound very loyal to your employers," I commented.

Gilley shrugged. "I'll get canned now anyway, probably. I don't owe them anything."

I changed the subject. "Just how often does he start up the plane before the passengers get in? Day before yesterday, he taxied over here and shut down."

"Usually he does. Shut down I mean. I think I remember one other time when we had to get in while the motor was running. That was another cold day last winter."

"Margolin just told the policeman that it was common for them to do that."

Gilley shrugged. "Alec's been flying with him longer than I have. He seemed to know his way around planes even if he wasn't a pilot."

"So you think Margolin is right when he says Alec knew better."

"Yeah. I guess so."

"What do you think?"

Gilley merely shrugged.

"When you went back there and Margolin was standing over Conrad's body, had he shut down the engine?"

"Oh, sure. I've never seen him get out of the plane and leave it running."

I saw Cpl. Nash bearing down on us, his craggy face grim, so I left Gilley to him.

I'd sure been taken for a fish! No one had paid the slightest attention to my reasoned explanation for not flying in the face of the coming storm. They'd only decided not to go because their competition hadn't gotten through either. But surely, they must have noticed the storm raging overhead only minutes after they'd settled into the motel. Nash stopped to confer with one of the other Mounties, and in the interval I turned back to Gilley to ask him one more question.

"Weren't you convinced that my advice was accurate after the storm hit?"

He stared at me, his face blank.

"What storm?" he asked.

"Didn't you notice?"

"Hell, we were too tied up with our own problems to notice the weather."

It must have been some session between the two equal — or perhaps very unequal — partners!

***

It wasn't Alec Conrad's death that preyed on my mind, but the unrealistic conception that Margolin must have had about the weather for his trip. I was curious enough that I called the Flight Service Station in Pine Hill. The specialist who answered was a friend of mine.

"Hello, Bill. I'm looking for some information."

"Okay, Robin. Fire away."

"Two days ago, just before the storm hit over here, a fellow was all set to take off on a flight to Georgetown. I couldn't talk him out of it, so I appealed to his passengers. One of them was his boss, and made the decision not to go. I'm curious about whether he filed a flight plan." I gave Bill the type and registration mark of Margolin's plane.

"Oh, that guy! Yeah, he filed all right, but not with us. We deal with him every once in a while, and he's always a pain in the ass. He subscribes to some computer service in the States, files his flight plan using a modem, to their headquarters. They're supposed to get your flight plan processed within a half hour, but they never do. We always have to call them. The plane will be in the air when the pilot calls us to open his flight plan, unless he's taking off from Exeter. Then the tower calls us at the last moment. We never have it, and have to phone the company in the States to get it. The company says they can't guarantee the thirty minutes for a Canadian flight plan. Sometimes we don't get the plan opened until they're half way to their destination."

"He did file day before yesterday, then?"

"Yeah. The plan came through about four hours after he'd filed it. He hadn't cancelled, so we had to track him down. I guess the weather scared him off, and he just forgot about the flight plan. We finally found him in the airport motel over there, and would you believe it, he was mad at us because he couldn't go?"

"Knowing him, I believe it."

"We don't make the goddam weather."

I chuckled, then asked, "Didn't he get a weather briefing?"

"We asked him that, too. He says he did, by computer, from this same company. Apparently all he asked for was current weather at Exeter and Georgetown. Exeter hadn't gone down yet. The front had passed through Georgetown already, and they were technically VFR — if you want to go Visual Flight Rules in five miles vis, in the mountains, under an eleven hundred foot ceiling, down in a valley, in moderate rain."

"Not very smart," I agreed. "Do me a favour, Bill. Save all the weather data from that day, and everything you have on that flight plan. I got the guy's boss to cancel the flight, but not without repercussions. The pilot is suing me for slander."

"You're kidding! The guy's got rocks in his noggin!"

"That's what I think, too."

"Well, good luck. We'll save all the dope."

The body was removed to the morgue. I wondered if they'd had to pick up parts of it with a shovel. The Mounties made arrangements with Rod to put the 182 into our hangar. Rod used a corner of the hangar to do the occasional small paint job, and had rigged up a curtain around the area to keep spray from drifting around the hangar. He put the plane in that corner and pulled the curtain. The aviation accident investigators would come later, and would go over every bit of that plane. They could have the job! There was a complete lack of interest in any of the local aviation people in looking at it. None of us wanted to see the results of a propeller accident.

Even idling on the ground, the prop must have been turning about 1500 RPM. Each blade of the prop is a heavy, solid piece of metal, attached at the hub to the governing mechanism. The result of the weight of the blade and the speed of its revolutions means that, at the tip, a tremendous force is applied. It can make instant hamburger out of a human body. This might be a ghoulish attraction to many people, but to those of us who work so close to this deadly force, it is unnerving to be reminded of its power.

It wasn't until I got home, ate my supper, and was sitting quietly with Cloud Nine in my lap, that the perception that all was not as it should be crept stealthily into my mind. Was this a straightforward accident? Something was wrong, but I couldn't pin it down. Or was I merely worrying about the lawsuit? Was that colouring my view of the entire incident?

This vague feeling stayed with me all through the evening. It wasn't until late that night, just when I was slipping off to sleep, that a scene flashed vividly into my mind and I knew what was bothering me. There had not been an accident. Alec Conrad had been murdered.

CHAPTER 6

I sat up in bed, wide awake, and turned on the bedside lamp. Two very clear images remained in my mind as I pondered what I should do. Obviously it was not necessary to call the police at this time of the night. It wasn't as if the perpetrator would do a bunk. My problem would be in getting the police to understand what I had seen and be willing to act on it.

I got up and made myself a cup of hot chocolate. Curled up on the living room couch with my slippered feet tucked under me, I considered several options. I decided that my best bet was to talk to Sergeant Bruce Jameson, whom I knew from previous investigations. Jameson, I was sure, considered me a reasonable sort of person; one who wouldn't come running to the cops with some wild idea that had just jumped into her head. I felt certain that Jameson would listen; but would he believe me? Carefully, I marshalled my thoughts, trying to remember every detail. One thing I couldn't pin down. Was the running figure I had seen headed toward the plane or away? If toward, then it was merely Sam Gilley running back after Margolin had called him. If away — I let the thought trail off into the air. I'd leave that part out. It might not have anything to do with the murder.

At eight the next morning, I presented myself at the RCMP detachment, identified myself, and asked for Sgt. Jameson. He wasn't in, I was told, but would be there at ten. Could I see him then? That could be arranged; what was it about? Not wanting to give my whole argument twice, and thinking that this guy at the desk was less likely to understand than would Jameson, who knew me, I declined to state what I wanted to talk about. I hoped this wouldn't diminish my chances of seeing Jameson, but the young constable at the desk didn't seem to mind. Come back a little after ten, he told me.

Since the church was within walking distance of the police building, I went there to wait. Douglas was just finishing morning prayer. Seeing me, he asked me to come into his office. Oh, oh! What now?

I went reluctantly, and when waved to a seat, perched on the very edge of a chair. Douglas picked up a newsletter from Idylwyld, an Anglican conference venue in central British Columbia, a three hour drive north of Exeter.

"I noticed a course being given this summer that I would like several parishioners from St. Matthew's to attend. It's the first of a series of training sessions for Lay Ministers of the Word and Sacrament. They're going to have courses over the next few years on such subjects as taking communion to the sick and homebound, leading morning and evening prayer, and conducting services with reserved sacrament. The one this year is on preaching. Actually, these courses are aimed more at members of isolated rural churches that don't have a priest every Sunday. But home communion, as you know, is a big thing here in Exeter because of our large population of retired people. Still, I think that the entire series would be helpful to people like yourself who are trying to learn more about the faith. Would you like to go?"

I frowned. It was hard to concentrate on this new prospect. On the surface, it didn't sound very exciting, and summer is a bad time for me to take off from my work.

Douglas continued, "I've asked Paul St. Cyr, but it's hard to get him to commit himself to anything these days. He's done so much in the past; he wants a rest. I also suggested it to Chris Whitney, but she feels she's too new to the church to get much out of it. I don't agree, but I couldn't persuade her to go. Besides, she says that summer is the busiest time for her veterinary practice."

"It's my busiest time, too."

Douglas glanced up, peering over the tops of his reading glasses. "Yes, I suppose so."

I was surprised that Paul wasn't interested. He was retired, so he had time, and was a life-long Anglican. Now, if Penny Farnham were to go...

"Have you asked Penny?"

"Yes, but she can't get away. Everyone with more seniority wants to take their vacations in July or August, and she has to take what's left over."

I felt sure that if Penny agreed to go, Paul would jump at the opportunity. I didn't say so to Douglas. I'm always tongue-tied in his presence, whether that is out of respect for his authority or because I'm not quite over my infatuation with him.

Dr. Chris Whitney, my cat's veterinarian, had only last year started coming to church. I had a trifling head start on her, having decided that there was a God a few months before I'd persuaded Chris to come to church with me. So if Chris felt too much of a novice, she and I shared that feeling.

"Are you getting desperate, or do you have others on your list?" I asked.

Douglas laughed, his warm brown eyes meeting my doubting green ones. Douglas is a man of average height, which means he's the same height as I am, since I'm tall for a woman. He has brown hair, greying at the temples. The bones of his face are prominent, and his visage displays both firmness of character and a sort of serenity. Not a handsome face, but a fascinating one, and one that always starts my heart beating a little faster.

"I'd like several people to go. I think it will enhance your spiritual life immensely. Do you want to know who's teaching it?"

"Who?"

"Bishop Michael and the Archbishop, John Radcliff."

I felt a stirring of excitement.

"Wow! They're both pretty potent preachers." My interest had been minimal but was now piqued. I hadn't met the Archbishop, but his prowess as a speaker was legendary. Our bishop, Michael Staines, had been to St. Matthew's several times since I had joined the church, and had always given sermons that were both practical and poignant. I wondered, though, whether such top-ranking men would really be good teachers. "Why such heavy hitters?" I asked.

"I think it reflects the importance they place on this training. The emphasis in the church these days is on lay involvement, and John Radcliff is one of the foremost promoters of it. What do you think?"

"I'm surprised that you're considering me. I thought I was in your doghouse."

"Robin! What made you think that?"

"Well, I just feel you don't trust me any more. All we have a chance to talk about any more is money, and you constantly challenge me over the way I handle the church's financial affairs."

He turned away, stared for a moment out the window and sighed. "I have the utmost respect for your ability as treasurer. You have had to learn some things about the church, mainly that there are traditions you just don't change. Since they're harmless, they're best left alone."

I didn't agree. There seemed to be a dual standard in the church. The old-timers could do what they'd always done, but no one else could do anything without jumping through all kinds of hoops. I was afraid to say this to Douglas. He might actually feel the same way, but he had to live with this congregation day in and day out. Had he surrendered, or was he biding his time? He was in his late fifties. Perhaps he hoped to reach retirement age without too much controversy.

My relationship with Douglas seemed to be falling apart, and my spiritual life had come to a standstill. I was procrastinating about daily prayer. When I'd first accepted the Christian faith, I had become very devout. Now, as a direct result of the differences with my priest, I was taking more and more time off from prayer, from reading scripture, and from looking for other ways to deepen my faith. It worried me. Had my initial piety been merely a result of meeting Douglas, so that when I had felt myself out of his favour, I'd lost my faith?

No, I didn't think so. But then why was I going through this dry spell? I hadn't dared approach Douglas about it. I'd stopped going to him for theological discussions. I couldn't take my troubles to him. We talked to each other now only when church business required that we must.

"I don't think I'm really competent to go to this," I said lamely.

"Of course you are. Why don't you think so?"

I couldn't answer that. I sat there looking and feeling miserable, and finally he changed the subject.

"I'm going to the other course that's being given at the same time. Betty will go along just for some R and R. If I know her, she'll spend all her time in a canoe out on the lake. You can ride up with us unless you'd rather fly."

"No. There's no airport closer than Raymond Bay and that's over on the other side of the lake."

"You will go then." His voice held a hint of expectancy.

"I don't know. Why should I learn how to preach? We don't need any lay preachers here." Besides Douglas there were several retired priests in the congregation who regularly took the services.

Douglas smiled. "Physically, we don't, but it never hurts to get a different point of view now and then."

"Would I actually have a chance to preach?"

"Certainly. But that's not the main reason for going. I'd like to see a few of you go for your own spiritual development. You're going to learn a lot more in those five days than just how to put a sermon together."

"What's your course about?"

Douglas picked up the newsletter and read, "'Change in the Modern Church.' It's led by Wilson Noble, the big evangelism guru."

Change! Wasn't that just what I wished Douglas could accomplish in this church? Three hours sitting with him in the car on the way back, hashing over what we'd learned! Perhaps by then my own flagging faith would have been given a boost, and Douglas would be ready to come back to St. Matthew's and make changes.

"Let me think about it. I'll call you in a few days."

***

The young constable at the desk spoke discreetly into a phone, waited briefly, nodded and hung up. He turned back to me. "If you'll wait a few minutes, Sgt. Jameson will see you."

I'd paced the floor about ten minutes, then was ushered into Jameson's office. He rose and shook hands, a friendly smile on his face. If he calls me "Robin," I thought, I'll know he thinks this is a social call. If he calls me "Mrs. Carruthers" he knows it's business.

"Have a seat Mrs. Carruthers. What can I do for you?"

Good, I thought. He's going to take me seriously.

I sat down in a straight-backed chair, and he seated himself opposite me, an expression of curiosity on his face. I'd never seen him in a uniform, though I presume he had one; at least the dress red serge and Smokey the Bear hat that identify the Mountie to most of the world. He dressed with impeccable taste. Today he wore a blue-grey suit, light blue shirt and a conservative striped tie. His dark hair, cut short, lay smoothly on his head, his lean, firm jaw cleanly shaven. I thought once again what a really handsome man he was, if it were not for those cold, grey, steel-trap eyes. It was hard to look into them.

"I know it's not a case you're working on, but I wanted to talk to you about the man who was killed out at the school yesterday."

"Walked into a propeller, I understand," Jameson said noncommittally. "Not my baby. Corporal Nash is on the case."

"I know. But it's not quite what it looked like, and I wasn't sure he would listen to me if I tried to tell him. Besides, I know you are in criminal investigation, so it might be your baby after all."

"You don't think it was an accident?"

"No."

Jameson frowned. "Nash seems to think it was a pretty straightforward case of a passenger walking into a whirling prop. He considers it to be the pilot's fault, since the pilot is supposedly in charge of the whole operation."

"I know that's what it was meant to look like."

Jameson leaned forward. "Look. If you're questioning Nash's competence, put it out of your mind. Nash was just recently promoted and assigned here. He's spent years in the Yukon, where you have to fly everywhere. He's not a pilot, but he knows aviation inside out. Inspector McBride is one for using the talents of the people he has, so anything involving aviation will be Nash's baby."

"I'm not questioning his competence. In fact, it was obvious the way he handled things yesterday. But I just realized last night that I know something that he doesn't, and I wasn't sure he'd listen to me. You know me, and know I'm fairly practical and level headed, so I thought I'd come to you first. If you tell Nash he should listen to me, I'm sure he will."

Jameson leaned back and grinned. "Okay, you've made your point. Fire away."

I edged forward in my chair and rested my elbows on my knees. "I'll have to give you some background, but I'll try to make it brief."

He nodded.

"Remember the storm we had three days ago?"

Jameson's face screwed into an expression of disgust. "I sure do! A tree fell on my garage and I'm going to have to replace the whole damned thing."

"Well, about half an hour before the storm hit, those three guys came out to the airport with the obvious intention of flying somewhere. They were headed for Georgetown, right into the teeth of the storm. When I saw that the pilot, Margolin, was about to fire up the plane, I tried to talk him out of going, and he told me to mind my own business. He would have knocked me down with the tail of the plane if I hadn't been fast on my feet. So I went into the office where Conrad and Gilley were waiting, and convinced them they shouldn't make the trip. Margolin was furious, but Conrad took charge and started giving orders, which seemed to surprise Margolin, who is supposed to be his partner. Gilley is just a gofer."

Jameson nodded noncommittally.

"Anyway, they went to the airport motel, and from what Gilley tells me, they had such a row that they didn't even notice the storm."

"That would take some doing," Jameson commented with feeling.

"I know. Gilley thinks Conrad was conspiring with Margolin's wife to squeeze Margolin out of the business, and possibly to take his wife away from him as well."

"Motive, in other words."

"Motive. Then yesterday, they came out again. This time only Margolin and Conrad were going to Georgetown. Gilley was staying here. But Gilley walked out to the plane with Conrad, who was giving him some last-minute instructions that he apparently didn't want Margolin to hear."

"What about?"

"I've no idea. I didn't ask. Anyway, Margolin had gone ahead and started the plane, supposedly to warm it up. He was sitting there in it, with the engine running while the other two were walking over.

"Now, I'll have to tell you where I come in."

Again Jameson nodded.

"I was going out on a commercial flight test. I was out on the ramp with the applicant, watching him do his pre-flight. I saw Margolin untie his plane, load some suitcases on board, and start it up. As we were taxiing out, I saw Conrad and Gilley walking toward the plane. We turned off on the taxiway, so that's the last I saw until I came back from the flight and saw the accident scene. I felt that something was wrong, but it didn't occur to me exactly what it was until late last night.

"Now, let me describe some things to you. When those guys didn't go on their trip the other day, Margolin taxied back over to the tiedown and just left the plane there, not straight, not tied down, with only the nose wheel chocked. Rod O'Donnell, my maintenance chief, and I went out there with a towbar and parked the plane properly. You have to know Rod to understand that when he had put it where he wanted it, that plane was exactly square on the parking spot, with its nose wheel precisely on the line painted on the asphalt for that purpose, the main wheels exactly opposite the wing tiedown chains and the tail right over the tail tiedown. Not an inch right or left, anywhere."

Jameson's squint showed that he was concentrating with interest in what I had to say. He ran a pencil through his fingers, first from one end, then the other. There was a kind of tension about him.

Good! I thought.

"Now, Conrad apparently was fairly familiar with airplanes. I understand that he and Margolin flew a lot. Whether or not he frequently had to get into the plane with the engine running is a subject of dispute, but I think I can tell you that he knew what he was doing yesterday. Do you know what a Cessna 182 looks like?"

Jameson shook his head.

"It's a high-wing plane with struts that connect to the underside of the wings about half way out. In order to get into the plane, if you were approaching it from the front, you'd have to go out around the strut, since it is in front of the door. A short person could duck under the outer part of the strut, but would still be outside the propeller arc. Conrad was tall; at least six feet, I'd say. He was familiar with the plane. He would know that he had to walk out around the strut to get in."

"Would he have been able to see that the prop was turning?" Jameson asked.

"Yes. Supposedly. Prop tips are painted some bright colour so you can see them when they're turning. Margolin's was painted yellow on the tip. Conrad would have been able to see this bright yellow circle, but it's surprising how people can overlook that. But whether Conrad noticed it or not, he wasn't walking toward it. As we taxied out, I could look straight across to where that plane was parked. Margolin had removed the tiedown ropes and chains, he'd pulled the nose wheel chock out. I think it was his, so he probably put it in the plane. The chocks around the mains were the type that is made from two elongated triangles of wood, held together by a section of rope. He'd left the chocks in back of the wheels, and swung the front chocks out to the side so he could taxi out.

"I looked across just as we taxied directly in front of the 182, a ways over from it. The plane was sitting there, chocked the way I just described, the engine running. Conrad and Gilley were walking across toward it. Gilley was headed toward the wing tip. Conrad was closer to the plane, but still far enough out to have walked around the strut if he'd continued on the same line. I didn't see them stop. But Conrad was definitely planning to walk around the outside of the strut, well clear of the prop.

"When we came back, after Conrad had been killed, the plane was in a different position. I'll describe the area. It's a taxiway that's on the edge of the ramp. It's wide enough that planes can be parked on the edge. We like to park planes where the nose wheel is on the pavement, so the prop doesn't pick up debris when the plane is started. That parking area, though, is on grass. The main wheels are back on the grass, and there are tiedown chains for each wing and the tail. There is a line painted on the edge of the pavement for you to line up the nose wheel when you're parking the plane. It was parked exactly straight when we left, but not when we got back."

Jameson's steel-grey eyes narrowed to mere slits. He stopped sliding the pencil through his fingers and held it motionless. He sat rigidly, intense concentration showing in all his body language.

I went on. "When I got back from the flight and went over to the accident scene, I was so shocked that the significance of what I saw escaped me. Besides, I had two other major problems on my mind."

"What were they?" His voice was sharp, his words clipped short.

"I'll tell you one of them. The man I was flying with has always been a real problem for me, and I was in the position of having to flunk him on the flight test. I expected a lot of trouble."

"And you're not going to tell me the other?"

I shook my head. "Not now."

"Had it to do with these three guys who were flying to Georgetown?"

I hesitated just long enough before answering that Jameson, I was certain, realized he'd hit the nail on the head. A tight smile touched his lips, lingered for a moment and was gone.

"Yes," I said. "But if you think I'm trying to make trouble for Margolin because of it, you're wrong. In fact it almost made me decide not to come."

"Okay. Go on. We'll come back to that later if need be."

"Anyway, let me describe the scene as I saw it when I got back. Your photographer will have recorded it, so you can verify this part."

"But not the 'before' part," Jameson quipped.

"Yes. You can verify that also. Ask Rod O'Donnell. He'll describe to you how that plane was tied down. Incidentally, I haven't discussed this with him, so if Cpl. Nash wants to talk to him, his answers won't be influenced by anything I've said."

Jameson nodded.

"When I went over to the accident scene, I saw a tarp obviously covering the body. I could see the outline of the body under it. It was right on the crown of the taxiway.

From what I've heard about his injuries, Conrad did not go anywhere after he was hit. He would have dropped on the spot. A spinning prop is an immensely lethal weapon. So that means that the prop on the plane was over the crown of the taxiway when it hit Conrad."

"Yeah, but maybe he'd already taxied into that position and was waiting there."

"But he hadn't. I saw the plane when Conrad was walking out to it."

"The pilot, what's his name, Margolin, could still have moved the plane after you'd turned away, or had his attention distracted so he accidentally let it roll forward."

"Let me finish."

Jameson nodded.

"When I went over there, the plane was on an angle on its tiedown. The nose wheel wasn't on the line, the right main was back against the very outside of the right chock, and that end of the chock had been pushed back. The left main was up on the edge of the paved area, quite a ways from its chock. The nose wheel strut was fully extended, which it was not previously. The tail was so far away from the spot it should have been that the tail tiedown chain wouldn't even have reached it. Incidentally, you can verify that the plane was exactly square on its tiedown by looking at the adjustment on all the tiedown chains. I doubt if Margolin changed that at all when he unfastened them. There'd be no need to."

Again Jameson nodded.

"When we went over to the plane to tow it into the hangar, I noticed that the luggage in the baggage compartment was all tipped over toward the rear of the compartment. We took it out and gave it back to Margolin, and I think Nash held Conrad's for his next of kin."

"He would have."

"The tail of the plane was almost on the ground, because of the fact that the nose was up on the taxiway and the nose wheel strut was fully extended. That could happen if the baggage compartment was overloaded. It wasn't though. What must have happened is that Margolin taxied forward, turning sharply to the right, then after the prop had hit Conrad, he'd cut the power and let the plane roll back onto the tiedown. It ended up crooked, and the jolt when one wheel hit the chock tipped the suitcases over. The combination of the sudden stop and the backward shift in the weight caused the nose wheel strut to extend. Margolin getting out of the plane wouldn't change that because the front seats are right in the area of the centre of gravity."

"It still could have been accidental if Margolin was doing something else and didn't see that the plane was rolling forward."

"No. The slope of the taxiway, which is for water to run off, by the way, is too great for an idling plane to run up it, especially when the mains were still on the grass. He had to increase the power quite a bit to get it moving."

"But ..." Jameson thought for a moment. I waited. "Those other guys would have heard the change in the sound of the engine."

"Not necessarily. The wind was making such a racket that you couldn't hear yourself think. I remember that because the fellow I gave the flight test to and I had to shout at each other even standing side by side. Also, the wind was blowing from behind the two men toward the plane, and would have sort of blown the sound away. I think what must have happened is that Margolin gradually increased his power, holding the brakes, while he was sitting there waiting for Conrad and Gilley to finish their talk. Then when Gilley turned away and Conrad started back toward the plane, Margolin released the brakes and the plane surged forward. He kept his foot on the right rudder pedal to turn it toward Conrad. When the prop hit Conrad, he cut the power and let the plane roll back. There's a fair slope to that taxiway. It would have taken power to roll up it, but the plane would very nicely roll back by itself."

Jameson turned his lips in between his teeth and rubbed a hand across his mouth. His eyes were fixed on a far corner of the room, narrowed in concentration. Suddenly he switched his attention back to me and said, "I'll talk to Nash. He'll probably come to see you and get a statement." He sighed. "I wish we could get that sort of description from witnesses at more accident or crime scenes."

"It's just a matter of special knowledge," I murmured modestly.

He grinned. "And a sharp proficiency at observation." I was flattered. Then a cloud passed over the ray of sunshine. I shifted uncomfortably.

"I'd like to ask you a favour," I said hesitantly.

"What is it?"

"That you not use my name. I know you have to tell Cpl. Nash. But I mean outside the police investigation."

"That may not be possible," he answered cautiously.

"But if at all possible. I'll tell you why. It's related to the other problem I had on my mind today. You see, Margolin was pretty sore about my telling his passengers they shouldn't fly into that storm. He's suing me for slander."

"I see. And if he knew you'd also accused him of murder … "

"Exactly!"

Cpl. Nash almost beat me to the airport. I'd stopped to buy a newspaper. I didn't subscribe because I felt that the local rag, The Chronicle, was not worth the cost of the subscription. But I wanted to see what they had to say about Conrad's death. As I parked my white Ford Ranger pickup with the red logo on the sides, a police car slid into the spot beside me. The young constable driving it and Cpl. Nash got out, greeted me and followed me into the office. I did a few of my normal beginning of the day chores, then invited them into my office.

The office was spare and functional. I spent little time in it. A plain desk was situated so that I could see out the window, across the ramp to the runway. There were three chairs of the stackable chrome and plastic type to be found in offices all over town, filing cabinets, a bulletin board with aviation notices pinned to it, and on the desk, a telephone and a basket for mail. I offered chairs to the two policemen and took the third myself. The constable pulled out a notebook and ballpoint pen. Throughout the ensuing interview, he never looked up from his task, but diligently recorded what I said.

Nash took me over everything I had told Jameson, occasionally asking knowledgeable questions. He certainly did know the aviation business, and was well aware of the most important regulation that pilots must learn; that the pilot-in-command is completely responsible for everything that happens in and around the aircraft. He hadn't bought Margolin's assertion that Conrad's death was his own fault.

Nash interviewed Rod O'Donnell and got the same information about the way Margolin's Cessna 182 had been parked. He did not express any opinion on whether he believed my allegation of murder. He asked me to drop by the RCMP detachment later in the day to sign a statement.

The men from the Ministry of Transport had been working diligently around the plane and on the ramp. They could have their job!

In the long run, everyone left and as weeks slid by, the public lost interest and turned their morbid attention to other accidents, tragedies, and crimes.

Life got back to normal at Red Robin Flying School. I did decide to go to Idylwyld with Douglas and Betty. My chief flight instructor, Terry McGregor, would take over for the week I was away. This would allow me to judge his ability to take command. Before long he would be applying for a job with the airlines, and a positive report on his ability to assume responsibility for the operation of the school would look good on his résumé.

Eventually the police charged Margolin with a crime, which sent a small shock wave across the airport. Aviation accidents are usually left to the MOT, and penalties enacted by that body. That the RCMP laid charges seemed to indicate that they considered this a more serious incident than usual. I had told no one about my suspicions, and my reaction was different from that of other people. I was disappointed, but I also realized that the police must not have had enough evidence to charge Margolin with murder. They charged him with criminal negligence causing death.

CHAPTER 7

The small maple tree I'd planted in my front yard five years before gave only sparse shade. Even in this shade, the mid-July day was like a broiler. How would you like yourself cooked? Medium rare? The temperature had already reached 40°C and was still climbing. It was one time I was glad I'd be getting out of the Devon Valley.

This interior valley has a semi-arid climate. Air is pushed up over the ranges of mountains to the west, losing its moisture. As the dry air descends into the valley, it heats up, creating Canada's hot spot. Summer temperatures in the upper thirties, and occasionally into the forties are not unusual.

It was Sunday afternoon. I'd left the social hour after church, gone home to change into casual clothes, and pick up my suitcase, which was already packed. I was waiting outside for Douglas and Betty Forsythe to pick me up and transport me to the cooler climes of Squilax Lake.

The Forsythe's brown Jeep Cherokee pulled up to the curb. Douglas got out to open the back and I deposited my suitcase beside theirs. Betty noticed Cloud Nine on the inside of the living room window, seeming to implore me not to leave him.

"Is someone taking care of your cat?" she asked as I climbed into the back seat.

"Yes. Grace DeBerg who lives across the street. She's a dispatcher for the RCMP. I think you've talked to her a time or two." This last remark was directed to

Douglas who nodded. "Grace is also going to care for my lawn. She loves Cloud Nine and spoils him hopelessly."

"Not that you don't." Betty turned and gave me a knowing grin.

"What have you done with Shadrach and Meshach?" I asked, naming the Forsythe's two young cats.

"They're staying with Chris Whitney. Douglas thought they'd be terrified to be boarded at a kennel, didn't you, Dear? But the little monsters seemed delighted to see Chris and didn't even give us a farewell meow."

We left the valley, climbing over a range of mountains and descending gradually along slopes densely forested with conifers, into the next, somewhat higher, valley. The climate here was more moist, the terrain greener, the weather marginally cooler. We turned northward along a lake created by damming the river. Our own Lake Devon is a natural lake, one of several along the course of its river.

There was no traffic at all on what appeared to be a major highway. We drove at a leisurely pace through groves of trees, around jutting points of rock, and through meadows where cattle grazed. We passed no one. No hurrying vehicle clamoured to pass us. Finally a speeding car approached from the opposite direction. It had barely whizzed by when along came another, then another. Several cars passed, all in a hurry. Then we passed a sedately moving pickup truck pulling a fifth-wheel camping trailer. As suddenly as it had come, the knot of traffic exited the scene, and we were again left alone in the beauty of the mountain valley.

Suddenly Douglas emitted a great guffaw.

"What's gotten into you?" Betty inquired.

"I think we just missed the ferry."

To punctuate his remark, around the next bend we passed a sign. "Ferry, 2 Km," it said.

"How often does it go?"

"Probably once each hour."

"Oh well. I guess it's as good a place as any to stop for lunch."

We pulled up just short of the wooden arm extending across the highway, shut down and got out. The ferry could be seen chugging slowly out into the lake, two hundred yards offshore. On a grassy knoll adjacent to the road, a picnic area had been built. We took a stroll through the trees to the rocky cliff on the water's edge, and stood admiring the view across the tranquil turquoise lake with its reflections of surrounding mountains and of the few puffy, white cumulus clouds that hung atop the peaks. Back at the picnic area Betty began to unpack a cooler, laying out sandwiches, salad and pickles, while Douglas set a large thermos on a picnic table and drew off drinks for each of us.

After we had eaten, Betty shooed us away while she cleaned up. Douglas and I found a shady spot on the cool grass and sat languidly, taking in the beauty of the day.

"I understand you're worried about this lawsuit," Douglas remarked neutrally. His voice conveyed the impression that if I wanted to talk about it he'd listen, if I didn't, he'd drop the subject.

The peace of the day vanished as if someone had punctured a balloon. I felt my muscles tense.

"Yes, I am."

"Why? I thought it was pretty clear that you warned these people about an oncoming storm that it wouldn't be safe to fly into, and that everyone agrees that you saved their lives."

"They don't think so."

"Surely, once that storm hit, they must have realized it."

"They apparently didn't notice. There was some big upheaval in their business, some power play, and when they went to the motel, they were so involved with it that they didn't even notice the weather."

"I find that hard to believe."

"It's possible though. If their rooms were on the bottom floor, facing inward toward the patio, they may not have realized the extent of the storm if they were distracted by their business problems."

"What is this power play you refer to?"

"According to the junior member of the threesome, the other two were partners and one of them was trying to take control of the business. He thinks the man who was killed was conspiring with the pilot's wife to take over, possibly to take the wife as well."

I saw Douglas' eyebrows go up. I continued, "So if that was true, the pilot who is the one suing me, could have been very distracted and not noticed the weather."

"But surely the judge or jury would look at things more objectively. Is there going to be a jury?"

"Yes. I'd have preferred to have it tried before a judge, with no jury. I think a judge would have enough sense to listen to the witnesses."

"I would imagine a jury would as well. What's worrying you?"

I found myself reluctant to tell Douglas my problem because it involved a parishioner of St. Matthew's whom I knew that Douglas liked. But I'd gone this far, so I might as well unburden myself.

"It's Lew Stern."

"He's representing you, is he?"

"Yes. I like Lew. Don't get me wrong. But I don't think he's the right lawyer for this case."

"Why?" Douglas' tone was non-committal, merely inquiring.

"He doesn't understand aviation. A lot of people think that flying a light plane is inherently dangerous, practically suicidal. They think you're apt to die any time you take off. He's like that, and can't understand what all the fuss is about. He can't see that you are in any more danger under any particular set of circumstances."

"Oh, you're exaggerating." For once there was animation in Douglas' voice.

"No, I'm not. He will go through the motions of defending me, but I know he doesn't really believe in what he's doing."

Douglas' face still wore a thoughtful frown. "But your witnesses should clear you."

"I'm not sure Lew is getting the right ones."

"Then why did you ask him to represent you?" There was a hint of challenge in his voice.

"I didn't at first. One of the pilots who flies with us is a lawyer. His wife is my accountant. He's a vigorous, go-getting type, and of course he understands aviation. But at the time when the case will come up, he's off to UBC to take some courses in a field he is interested in, and won't be available. He suggested two other lawyers who he felt would be good and who know aviation. The first one I called didn't return my call. Several days later, his office called and told me he had suffered a heart attack, and though he survived, he will be forced to retire. The other is Mortimer Thurlow. He's a pilot and a well-known trial lawyer. He's the type of pilot who gives aviation a bad name, like the man who is suing me. He thinks he can set his own rules, considers the controllers at the tower his lackeys, and makes life difficult for other pilots. When I was safety officer at the airport, I had more than one run-in with him. I couldn't have gone to him. But besides, he is the attorney for Harris Margolin. He's probably licking his chops."

Douglas gave a snort of laughter, but there was no amusement in it.

"So, I was left to find a lawyer, and since I hadn't had need for one for years, except to make out my will and the papers on my house, I didn't know where to turn. Lew had handled those things for me, so I asked him. Now I'm sorry I did."

"What about your insurance company? Have you asked them to recommend a lawyer?"

"Yes, but they're being very difficult. If I'd run a fuel truck into Margolin's airplane, they'd have been right out there helping me. But they don't like this slander business. It's not specifically in my policy, and they're trying to weasel out of covering me."

"So if you lose, you may have to pay the judgment yourself?" There was alarm in Douglas' voice.

I nodded. "It could ruin me. Unless I can get the insurance company to cover me after all. But they also insure Thurlow and Margolin."

"Oh, oh!"

"'Oh, oh' is right." I felt my muscles relax as I talked to Douglas. I felt at ease with him again. I used to be able to discuss my problems with him. It had only been in the last few months that I'd found myself reluctant to confide in him. I'd thought that his attitude toward me had changed, but now he seemed his old self. Maybe he hadn't changed at all. Maybe it was me.

"You said something about not having the right witnesses." There was now definite concern in Douglas' tone.

"The controller at the tower and the Flight Service specialist will give factual information, which will confirm what I'm saying about the weather, but they won't express opinions on my actions. They still have to live with Thurlow. They'll be pretty reticent. The key witness will be a person from Transport Canada who works in the area of pilot licensing and enforcing flight standards. Those people are the ones who decide on punishment for breaking the aviation regulations. Margolin is probably going to get hit with some penalty from them for running into his partner with the propeller of his plane."

Betty had joined us, and at the mention of the propeller accident, she gave a squeamish shudder.

"Normally, Transport Canada would back its flight instructors to the hilt. In fact, I've talked to them and they're solidly on my side. But the person they're sending is the worst possible choice of all their inspectors. She is the one woman in the office; her name is Candy, she is tiny and tries to look bigger by piling her hair on top of her head and wearing high-heeled shoes, and she speaks in a small, high-pitched voice. Thurlow will walk all over her."

"Are you sure?" Douglas asked.

84

"He'll wipe the floor with her. He's a male chauvinist of the worst kind. He might have listened to a man, but he wouldn't think of taking advice on flying from a woman. I know Candy. That kind of man can fluster her, and don't think Thurlow won't take advantage of it!"

"Then why don't you ask them to send someone else? Or have Lew ask?"

I ran a nervous hand through my hair. How could I explain my feelings to Douglas? I replied hesitantly, "Because she is a woman."

As I expected, he frowned with incomprehension. It was Betty who said, "Of course."

Douglas looked from one of us to the other, trying to decipher the bond of feminine knowledge that passed between us. Betty said, "Never mind. I'll explain it to you later."

Douglas sat for two or three minutes in deep concentration, his arms wrapped around his knees, his head bowed. Then he straightened up and scrutinized me, an expression of care and concern on his lean, firm-jawed face.

"In the first place, Robin, remember that you are not the only person to have been persecuted unjustly."

The impact of what he had said knocked the stuffing out of me, as a vision of Christ on the cross seared itself into my mind. I couldn't look at Douglas. All I could manage was a weak exclamation. "Oh!"

He watched me for a few moments, then spoke with compassion in his voice. "That does not mean that it is wrong to be concerned. It's human nature. But don't turn in on yourself and wallow in your grief to the point where you lose sight of God. God is with you, whether you recognize it or not. Let Him take some of the load."

I nodded, afraid to speak.

"Don't overlook the value of prayer. Don't be afraid to share your concerns with others so they also can pray for you."

I found my voice. "I don't like to just go to God with a list of things I want. God, do this. God, do that."

"Some people do pray that way. Sort of reading a grocery list of things they want. There is a saying that you should be careful what you pray for, you might get it.

"But that doesn't mean that you can't pray to God for His help. Petition is one of the important elements of prayer. It's not the only one. Thanksgiving is another, as are penitence and adoration. The Lord's Prayer, the great prayer that Jesus gave to his disciples, has all these elements. It starts with praise, adoration. 'Our Father in heaven. Hallowed be Your name.' It moves on to petition. 'Give us this day our daily bread.' Then penitence and forgiveness. 'Forgive us our trespasses as we forgive those who trespass against us.' And thanksgiving. It's all there. It is not complete without all its parts. So don't be afraid to ask for God's help. Open your heart to Him and let Him help you."

I managed a weak smile and quoted, "'Blessed are the poor in spirit, for theirs is the kingdom of heaven.'"

He nodded. "When you need Him most, He will be there."

The throb of a diesel engine broke into our thoughts. The ferry approached the dock; a line of cars had now formed behind ours. We gathered up our picnic paraphernalia and prepared to continue our journey. A journey in a bobbing boat on a tranquil lake, surrounded by God's mighty creation. The symbolism was not lost on me.

CHAPTER 8

Idylwyld teemed with people flocking to the courses. Campers searched for their sites and busied themselves in setting up. Those staying in the residences found their rooms, many wondering what their roommates would be like. Children ran everywhere. There was not enough space for everyone to have a single room, so doubling up was inevitable.

The Forsythes were given a room in the newest of the buildings. Mine was in an older one, but this came with the advantage of afternoon shade from huge cottonwood trees.

The woman handling the registration had been at it for several hours, and was hot and flustered. She looked around her as if expecting a replacement as she explained to one registrant that no, she had not forgotten to give her a key. There were no locks on the doors.

"No locks? Do I have to take everything with me wherever I go?"

"I don't think you need to. We've never had any theft."

"I think it is very strange that one cannot lock one's door. I shan't be able to sleep. Perhaps I will get a motel."

"You're welcome to if you want, but there is only one in the town, and it's always booked solid at this time of year."

"I will expect a refund."

"Of course. But be sure you can get a room first."

The registrant jounced out in a huff, just as Idylwyld's secretary hove into view. The woman at the desk explained what had transpired and the secretary, whose name, according to the tag she wore, was Nell, shrugged and seemed unconcerned.

"She's been a problem all along. She insisted on a single; absolutely refused to share a room. Actually, I think she will probably get in at the motel. They often save one room for last minute emergencies. I think I'll call and tell them she's coming." Nell bustled into the inner office.

The receptionist turned her attention to me, the tension draining out of her face. "Your name?"

"Robin Carruthers. Here. This says I'm in number ten in Pine Lodge." I passed my registration form across the counter to her.

She ran her finger down the master list until she reached number ten, then gasped. The first of the two names listed opposite that number was not mine. She studied the name for several seconds then blushed beet red. "There must be a mistake."

"Why?"

"Your roommate is listed as Colin Broadstreet."

"Colin? As in Mr. Colin Broadstreet?"

She nodded, looking as if she expected me to slap her. Nell scurried over.

"What's the problem?" she asked.

"Robin here has been put in the same room as Colin Broadstreet."

Nell peered at the list, then raised her head and looked me over. "Are you Robin?" She made it sound like an accusation.

"Yes, I am," I replied, not trying to hide the annoyance in my voice.

"I'm sorry. We thought you would be a man."

"Why?"

"Because when you called and left your number on the answering machine, you said to call you at some flying school but you'd be out flying until some specified time, so we assumed you were a man."

"Again the question is, why?"

"Well, pilots are men."

"Not all of them. I happen to own Red Robin Flying School, and have done so for over twenty years. Also, when you did call back, I was the one you talked to. My voice is recognizably female."

"Oh, but we assumed you were the secretary."

The receptionist cut in. "What are we going to do?"

"The motel did have a room, so that last woman will be out of her single. We can put Robin in there." To me she said, "It's sort of tiny, but it's the only place we have left."

"And what are you doing with Mr. Colin Broadstreet?" I asked, emphasizing the name.

"He can stay in number ten."

"A double room all to himself?"

Nell squirmed, then nodded. "Yes."

"Why can't I have the room I was scheduled for way back in March?"

"Well, Mr. Broadstreet has already moved in."

"Does he know who his roommate was to be?"

"I... I don't think he asked," the receptionist said tentatively.

"Please don't tell him. I don't want to be the butt of jokes. I'll take your single."

Nell gushed with relief, falling all over herself to make me welcome. I found the room. It was indeed tiny, but neat and pleasant, with a private bathroom with shower.

I had envisaged a communal washroom, but this was like a motel. No TV though. There wasn't one anywhere on the grounds. My smouldering anger dissipated as I viewed the compact but attractive unit.

I unpacked, then went in search of the Forsythes, finding them on the deck of Spruce Lodge. I told them about the mix-up, which by now seemed funny. I'm always annoyed by people who assume that anyone who flies, especially anyone who makes a living at flying, is a man. I usually let my annoyance show. It's partly an act, to make them think twice before they make another assumption about what is suitable for a woman to do. But I could also put myself in the place of the poor receptionist who had found herself faced with five feet ten of angry redhead. The Forsythes also saw the humour in the confrontation. I swore them to secrecy.

We walked up to the village of Mallard Beach for a light snack, since we had arrived too late for supper in Idylwyld's dining hall. The coffee shop was packed, and we played a game of guessing why each group of diners was there. One family group, we decided, was at the end of a day's travel, had a room at the motel, and because the father seemed to be one of those well-organized types, we assumed they'd be up at the crack of dawn to be on their way. The two squirming children responded to a quick word or a meaningful glance from the mother. When she rose to leave and turned around, all our calculations went right out the window. She was wearing a clerical collar, and was obviously one of our fellow scholars at Idylwyld.

Hers was the only clerical collar I saw all week, and it was gone the next day. She, like all the rest of us, turned out in shorts and T-shirt. Even the two bishops wore casual clothes.

I was up and dressed by five the next morning. The sun coloured the mountaintops but its light had not yet dipped into the valley. A chill to the air sent me reaching for a light jacket. I wasn't the only early bird. Douglas also was up, and I met him at the top of the trail down through a thick cedar forest to the shore of the lake. I felt a bit embarrassed at meeting a married man and going for a walk with him that early in the morning, but we weren't the only ones up and about. Douglas didn't show any reticence, so I decided to act casual. There had been a time when I'd have been very nervous about meeting Douglas like that. What would I say to him? Would he spot my feelings for him? What would Betty think? But it had not been long after I had met them when I realized that marital infidelity was not something Betty suspected in her husband. Besides, clergy wives must be used to female parishioners talking to their husbands about very intimate things. A jealous wife wouldn't last very long. Betty and I had become fast friends.

With Douglas in the lead, we made our way down the switchbacks on the trail, walked across the broad, gently curving beach, which appeared to extend off endlessly in both directions, and drank in the tranquil setting. Not a breath of wind rippled the surface of the water. A mother duck with four ducklings in tow glided by, paying us not the slightest heed. A short distance from the shore, the still water was explosively disrupted by a surfacing loon. The bird skimmed across the water for a minute or two, then dived again. Long minutes passed. Then it reappeared, far from the spot where it had dived.

The line of sunlight marched relentlessly down the opposite mountainside and touched the far shoreline. A puff of wind disturbed the reflection of the mountains. Then the distant sound of a motorboat reminded us that this was a much different lake in the middle of the day.

We climbed back up the hill and ambled lazily over to Spruce Lodge, where we found Betty, still in her dressing gown, brewing a pot of tea.

"I don't know where Douglas gets his energy," Betty said, yawning. "This is early for me."

At seven thirty, we were among the early birds in line for breakfast in the dining hall. We were served pancakes and sausages, then took our trays to a large table laden with cereal, fruit, sweet rolls and assorted condiments. I ladled out a large helping of porridge and covered it with milk and brown sugar, poured syrup over my pancakes, then picked out pieces of melon and orange. I seldom eat breakfast, but having it spread out before me, being relieved of doing the dishes, and not having to rush off to work, combined to give me an appetite. I'd better spend my afternoons doing active exercise, I told myself. Otherwise I'd gain ten pounds!

A young woman well along in pregnancy was just ahead of me in line. She carefully chose fruit and yoghurt then looked longingly at the sweet rolls. A large, flabby man with blond hair and a bushy moustache bypassed me in the line, and sidled up to the pregnant woman, casually bumping into her. She looked up, murmured "Sorry" and went on about her deliberations. She reached for a sweet roll.

"Good morning, little lady," said the flabby man. His eyes went up and down her body in a way that reminded me of a male cat detecting the odour of a female on someone's clothes. I could almost see him curl his lip back. His eyes rested on her protruding belly. "You're looking great."

Her discomfort was clearly evident. He had her wedged in between himself, the table and the person ahead in line.

"Excuse me," she said softly, pleadingly, as she tried to manoeuvre around him. He stood his ground. I stepped forward and muscled my way toward the table in front of him. The woman made her escape. I caught up with her.

"Come sit with us," I invited, indicating the table where Douglas and Betty were unloading their trays. She looked quickly over her shoulder. The big man continued to eye her. She followed me to the table.

"I hope he doesn't come over here," she said.

He did though.

"Looks like there's still room at this table," he said in an overly loud, blustering voice.

"We're saving it for someone," was my firm reply.

Miffed, he moved away.

I looked around for some other isolated soul and spotted a sprightly-looking little woman with snow-white hair peering around as if deciding where to sit. I caught her attention and motioned her to sit with us.

"Hi. I'm Lucy." The white-haired lady must have been in her seventies but was chipper as a bird. She set her tray on the table and cast a quick glance around the room. "I was looking for friends, but they aren't here yet."

"I'm Robin. This is Betty… and Douglas. I don't know your name," I said, turning to the pregnant young woman.

"Kathy," she replied.

Lucy acknowledged the introductions. "I think we're supposed to have name tags, but they weren't ready yet." She surveyed the room, her eyes first sliding over the flabby man, then coming back to rest on him. "Good grief! There's Colin! I wonder what he's doing here?"

"Colin?" I asked, alarmed.

"Yes. Colin Broadstreet. He's a joke around our church. Everyone says he just comes to church because he heard that there are three times as many women as men. I guess he figures that the same will apply here. He's always on the make. Doesn't do him any good, though. None of the single women pay him any attention."

Kathy shuddered. "I can't stand him."

"Don't worry, honey. He's harmless."

I glanced across the table at Douglas and Betty. They had their faces buried in their coffee cups, trying their darndest not to break out laughing.

Lucy was in my course and sat beside me. She wore white shorts and a sleeveless red blouse. Her white hair, done up all over her head in curls, surrounded her face like a halo. Her carriage was erect, her movements quick and decisive. You had to see her up close to be aware of her age. Her deeply tanned face was wrinkled, the skin on her hands thin with prominent veins showing.

"That was a lovely worship service this morning. Very pastoral," she said. "I like the morning services here. They're so much more relaxed than in church."

We'd been in an outdoor chapel, with people sitting in lawn chairs or on the ground. The female priest we had seen the night before was the celebrant. She was in casual clothes, the only concession to the conventional being the green stole draped across her shoulders. Two communion stations had been set up, one in the front and one in the back of the assembled throng. Youth workers administered the bread and the cup. The hymns, to the accompaniment of two guitars and a recorder, were modern and upbeat.

"I just hope they don't make us sing She Flies On," Lucy remarked. "I'm not into this feminist stuff."

"Me either," I replied. "Father, Son and Holy Spirit is just fine with me."

We were interrupted by the entrance of the two bishops. We rose as they entered, but Bishop Michael, looking embarrassed, pleaded, "Don't do that. Treat us like anyone else here. This is a very informal place, as you will see. As to what to call us, I'm Michael and this is John." Archbishop John Radcliff was a tall, heavyset man with a shock of wiry black hair speckled with grey, a square face, ruddy in complexion, wearing blue jeans and a short-sleeved polo shirt, stretched in front to cover his protruding stomach. Michael himself wore neatly creased off-white trousers, and a pale blue checked shirt. He looked very tidy. I remembered that he was always an extremely neat dresser, and wondered if he'd become more relaxed and grubby as the week wore on. He was a tall, thin man with pale blond hair, rimless spectacles, and very pale blue eyes. His clear tenor voice contrasted with the Archbishop's deep rumble.

"Let me outline the way this course will proceed," Michael explained. "I'll do the morning sessions, giving you the meat and potatoes. John will lead the evening sessions. He'll provide the dessert. He will be telling you how to put together a sermon. I will be trying to tell you how to analyze the scriptures." He paused for effect. "All in five days," he added. We laughed.

A man who I had not seen before entered the room quietly and sat down in an empty chair beside me. "Sorry to be late," he whispered. "Had to do some village business before I could come." Later when we paired off for discussion, he introduced himself as Gordon Saunders. He lived in Mallard Beach and served on the village council. He was a teacher in the local junior secondary school, now out on holiday. He attended the local church, St. Aidan's, which was one part of a three-point parish. Lay people frequently played roles in the services; roles that were unknown to those of us from larger churches. He was a veteran preacher. All this came out when we formed into small groups and became acquainted with each other. His slender frame was well muscled. He wore Spandex and carried a bicycle helmet. Considering the hilly terrain in the area, he must have been a dedicated athlete.

At the conclusion of the morning session, Michael asked for volunteers to preach sermons. Only a few of us could have the opportunity, as there were sixty in the class. There were two possibilities; to preach to the class on Wednesday or Thursday evening, or to preach to the entire ensemble at the morning services. He asked for an experienced preacher to do the Tuesday and Wednesday morning service. Gordon Saunders volunteered for Wednesday. Several others agreed to preach to the class.

"I need more people to preach at the morning services. Just short homilies, five or six minutes long." He looked around expectantly.

I don't know what got into me. I'd been a Christian for only a couple of years. I felt that my knowledge of scripture was very weak. I really hadn't come here to learn to preach, but to have my spiritual batteries recharged. St. Matthew's, Exeter did not need an amateur lay preacher. So what was I doing raising my hand?

"Robin." Michael gestured in my direction.

"I'll preach if it can be Friday morning."

"Fine. You're on. Anyone else for the other days?"

Lucy, encouraged by my example, volunteered for Thursday, and another experienced preacher agreed to do Tuesday.

"Now!" Michael rubbed his hands. "I'll tell you what I want you to do. We have chosen several significant times in the Christian year and will ask you to preach a sermon appropriate to one of these days. They are Advent One, Epiphany, Lent One, Trinity, The Reign of Christ, ..." He went on naming specific days from the Christian calendar, then put slips of paper in a hat and had us pull out one at random.

I groaned when I saw mine. First Sunday in Lent, year C. The slip went on to say, "The temptations of Christ." One of the most difficult subjects to deal with in all of scripture, judging by the misinterpretations that many people have about it. I was to preach on this in front of a bishop, an archbishop and several clergy, including my own rector! What had I gotten myself into?

After lunch I stretched out in a lawn chair for a few moments' relaxation before going to the library to study. A variety of reference books had been left for us to use. I'd better start boning up on temptations.

Douglas and Betty came out of the dining room and headed my way, but before they got to where I was sitting, they were waylaid by Bishop Michael and his wife, Gerry. They all greeted each other with exclamations of joy and with generous hugs. Sitting alone, I felt definitely left out.

"Hi! Your friends seem to have made a hit with the bishop." Lucy flopped into a chair beside me.

"They're old classmates. Douglas is our rector. He and Michael were seminary classmates, and Betty went to university with them as well."

"You look glum," Lucy observed.

"I'm always the third person. I never quite fit."

"You don't have any family?"

"No. I've been divorced for years, I didn't have children, and my parents are dead. I don't have any close relatives, and the ones I do have live back east."

"How about people you work with?"

I shook my head. "I run a flight school. Most professional pilots are men. I don't fit in. When we have a social gathering, I'm not one of the boys and I sure don't belong with the wives. I have friends in church, but they are either married with families, or single with families, or single and on the lookout for male companionship."

"Well, you don't have to feel left out here. This is your first time at Idylwyld, isn't it?"

I nodded.

"You'll find that this is your spiritual home, and every time you come it will be like a family reunion. I know a dozen or so people here from previous conferences. You'll be one of the crowd the next time you come." She reached out an arm and put it around my shoulder. "See! You've already got one spiritual sister."

I grinned. "And I don't even know her last name."

Lucy laughed. "Merriman," she said.

"It suits you. But it should be Merriwoman."

"Remember, we said no feminist language."

The Forsythes had parted from the bishop and his wife and headed my way. "Let's take a walk around the grounds to help our lunch settle," Betty suggested.

"I've got to hit the books. The bishop gave us homework."

"That's right," Lucy agreed. "But first I'm going down into the canyon. I hear there's a new trail."

"Canyon?" Betty asked.

"Over there on the east side. There's a little stream that flows down through it. It's very wild."

"Umm. I think just a gentle walk around the place is more my pace right now."

"Okay. See you later." Lucy bounced off. What energy for a woman her age!

I decided that a little exercise wouldn't hurt, so Betty, Douglas and I strolled around the periphery of the estate, keeping to the shade, smelling the scent of trees and flowers, trying to identify the birds. At the top of the grounds, we came upon one of the youth workers sitting on a log and calling to a large, longhaired ginger cat. The boy was probably sixteen, tall already, with full lips and curly black hair tumbling down his forehead. His facial features were not yet mature, but in a few more years, he would be a handsome young man.

The cat ambled sedately over toward him. It was extremely fat. The boy held out his hand and talked in a soft voice.

"What is this? Is this a cat? This is a cat. This is a very fat cat. What is a cat? A cat is a furry creature with four legs. It is sharp on all four corners. It has a tongue that was used as a model for sandpaper. A cat is … What else are you, Cat?"

The cat having reached the boy, turned to rub on his leg, arching its back and making kneading motions with its front feet. Saliva drooled from its mouth, forming long ropes that hung from the hair on its chin.

"You're a mess, do you know it?" the boy said, wiping his hand on his jeans. He saw us and scrambled to his feet.

"Don't get up," Douglas commanded. "You seem to have a friend there."

"This is Paprika. She belongs to the cook."

"That's an appropriate name. We have a cat the same colour, but he's long and lean."

"I think Paprika gets special handouts," the boy said. He wore a nametag. It said "Todd."

"Well, Todd. We'll leave you and Paprika alone. We're just wandering around."

As we walked along the eastern boundary of the estate, we realized what Lucy had meant by "the canyon." What from a distance appeared to be a wall of trees, was instead the top of a deep cleft in the ground. It couldn't have been more than fifty yards across at the top, but was quite deep. We could hear the sound of a small creek, but could not see it. The walls of the cleft were nearly vertical, but trees grew out of them, the trunks bending upward once the trees had grown out far enough from the steep slope. They were predominantly cedar and pine, but interspersed were a variety of deciduous trees. Some had lost their hold on the side of the canyon and toppled across it. The result was a dense mat of growth. The canyon formed a gentle curve, the upper part angling away to the east.

We strolled downward toward the beach. Ahead of us, a head of white hair appeared, then Lucy's torso seemed to rise up from the ground like Erda in a performance of Wagner's Ring. Finally her whole body appeared. She stopped, placed her hands on her knees and panted for breath.

"I've been all the way down and back. There's a new trail, but it's still quite steep." She took a few more deep breaths. "Whew! It's worth it though. It's so serene and tranquil down there. It's incredibly beautiful. You'll have to go down. Pardon me, though, if I don't go with you. I'm out of shape."

The three of us exchanged glances. "Shall we?" I asked.

"Do go. You'll love it," Lucy by now had her wind back.

"Let's," said Betty eagerly.

"I'm going to go down there every day for meditation," Lucy stated. "By the end of the week, I'll be able to climb back up a lot easier."

We headed down the steep, narrow trail, carved out of the hillside and held in place on the outer edge by long, slim logs. Logs had also been used on the outer edges of occasional steps. The descent was steep, the trail switching back half way down. A bench had been placed at this point.

We were near the bottom before we saw the creek. It was a small stream, rushing restlessly downward, splashing recklessly over its rocky bed. A tree had fallen into the stream a few yards upstream, forming a waterfall. The scouring effect of the water had produced a pool below the falls, and at this point, the floor of the crevasse widened to about fifteen feet. On the edge of a small area of flat ground, a bench had been made from a half log resting in notches cut into two trees.

There was just room for the three of us on the bench. In front of us, moss spread across the floor like a green carpet. The brook gurgled around the far side of the flat spot, the water clear, the stream bed lined with small, multi-coloured pebbles. No sunlight penetrated more than half way down the walls, even though it was mid-day. The air was blue, the temperature at least ten degrees cooler than on the surface. We sat languidly, not wanting to leave, to climb the steep trail to the top. It was one of the last peaceful moments we would have.

CHAPTER 9

The library was crowded; piles of books strewn across the tables. Students from my class read silently or conversed in pairs, a low hum of conversation permeating the room. At one point, Bishop Michael entered, halted, and viewed his students with amazement, then quietly withdrew. I found a New Revised Standard Version of the Bible, and looked up the passage in the Gospel of Luke that had been appointed for the first Sunday in Lent of year C. I read it twice, then read the corresponding passages in Matthew and Mark, those being the ones for years A and B of the liturgical calendar. Then I read the verses in a King James Bible, and studied the material again. My dismay at this assignment slowly evaporated. I passed through a feeling of contentment, like curling up in a comfortable chair to read a good book. Then a fire seemed to light itself deep within me, as a new, more profound awareness came out of my quest.

What was this about? Trust, I decided. Trust in God. Wasn't this what Douglas had talked about as we waited for the ferry?

I finished my session of study with a perception that I had passed a milestone in my spiritual journey. The material for my sermon was laid out before me; now to put it in proper form.

To help us do that, Archbishop John Radcliff was our mentor. As a way of loosening us up, he started the evening session by reliving some of his own early experiences as a preacher, emphasizing the gaffes as well as the little triumphs. He exhibited a wicked sense of humour, and soon had us roaring with laughter.

At twenty to eight, Gordon Saunders quietly slipped out of his chair and whispered to me, "I have to go to the village council meeting. We're voting on casinos. I'm not in favour, but I'll be outvoted, and I want to at least limit it to one."

The students entered into the exercises with enthusiasm, and often with hilarity. I could not remember attending a class where I had learned as much in as short a time, and had as much fun doing it. Being in the teaching trade, this made a profound impression on me. How could I capture the essence of this course and apply it to flight training? Budding pilots groan at the thought of ground school. I'd have to re-evaluate how we taught it.

Before the worship service each morning, Bishop Michael explained to the gathering that the sermons would be given by students in the class on preaching, and that the topics had been selected as part of the assignment, and were not relevant to the readings for the day. He gave a brief summary of the text from which the sermon would be taken. We knew the topics well enough to understand the sermon without hearing the entire reading. On Tuesday, the text was the passage from Exodus that related the crossing of the Red Sea. A woman from one of the small parishes in the diocese — this one had nine members — who was already an experienced preacher, gave an interesting and well thought out interpretation of this famous passage. I would have to work hard to reach the level of competence that this woman had shown.

We had a half hour before the courses got underway. Lucy wanted to go down into the canyon, but I declined. She might be thirty years my senior, but the thought of going with her on that strenuous a jaunt didn't appeal to me so soon after breakfast. I found Douglas and Betty discussing another stroll around the grounds.

"Let's do it while it's still cool. Today is going to be the usual scorcher," Douglas suggested. We started up the dirt road along the edge of the canyon. The road consisted of two tracks with a centreline of grass. Delivery trucks, bearing food for the kitchen, used it, but all other traffic traveled over the main entry road. This track had once been a route to the beach, but a barrier crossed it at the point where it began a steep descent down the hill from the level bench occupied by Idylwyld's buildings. Hikers used it as an alternate to the more gentle trail through the forest. I had come up this road the previous afternoon, after a quick afternoon dip in the cold waters of the lake.

As we started up the track, we were barely aware of the sound of a truck, driven slowly in a low gear. The loud cracking of tree branches caught our attention. Ahead of us, on the dirt track, a truck pulling a trailer with half of a doublewide mobile home had tried to get under an overhanging maple tree, and hadn't made it. The driver exited the cab amid loud cursing, spreading his arms, then letting them drop to his sides in an expression of helplessness. He grabbed a mobile phone from his belt and hastily dialled a number. The ensuing conversation was loud and heated. Out of the corner of my eye, I caught sight of the youth worker, Todd, sprinting toward the offices.

"Well, goddam it, you told me to take the old road to the beach," the truck driver shouted. He listened for a moment. "Go fuck yourself!" he bellowed, turned off the phone, and threw it onto the seat of the truck.

The mobile home was stuck solid, the top corner wedged tightly against a large limb of the tree. A section of roof had been peeled back like the lid of a sardine can. The walls at the corner had buckled inward. We waited and watched, not being able to help in any way, and not wanting to get in range of the angry driver. Idylwyld's maintenance man appeared on the scene. As he conversed with the driver, it was evident he was trying to calm the man down. Soon the Director, Dr. Evelyn McNaughton, came hurrying over. She consulted with the maintenance man, then spoke in a kindly voice to the driver, whose belligerence was rapidly evaporating in the calmness that the others brought with them.

A car roared down the lane, screeching to a halt beyond the mobile home, throwing up a spray of dust and small stones. Its driver flung open the door, and charged toward the trio beside the truck. The trucker's back was to me, but I could see him tense his shoulder muscles and bunch his hands into huge fists. The newest arrival, though tall, was a pudgy young man and probably no match for the truck driver. He'd better watch what he says, I thought.

The conversation was heated and animated, the trucker defending himself against the new man's accusations, his fists still clenched.

"Now calm down, everyone," Dr. McNaughton remonstrated. "You," she indicated the newest arrival, "come with me to the office." She turned toward the trucker. "Bill here will help you get your truck out. If you can back it up and get free of the tree, you may drive across the lawn to the entrance road. The ground is dry enough, I don't think it will hurt it any. That will save you having to back clear out to the highway."

The trucker nodded. "Thanks ma'am." He and Bill, the maintenance man, turned their attention to the problem of extricating the mobile home.

The other man returned to his car. I saw him sitting there, dialling numbers on his cell-phone. It appeared that nobody was answering. By the third call, the man was punching numbers as if punishing the phone for not making the connections he wanted. After three calls, I saw him slam the antenna back into the phone and throw it on the seat. The car dug dirt and gravel as he backed up to a place where he could turn around. A while later I saw him coming down the road to the office.

The trucker climbed back into the cab, put the truck in reverse and slowly backed the trailer out from under the tree. As the large limb that had caught the corner of the mobile home let go, it took a piece with it, the screech punctuating the morning air.

"What on earth is going on?" We turned to see Lucy, wide-eyed with astonishment, standing at the top of the trail into the canyon. We explained.

"I don't believe it," she said. "Here I am coming up from a time of quiet meditation — you can't hear anything from the outside world down there — and the first thing when I get back up here, I hear this poor tree screaming."

"I don't think it was the tree," I replied. "It was metal on the trailer ripping."

"Whatever! Anyway, it sure broke my peaceful mood!"

It was nearly time for our courses to begin. We trooped over to the main building, where the lecture rooms were located. This took us past the office. The pudgy young man stood facing Dr. McNaughton, who leaned against the counter with her arms folded and a frown on her face, as she listened to a long-winded explanation given too rapidly, in a voice that lacked conviction. We stopped to listen.

"You will have to pay for damage to the tree. It appears to be substantial," Dr. McNaughton was stating firmly.

"Of course, of course. The trucking company will have insurance." He was about thirty years old, tall, overweight, with a shaggy brown beard that needed a trim. His trousers and shirt could stand pressing; he was sweating profusely, moist patches showing under his arms and down his back.

He seemed vaguely familiar, but I couldn't place him. Maybe someone I'd seen at the cafe on Sunday night, when we were doing our guessing game about our fellow diners.

As I was thinking this, Colin Broadstreet bumped up against me. "Hello there. You're here alone, aren't you?"

I moved away from him and gave him a frosty glare. "No," I answered curtly.

"Oh! I thought you were."

I turned my back. Now I knew who the man talking to the Director looked like, I thought. He had the same build, the same whining voice as Colin Broadstreet.

Broadstreet, recognizing a cold shoulder, or a cold back, when he saw one, moved away.

Lucy divided her attention between the scene in the office and that being played out between me and Colin Broadstreet.

"Brrr!" She shivered as if a sudden gust of cold wind had blown down the hallway. "I can feel it! Can't you just feel the presence of evil?"

CHAPTER 10

Gordon Saunders didn't arrive until shortly before the mid-morning break. I had saved a seat for him, since he seemed to enjoy my company, and I found him interesting. In the back of my mind there was also the thought that when I was with him, I'd be free from the advances of Colin Broadstreet. Gordon looked like a cat that had just dined on canaries with cream. As he parked his bicycle helmet under his chair, I couldn't wait for an opportunity to quiz him.

"How'd it go last night?" I asked as we lined up for coffee.

"The council approved casinos, but I was successful in limiting it to one."

"You look tickled with something. I thought maybe you'd gotten them banned."

"Not a hope! This council is into grabbing tax revenue from any source it can."

"What's got you grinning then?"

He chuckled as if telling himself a joke. "I heard what happened here this morning. I guess old Harris got himself thoroughly scotched."

"Does that have something to do with this casino issue?"

"Yep! That was the end of the more unsavoury competitor."

Gordon filled a coffee cup and passed it to me, then got one for himself, spooned sugar into it, and poured in a dollop of milk. We found a table in the shade on the north side of the building and sat down.

"There were two competitors for the casino. When we agreed to letting only one set up, the two of them wanted to know how we would decide. We argued about that for half an hour, and couldn't reach an agreement.

"One of the outfits is run by a reputable businessman. He owns the Hilltop Steakhouse, which, by the way, is an excellent place to eat if you're looking for a change from Idylwyld's chow. We would like to see it go to him, but this other outfit has a lot of money behind it. What we finally decided on was that the first one to be able to set up and start operating would get the nod. We thought that would give the advantage to Hilltop, because they had bought up the old supermarket building that has been empty since the grocery chain moved into a larger store.

"This other outfit had some lake-shore property and were just holding it, waiting for something good to come along. That something turned out to be the casino issue. When they first heard of it, they went out and bought some equipment from a town down in the Lower Mainland that had to close its casino when there was a change in government, and the new one threw the casinos out. So they were sitting here with several bays in a mini-storage place full of gambling equipment, and no place to use it. Hilltop made a deal with an outfit in Georgetown that manufactures slot machines and other stuff to supply them whenever they got the go-ahead."

Gordon stopped to drain his coffee cup, went for a quick refill, then went on with his tale.

"Well, one outfit had the building but not the equipment, the other had the equipment but not the place to put it. Hilltop's owner, Demmy Scropos, got on the phone to the president of the company that was making their stuff — got him at home — and had him load a bunch of slots onto a rented truck, and send it up here overnight. In the meantime, the other guys got the local mobile home dealer to deliver a doublewide to their land down on the lake. It looked as if they'd gotten the jump after all.

"We'd secretly agreed to be available for Demmy once he got his equipment delivered. We all just happened to come into the Town Hall this morning, and all go out to coffee together. When we heard about this half of the double-wide getting stuck on a tree down here, and connected it up with these guys who are trying to get a license for a casino, we scattered out of there like a covey of quail being flushed by a dog. We didn't want to be available for those guys!

"The mayor went down to the beach, when they finally got the thing down there. He took a look at it and decided that it was uninhabitable. The young fellow who'd been in charge of the moving operation came to the mayor and objected, saying they could repair it in no time. The other half had already been delivered, by another road that's not well known except to the locals. They didn't want to make a show of it by taking it down the main access road."

Gordon leaned back, drew his feet up to the edge of the bench and wrapped his hands around his knees as if hugging himself. "The mayor decided that the building inspector should be called in to pass on the structural integrity of the mobile home, but the building inspector doesn't want to get caught in the middle on this, so he's been strangely absent. No one can find him. In the meantime, Hilltop's load of goods came in, and they're busy installing it. They say they'll be open for business tonight."

"Good grief! What a mix-up. Will you give them the license?"

"Probably. I'll give you the next instalment tonight."

Colin Broadstreet made himself a nuisance again at lunch. Gordon wasn't around to act as a buffer. Colin managed to sit at the same table I was sharing with some of the course participants. Douglas and Betty were having lunch with Wilson Noble, their course leader, and Bishop Michael and Gerry, so our little table group was broken up. As we finished our meal, Colin leaned across the table and suggested, "How about you and me going for a drive this afternoon. I'm getting kinda tired of this place. There's not even a TV set anywhere."

"No thanks. I have to study."

"Ah, come on!"

"No."

I made a hasty departure, and partly to get away from him, I decided to go down into the canyon. It would be a good place to quietly meditate upon my sermon topic.

I was about fifty yards away from the top of the trail when I heard a long, wailing scream rising from the depths of the earth. It increased in intensity, until suddenly Lucy Merriman's white head popped up over the rim. By that time, I had reached her, and others, Gordon among them, were also running toward the sound. I caught her in my arms and asked, "Lucy, what is it?"

She emitted one last great sob, her body shaking. Then she raised her head, stared into my face and wailed, "There's a dead man down there!"

Someone said, "Are you sure?"

"Yes. He's wedged in the fork of a tree. I think his neck is broken. His body is hanging down one side and his head down the other. Ohhh! It's so horrible."

I felt her body go limp in my arms. I eased her onto the ground on a grassy spot in the shade. I felt her pulse. It was rapid, but strong and regular. She'd fainted then, not had a heart attack. I had a vague impression of activity around us, but didn't pay much attention to it. Words came to my ears, and later I found that I could remember them, but at the moment, my attention was entirely on Lucy.

"Let's go see," one of the men suggested, as he headed toward the top of the trail. But Gordon interposed himself between the man and the trail.

"No! If he's dead we can't help him, so we should leave everything alone and not trample all over the place. Someone call 911."

"I think someone has."

The cook, a young woman with the approximate shape of Paprika, her cat, appeared on the scene with a cold, damp towel and placed it on Lucy's forehead. Douglas arrived and knelt beside us. "What happened?"

"She went down to the grotto and found a dead man there. Apparently he's caught in a tree. She thinks his neck is broken."

Douglas stared in disbelief. "Caught in a tree?"

"I think he must have fallen into the canyon."

"Yes. It's steep enough. Does she know who it was?"

"I don't think so. She didn't say, but I got the impression that she didn't."

Lucy began to stir. She moaned, and tried to push the damp towel away. The cook removed it and asked, "Are you feeling better, love?"

Lucy struggled to sit up. Douglas moved over to support her, putting an arm around her shoulders. She leaned against him. Gordon still held his ground, guarding the top of the trail. A siren sounded in the distance, then another, their sound gaining in intensity. Tension seemed to emanate in waves from the silent crowd.

A white RCMP car arrived first, followed closely by an ambulance. The two constables spoke to Gordon. They obviously knew him, and treated him with respect. He explained what had happened in terse sentences, and gestured toward Lucy.

"Stay here," one Mountie said to Gordon. "I'll go down." He turned to the ambulance men. "You'd better come, too, in case he's still alive." They unloaded a basket-type stretcher and headed down the trail in the wake of the Mountie.

The other constable came over and squatted in front of Lucy. In a compassionate voice, he said, "I know it's a shock to you, but can you tell me how you happened to find this dead man?"

Lucy took a deep quavering breath, then rubbed her hands over her face. For once her face and her body looked like those of a seventy-year-old. In a weak voice, she replied, "I like to go down there. It's so peaceful and quiet. There's a bench to sit on by the little creek."

She buried her face in her hands and sobbed.

"Take it easy," the constable said, gently. He lifted his gaze to take in the crowd gathered round. "Did anyone else go down there?" There was a general shaking of heads.

"No, I went alone," Lucy replied. "I didn't see anyone else."

"Do you know who the dead man is?"

"No."

"Do you think it was someone from this place?"

"I don't know. I don't think so. He was on the other side."

"What do you mean, the other side?"

"The place he was caught was part way up the far side."

"You're sure he was dead?"

"He was caught in a notch where one tree fell against another. His body was hanging down one side, and his head down the other. His body was just dangling there limp. His head's at a right angle to it."

She seemed to be getting some strength back, her voice becoming gradually more firm. Rather than leaning on Douglas, she now sat on her own. Someone brought a lawn chair; she got shakily to her feet and moved over to it. She grasped Douglas' hand and smiled up at him. He and I continued to hover over her. Her colour was better; she was going to be all right physically, but I thought she was going to need all the emotional support she could get.

The constable who had gone down into the canyon now appeared again, his face a few shades paler than when he had left. The two officers conferred, and one went to the police car and spoke on the radio. Then they walked over to the edge of the canyon, peered into it, moving slowly up the slight slope of the lawn, staying along the edge of the chasm. Lucy seemed much more her old self. So, out of curiosity, I followed the two policemen as they moved up the rim of the canyon, staying a few yards away from them, over on the lawn, hoping they wouldn't notice.

"About here," the one who had gone down the trail remarked. "You can see the tree that's leaning across the canyon." He pointed. "It's being held up by the other one. There's a deep V between them. He fell from the other side and got caught in the notch."

They lifted their eyes and peered across the top of the canyon. The second officer moved over a few feet. "There! You can see it. I think it's the middle house."

I moved to where I was in line with the direction in which he was pointing. Through the thick growth, I could make out a portion of a dark brown wall, and below it a railed porch. I'd never noticed them. I hadn't even thought of the possibility of anyone living on the other side of the canyon.

I went back to Douglas and Lucy. The cook had taken charge and was shooing everyone else away. I gestured to Douglas; he walked over to where I stood a few feet away from the crowd. A Mountie had relieved Gordon, who joined us.

"Apparently there are houses on the other side. They seem to think the man fell from the middle one."

"That's right. There are several right on the lip of the canyon," Gordon affirmed. "I wouldn't want to live there, but the guy who's putting up the double-wide does. It's probably his house they're talking about."

Other police cars arrived, and the Mounties moved people back from the area around the canyon. They asked us to go on about our business, and to stay out of their way. I saw them speak to Nell, the secretary.

"I wonder where the Director is?" I asked.

"I think she's away for the day." Gordon seemed to know everything that went on. "Anyway, that's probably the end of our little race."

Douglas looked perplexed, "What race?"

"Oh, that's right, you don't know. Ask Robin." He got on his bike and rode away.

The cook had taken Lucy to her room. The crowd began to thin. Douglas and I drifted with the others back toward the buildings. Suddenly, I stopped in my tracks, and as I did so, I inhaled a great gasp of air. Several things had slotted themselves together in my mind.

"What's the matter?" he asked.

"I just thought of something," I answered vaguely. I tried to focus my mind, then turned to Douglas.

"Will you come with me? I think I know something, and I want an answer. It has to do with the race Gordon was talking about. I may need some moral support."

CHAPTER 11

We walked up to the highway, across the high bridge over the little creek, then another hundred yards or so, before we found a street leading off to the left. It was called Lakewood Drive. It sloped gently downward, and could be seen curving to the right near the far end of the bench land. The forest beyond signified the edge of the steep slope down to the lake.

I stopped and frowned. "None of these houses look as if they overhang that creek. They're too far away."

"You're looking for the house the man fell from?" Douglas asked.

"Yes."

"Let's walk down this street a ways. Maybe we'll be able to see where it is."

He was right. A block down Lakewood Drive, another street turned off to the left, its sign blocked from our view by a fat fir tree on the corner. This was Lakewood Crescent, according to the sign, and it curved around by the brow of the little canyon.

There were three houses that backed on the ravine in the concavity of a gentle semi-circle. The first was a sprawling ranch-style abode in light green with manicured lawns and a neatly trimmed hedge. The last one was a tall, awkward structure in a modern, unfinished style that made it look like a half completed barn. Painted in battleship grey, all angles, with no windows in the near wall, it did not impress me as a comfortable place to live.

Between these stood another ranch-style house, smaller than the first, its board walls stained dark brown. This must be the one I had seen from the other side. I could have picked it out without having previously seen it, however, as there were two white police cars, with the multicoloured stripes of the RCMP, parked in front. One officer stood at the door ringing the bell. Another peered over the backyard fence at the lip of the canyon. It looked as if no one was home.

We had almost reached the house when a large black Chrysler screeched around the corner behind us, swung into the driveway of the brown house, braking to a stop with such suddenness it almost gave me whiplash just watching it. The driver's door was flung open and a tall, blonde woman swung her feet onto the sidewalk, slid aggressively from behind the wheel, slammed the door, and marched toward the policemen.

"What the hell are you doing here?"

A man wearing sergeant's stripes stepped forward. "Are you Mrs. Margolin?"

"I'm Diana Lovelace," the blonde woman replied, her hard face contorted into a scowl. She had been to the beauty parlour, her hairdo was perfect, her nails manicured, even and neatly polished. Her attire was classy and blended well with her colouring. But she could have skipped all the beauty treatment. The lines of displeasure that creased her glowering face had the appearance of being chronic.

"Are you Harris Margolin's wife?"

"Yes. What's it to you?"

"Let's go into the house where we can talk in private," the sergeant suggested. He flicked a glance toward

Douglas and me, then indicated with a jerk of the head that one of the other officers should take care of us.

"I don't have anything to talk to you about." Diana Lovelace snapped.

"Well, we have something to tell you. Come along."

The sergeant's voice was neutral, calm. Would it be easier for him to break the news to this woman than to one who responded in the normal way, with anxiety at the sight of two police cars in front of her house?

I appreciated the way Douglas had calmly stood his ground, giving me his support during this scene, in which we seemed to be interlopers. I wasn't about to leave!

"Well, my question is answered," I told him.

"Yes?"

"Apparently the dead man is none other than the person who was suing me for slander."

His jaw dropped. "How extraordinary," he exclaimed. "It is, isn't it?"

The sergeant, one other officer and Diana Lovelace went inside, leaving the other two officers on the front lawn. One of them was the constable who had talked to Lucy. The other, a giant of a man, must have been nearly seven feet tall. The sergeant, by contrast, was so short he must have stood on tiptoes to reach the height mark required for acceptance into the Royal Canadian Mounted Police. I wondered whether there was an upper limit.

The constable who had talked to Lucy came over. "You were with the woman who found the body, weren't you?"

We both nodded.

"Is there anything we can do for you?"

I answered his question with one of my own. "Was Harris Margolin the man who fell into the canyon?"

"Yes, we think so."

"I know something about him, then."

"About this casino business?"

I shook my head. "All I know about casinos is what Gordon Saunders has told me. I know Margolin from another affair. It probably has no bearing on this, but I thought it strange that I should run into him here, and wanted to find out for sure whether he was the dead man."

"What is your name?"

"Robin Carruthers."

He wrote it down. "Do you live here in Mallard Beach or are you a guest at that conference place?"

"We're at Idylwyld for the week. This is the Reverend Douglas Forsythe. We're from Exeter."

"Wait here a minute," the constable commanded. He spun on his heel and went into the house. In about two minutes, he came back out and asked us to follow him. "Sergeant Simchuk would like to speak to you."

We stepped into the entryway of the Margolin house. In a room to our right, we could hear Diana Lovelace's voice, loud and angry, and the calm, low-pitched tones of the sergeant who was standing just inside the room. We were told to wait in the entry, while the officer stepped into the living room, trying to get the attention of the sergeant who, with a slight flick of his hand, indicated that he did not want to be interrupted.

"I told you, he was out in the kitchen supposedly installing a dishwasher when I left."

"Are you telling me that on a day he was busy trying to get his casino up and running, he was here doing chores?"

"Well there wasn't very goddam much he could do until the mobile home was put in place. He had everything all ready to go. As soon as those lunk-heads got the mobile home set up, and the stuff moved in, he'd have been down there."

"He wasn't supervising the moving of the double-wide?"

She snorted. "That was Sam's job. Fat lot of good he did!"

The sergeant remained silent.

"It's a great big waste now, anyway. They can't find the goddam building inspector. It's a damned conspiracy to keep us from getting a license."

"How did you know the building inspector couldn't be found? I thought you said you went to Castleton to do your grocery shopping."

"Sam called me. What do you think I am? Out of touch with everything?"

"Where did he call you?"

"On the cell-phone, of course."

"Why did he call you?"

"Why do you think he called me? Because he couldn't get hold of Harris, that's why. He tried to call Harris, and when he couldn't get him on the phone, he came over here. No one answered the door and the car was gone."

Sgt. Simchuk changed his tack. "Did your husband have dizzy spells or a bad heart or anything?"

"Not that I know of. I suppose he leaned over the railing for some reason and fell. I don't know what he'd be doing out there. He was supposed to be installing the goddam dishwasher. I've been bugging him about it for weeks, so he finally got around to it this morning, while he waited around home for reports to come in. He didn't want to go out in case someone who didn't know the number for his cell-phone called.

"He was supposed to build us a house on that land down by the lake. That's what he said he bought it for. He bought this rat-trap just to live in until he'd built the new house."

"That property down on the lake is zoned commercial. You can't build a house on it," Simchuk explained.

"Well how was I to know that? He told me he was going to build us a house. Now I'm stuck with this dump that doesn't even have modern conveniences."

I said to Douglas in a low voice, "I wonder where the outhouse is?" He allowed himself a smile.

The constable had been restively drumming a tattoo on the door frame while awaiting a chance to speak. He broke into the conversation. "The two witnesses are out here."

"Thanks. I'll see them out on the deck. Tell them not to touch anything."

The constable beckoned to us; we followed him through the house to the deck overhanging the canyon. It was a wide, covered deck, built of two-by-sixes with slats between them for water to drain through, and a roof of corrugated green plastic. Around all three sides, a railing reached from about three inches above the floor to a height

125

of about three and a half feet. The top of the railing was a flat two-by-six, and at intervals along it stood potted geraniums. Everything was stained the same dark brown. It was hot on the deck as the mid-day sun beat down. The canyon wall was not as heavily forested on this side, but the tops of several small trees showed above the railing, several large trees rose from the depths of the cleft, and the dense wall of vegetation on the opposite bank seemed close enough to touch.

A dark green plastic patio table stood against the wall of the house, a multicoloured umbrella protruding from the centre. Three matching chairs were arranged around it. A cellular phone lay on the table. Beside the door, under a wall fixture, a two-step stool had been placed. There was no bulb in the socket, and the yellow glass shade that fitted over it lay on the table. Someone had been changing the bulb and hadn't finished the job.

"His wife doesn't seem to be grieving much over his death," I remarked.

The constable started to say something, then thought better of it. "Stand back near the wall," he ordered. We did as we were told.

I heard other vehicles pull up. Two more Mounties came through the house carrying cases, which they set down on the deck. At the side of the house, men from the local search and rescue organization began unloading gear. They looked at the fence, testing it for soundness. The tall officer, who now was on the deck, said to them, "Its got metal posts set in concrete. It looks pretty substantial."

"Okay, we'll go over it, not take it down."

They began to secure ropes to a maple tree in the side yard, stringing one around the deck to some unseen mooring on the other side. One of the search and rescue crew, and a Mountie who had just arrived, strapped on harnesses and fastened wicked looking spikes to their feet. The sergeant, who had joined us on the deck, leaned over the rail and spoke to them.

"Evans," he said to the officer who was strapping on the harness. "Check the fence and see if you think he might have been trying to climb over it."

"Okay."

The tall officer said to the sergeant, "I think he fell from this corner of the deck. It's right above those trees where he got caught. He'd have fallen straight down." The sergeant looked, then nodded.

"I expect you're right about that, Phillips." To the two who were ready to rappel down the hillside, he said, "Pay most attention to the area below this corner of the deck. He probably fell from here. Look at each area before you go into it. What's your name?" he asked the search and rescue man.

"Luc."

"Okay, Luc. If you see anything, don't touch it until you've showed it to Evans. Evans will pick up all the evidence. We'll throw a rope straight down from this corner post so you can keep your bearings. Okay, on your way."

The men climbed over the fence and began to lower themselves down the hillside. Just below the deck, Luc began carefully to traverse across to the other side. The officers on the deck leaned over and watched intently. It occurred to me that they didn't seem at all nervous about falling. The reason was obvious. The top of the railing hit the sergeant well above his waist. Even if he slipped, he wouldn't have fallen over.

They seemed totally oblivious to our presence, as we pressed ourselves against the wall of the house, staying out of their way. So much was happening all at once, they must have forgotten us. I got the impression that the police thought it a straightforward accident. If they'd suspected foul play, they probably wouldn't have let us stay.

Phillips got out a tape measure and a pad of paper. He measured everything on the deck, recorded it, and drew a rough map. Another man waited with his case of gear, helping with the measurements and listing everything on the deck.

"Yo!" called Luc.

"What have you got?" the sergeant asked.

"There's an outcropping of rock here, and it looks like blood on it. Also, there's a small tree here that's nearly uprooted."

Evans traversed across and examined the rock. He carefully scraped a specimen into a plastic bag.

"Blood?" the Sgt. Simchuk asked.

"Yeah. And some hair and skin. It's dried up in the sun, but it's fresh."

"Right below this corner of the porch. Good. Take measurements."

By the time Evans had collected his specimen, Luc had another find. "Don't imagine it's anything important, but there's a length of copper pipe here."

"Don't touch it until Evans gets there. And everything is important."

The two men measured the location of the pipe, then Evans worked a stout cord under it, tied a secure knot, and wrapping the cord around his hand, lifted the pipe free of the grass on the hillside. He traversed back across and the men above pulled him up the steep slope to a point where Phillips could reach down and take the cord. The three on the deck gathered round their find, examining it from every angle.

"It's fresh. Hasn't been lying out there long. Even has the price tag on it. Store in Castleton. Let me print it before you touch it." The forensic expert opened his case. "There are some threads here on one end. Probably from a towel."

"There's a towel on the counter just inside the back door. Looks like someone just dropped it there. Would this be something a person would use in installing a dishwasher?"

"Oh, sure. That's what it is. Water pipe."

Prints sprang to life on the pipe as the forensic man, whose nametag identified him as Hendrickson, puffed powder onto it. "None on this end though. He picked it up with the towel."

"I suppose he was working on the dishwasher and for some reason went out on the deck. He dropped the towel on the counter on his way out, but carried the pipe out with him. Then he set it down or leaned it against something here, right near the door, it fell over and rolled across the deck and off. It was right below here." The sergeant walked directly from the door to the rail and looked over. "Yeah. That fits. Does the deck slope?"

Phillips found a small level and applied it to several areas on the floor. "Yeah. There's a slight gradient, for drainage probably."

"Maybe he leaned over the rail to try to catch it and lost his balance," Hendrickson suggested.

"No. Because he fell off over there at the corner. I wonder what he came out here for?"

"Maybe he heard the commotion over there where that trucker drove the double-wide into the tree. I hear there was a lot of shouting going on." This from Phillips, who peered across the ravine and pointed. "You can see the broken tree from the corner here. There's a sort of gap in the trees and you can see across."

Simchuk and Hendrickson took turns at the corner, searching the far bank with intense eyes. Each stood on tiptoe to better see across the canyon.

"You can see across," Simchuk said. Everyone laughed, their demeanour showing that Phillips was used to being ribbed about his height by the others. "Margolin couldn't have."

"He might still have been drawn out here by the noise," Phillips suggested.

"Could be. We'll have to find out what time he died. Well, speak of the devil! Here's the coroner. Hello, Dr. Jackson."

A new arrival stepped onto the deck. "Just stopped by to tell you we've removed the body and the place is all yours."

"Got a time of death for us?"

"Somewhere between eight-thirty and nine-thirty this morning, I'd say, Sgt. Simchuk."

"It was after nine."

Everyone turned and stared at me. I'm sure, in the excitement of all that had been going on, they had forgotten we were there.

"What makes you say that?" Simchuk asked.

"The woman who found the body was down in the sort of grotto at the bottom of the canyon this morning as well. She came back up just as the truck was backing out from under the tree. It was after nine already, probably about nine-ten. I don't know how long it would take her to climb the trail. Probably about five to ten minutes."

"You don't think the body could have been there then and she didn't notice it?"

"No way," said Dr. Jackson. "It was staring you right in the face."

"And," I added, "if he'd fallen while she was there, she'd have known it. It was very quiet down there, and I'm sure there would have been a lot of racket involved in a man tumbling down through those trees."

"Doctor?"

"Yes. I'd agree with that. You could see the broken limbs where he had crashed through some small trees. By the way, he got a bash on the back of his head somewhere. Also a fractured arm. You'd think he would have cried out, too."

"If he did, no one seems to have heard him." Simchuk turned to Phillips. "We'll have to check with the neighbours."

Phillips nodded.

"But," he said, "if he hit his head on that rock right below the deck, he was probably unconscious during the rest of his fall."

"Lucky for him," said the doctor. His eyes dropped to the piece of pipe Hendrickson was holding. "If you're thinking he might have been hit with that, forget it. The whole back of his skull was caved in."

131

"Then that's what killed him, not the broken neck?" Simchuk asked.

"Don't know. The pathologist will have to tell you that. Either injury would have been fatal. The blow on the head might not have killed him instantly. The broken neck would have finished him off."

Diana Lovelace walked to the back door, stood there for a moment, pouting, her lower lip thrust out. "Well, if my house is going to be turned into Grand Central Station, I might as well get out of here."

No one told her not to, and soon we heard the squeal of her tires, and the angry honk of a horn from another motorist.

Simchuk turned away from the door and stared at the deck railing. He stood for a moment, his weight on one foot, the other toe tapping on the floor, his hand cupped under his chin, a frown wrinkling his forehead. He might be short for a policeman, but he was powerfully built, with broad shoulders, a large chest, and arms like logs. Probably about fifty, he was bald, with a fringe of salt and pepper hair, heavy eyebrows and a neatly clipped grey moustache.

"You know," he mused, "I can't figure out how the hell he managed to fall off!"

CHAPTER 12

The three policemen stood at the corner of the deck surveying it carefully.

"I don't suppose he could have stood on a chair. Or that stool?" Simchuk pointed to the two-step stool beside the door.

"Not unless someone came in and put it back. It wouldn't have slid over there so neatly on its own," Phillips observed.

"Mrs. Margolin might have tidied up if she'd come home sometime during the morning. She says she didn't."

"You mean Ms. Lovelace," Phillips commented with a grin.

"Mizzz Lovelace then." Simchuk drew the sound out to emphasize it. "Hendrickson, is there any possibility of getting prints off this rail and the corner post? He might have grabbed something as he went over. There might be prints in some unusual place."

The forensic man shook his head. "The wood is rough and it's stained, not painted. I didn't see any scuff marks either."

"Humph! Nice little problem."

"Yeah, isn't it?"

I don't know about Douglas, but I was getting pretty tired of standing in one place in the intense heat on that deck. Still, the police seemed to have forgotten us again, when they saw the coroner off. Curiosity kept me rooted to the spot.

Sgt. Simchuk sighed deeply, rubbed a hand across his bald head which was beginning to show beads of sweat, and turned to the other two officers. "Then we have to think of the possibility that someone gave him a boost over that railing."

"Not Mizzz Lovelace, though," said Phillips. "She wouldn't have the strength. He weighed maybe 180 or 190 pounds."

"What about that young man who worked for him?"

"Sam Gilley? He'd be big enough to do it."

"I'd think Margolin would put up a fight, though."

"Unless Gilley caught him by surprise. If he grabbed him by the legs, below the knees, and gave a quick heave, he could probably boost him over."

"I wonder…" Simchuk turned to Hendrickson. "What kind of evidence would that leave?"

Hendricksen replied. "I can check for threads from the fabric of his clothes which might have got caught on the railing. Of course you wouldn't be able to tell when the threads got left there. You might have the pathologist look for scratches or slivers on his hands."

"If I know Dr. Dannenberg, he'll do that without being asked. He's very thorough. Who else might have it in for Margolin?"

Phillips laughed. "Who wouldn't?"

"Not well liked, eh?"

"No. People didn't like this outside sharp-shooter coming into the community and trying to take things over."

"Then this casino issue wasn't his only interest here?"

Phillips shook his head. "I don't think so, but I don't know for sure what else he had his hand in. I just have the feeling that there was resentment toward him before the casino issue came up."

Simchuk nodded. "Who in particular might have had it in for him? Scropos?"

"Yeah, but I can't see Demmy Scropos losing his cool like that."

"You never know! He'd have the strength to do it, though."

"Yeah. He's pretty fit. Does mountain climbing. Or used to when he was younger."

"Who else?"

"Most of the guys on the village council."

Simchuk laughed. "We'll have to leave out the three guys who are gals, but do you seriously think any of them would resort to murder?"

"Not really," Phillips agreed. "There are probably a few other people in town who have it in for him in one way or another."

"We'll have to check up on that. No mention of the possibility of murder, though, until we know more."

Suddenly, Simchuk appeared to remember us and whirled around. "You're a priest," he said to Douglas. "You know about confidentiality. I don't want any rumours spreading around, any more than the usual stuff people say."

"I understand. I won't say anything," Douglas replied.

Simchuk levelled his intense gaze at me. "And you. The same thing."

"I won't talk about it."

"You can trust Robin's discretion," Douglas told the sergeant, who nodded.

Before Simchuk could say anything more to us, we heard another call from down the hillside. Simchuk looked over the railing. "What have you got this time?"

"Nothing much," Luc called. "An old shoe. Also a new plastic bag from the Shop and Save. It's caught in a tree. Probably just blew there."

Evans examined the shoe and remarked, "It's been here a long time. Half buried. It's a blue man's boat shoe, pretty well decayed, about a size ten I'd say."

"Okay. Keep looking."

I'd better get it over with, I thought, so when Simchuk turned back toward us, I dropped my bombshell.

"If you are looking for people with motive to murder him, I had."

The three policemen all turned toward me as if jerked by a string. I went on, "I came over here to find out whether the man who had fallen was Harris Margolin. I had no foreknowledge that he lived here, but several things came together in my mind. This morning when that trucker ran the trailer into the tree over there, I thought the man who came to take charge looked familiar. I would have recognized him as Sam Gilley, but he's grown a beard since I last saw him. Then Gordon Saunders referred to one of the men trying to get a casino license as 'Harris' and talked about him buying land for speculation. I assumed this was a last name, and since it was a common one, nothing clicked. But when Gordon told us, in a roundabout way, that 'Harris' might be the dead man, everything gelled. So I wanted to find out for sure."

"You knew Margolin from someplace else?" Simchuk asked.

"Yes. Do you know about the death of his partner?"

Simchuk shook his head. "Do you?" he asked Phillips.

"I'd heard something about it. Some accident, I think. Down in Exeter. If I heard right, it was a plane crash."

"Not a plane crash. Margolin ran into him with the propeller of his plane. It happened on the ramp at the flight school I operate."

Hendrickson exclaimed, "Oh, yeah! I remember that. Guy walked into the prop."

"He didn't walk into the propeller," I stated firmly. "Margolin ran his plane into him."

"On purpose?" Simchuk asked.

"On purpose. Deliberately. With malice aforethought. He murdered his partner."

I could see the shock registered on Douglas' face. "Robin, you didn't tell me this."

"I didn't tell anyone except the police. I was in enough trouble with him, anyway."

"With Margolin?" Simchuk wanted to know.

"Yes."

"Why?"

"Because he was suing me for slander."

"Before you accused him of murder?"

"Before."

"Why was he suing you?"

"Do you remember that big storm we had back in early March?"

Simchuk grimaced. "I most certainly do. It blew a tree down on my son's car, and of course his Dad had to buy him a new one."

"On that day, Margolin, his partner Alec Conrad, and Sam Gilley were going to fly from Exeter to Georgetown.

That storm front was about to hit us. No one in his right mind would have flown into it, and if Margolin had gotten a proper weather briefing, he'd have realized it was suicide to try to fly to Georgetown.

"When I saw him going out to the plane, I followed him and tried to talk him out of flying. All I got from him was some rude comments, and he nearly knocked me down with the tail of his plane."

The three policemen exchanged glances.

"You say you run a flight school?" Simchuk asked.

"Yes. Red Robin Flying School in Exeter. I've operated it for over twenty years. I used to be the safety officer on the airport. Anyway, when Margolin wouldn't listen to me, I went back to the office where the other two were waiting and put it up to them. Conrad made the decision not to go, and that made Margolin angry. He's suing me. Or he was. I don't know what will happen to the lawsuit now."

"I expect it will be invalid. I don't think that's anything the heirs could take over."

"Exactly. So I have motive, but I didn't have opportunity. As I told you, he couldn't have fallen down that hillside before nine and I was with Douglas, Douglas' wife, and later a whole classroom full of people. I would have been strong enough to boost him up over that rail though, but I didn't."

"Thanks for your frank account, Mrs. Carruthers. Now let me get this straight about Margolin killing his partner. You said that the partner decided not to go on the trip? So how'd he get out on the ramp with the airplane?"

"He wasn't killed at that time. That happened two days later, when the weather broke enough for them to go."

"Why do you think he did it?"

"Conrad was trying to take over the business. I saw it myself, but also Gilley told me that when they went to a motel after Conrad called off the trip, they had a big fight. Apparently Conrad called Margolin's wife. It had something to do with the business. I gather from what Gilley told me, Conrad owned half the shares, and the Margolins jointly owned the other half, and that Conrad was trying to get Mrs. Margolin, or Ms. Lovelace, or whatever she calls herself, to throw her shares in with his and squeeze her husband out."

"Nice people, eh?" Simchuk remarked. "So how come Margolin was chasing this Conrad around your ramp in his airplane?"

"Chasing isn't quite how I'd put it. Margolin had gone to start the plane and warm it up. While he did, Conrad and Gilley were walking across the ramp. Gilley wasn't going on the flight. Conrad was giving him some last-minute instructions. Gilley turned around to walk back to the terminal, and when his back was turned, Margolin taxied forward and hit Conrad with the prop, which is a very lethal instrument, in case you wonder. It was meant to look like an accident, but it wasn't."

"Did you see it happen?"

"Not the actual, uh, incident I think you say. I saw the circumstances just before and shortly after it happened. What I saw told me what had happened."

"Hmm! I haven't heard about this murder."

"I told the police in Exeter. The ones I talked to were Cpl. Nash and Sgt. Jameson. You can check with them."

Simchuk nodded. "I'll do that. It's interesting. Adds some more people to the list of those who might want

Margolin dead. Do you know anything about Conrad's relatives?"

"Not a thing."

"I wonder how many other toes this pretty pair has managed to step on?"

It was a good question, but before it could be pursued further, a shout from below signalled another find.

"Finders keepers," came Luc's jocular comment.

"No way," shouted Evans. "The police get first dibs, don't we Sarge?"

"Well, since it's not enough to buy a ticket to Acapulco, I'll let you take it."

"Thanks a lot."

"What are you guys fighting over?" Simchuk called down to them.

"The dude spilled some change out of his jeans when he hit this tree here," Luc explained.

"And a pocket-knife," Evans added. "The tree's nearly uprooted."

"Okay. Save everything you find and record the position of every broken or uprooted tree or anyplace things are disturbed."

"Sure thing."

Simchuk watched thoughtfully for a few moments. Hendrickson asked, "What about suicide?"

"It's not likely, I don't think. He doesn't sound like a suicidal chap, not right while he's trying to put over some big deal. And if he wanted to kill himself by jumping off something, why not the railroad trestle?"

"You'll have to admit, though, that it was effective."

Simchuk gave a curt nod. He walked around the deck, looking things over. "How's this for a scenario. Margolin is installing the dishwasher. He may or may not have had someone with him, someone who dropped by after his wife left. He hears the commotion across the way, gets up and goes out on the porch. He still has the pipe in his hand. He grabs a towel to wipe his hands and sets the pipe down when he walks out the back door. He tosses the towel on the counter. The pipe rolls off the deck. Then…"

"The sequence seems wrong," Phillips interrupted. "Why would he carry the pipe out with him? And if he'd wanted to wipe his hands, he'd have set the pipe down first. It would be more logical to set the pipe down where he was working and pick up the towel. The pipe should be in the kitchen and the towel on the porch."

"Yeah, you're right."

Hendrickson suggested, "He probably did set the pipe down. Whoever was with him probably picked it up, using the towel so as not to leave any prints, came up behind Margolin while his attention was diverted by the racket over across the canyon, whacked him a good one, knocking him out, then lifted him over the railing. That would account for him not crying out, and the bigger bash would cover up the first one."

Simchuk thought a moment, then said softly, "Yeah. That makes sense."

"We're still looking for a pretty strong man. He'd be even harder to toss over the top if he was a dead weight."

Sgt. Simchuk heaved a big sigh. "Okay boys, we go looking for a murderer."

CHAPTER 13

The dining room was abuzz with talk of the death of Harris Margolin as we carried our trays to a table. We had stopped by Lucy's room to see how she felt, and had persuaded her to come have something to eat. Kathy, the pregnant young woman, had the same idea, and as we trooped over to the dining room, requested of the rest of us that we not talk about Margolin's death. We readily agreed.

Lucy picked listlessly at her lasagne and Caesar salad. Kathy became solicitous, assuring Lucy that she would feel better if she ate. Lucy watched Kathy put away her portion of food with good appetite and remarked, "You're lucky you can eat like that. When I was pregnant, I was so sick I could hardly eat a thing. I didn't just have morning sickness, I had afternoon sickness and evening sickness as well. I couldn't keep anything down. I ended up in the hospital twice, getting IVs."

"Was that just in your first pregnancy?" Kathy asked.

"My first, my last and my only pregnancy. I never wanted to go through that again." Lucy was getting her old exuberance back, I noted with approval. Kathy skilfully kept the conversation on the subject of babies. Lucy got into the swing of it.

"I got so sick, they induced labour early, which wasn't done so often in those days. It was a blessing in one way because I had an easy delivery. The baby was small. He only weighed five pounds. You'd never know it now. You should see him! Once that kid figured out where dinner came from, there was no stopping him."

"I'm trying to eat a balanced diet and stay away from harmful things. Fortunately, I haven't had any trouble with morning sickness."

"Good for you." Lucy ate a few bites of salad. "You know, I can remember looking at my son when he was about three days old. He was still beet red, with his little head sort of coming to a point (though it got its normal shape later) his face all screwed up from howling, and I thought of the name we'd given him. We named him after his father and both grandfathers. My father was a dentist, and was at that time president of the provincial dental association. My husband's father was a judge, and my husband was a young lawyer starting out with his dad's firm. He never became a judge, but he was a QC. Here we'd hung a name on the little mite that showed that we expected him to amount to something big in life. I remember saying to my husband that we might be inflicting too great a burden on the poor kid. What if he decided he wanted to be a plumber, or a jazz drummer, or something. My husband, God rest his soul, said to me, 'Don't worry. He'll be all right.' He was correct of course. My son went into the diplomatic service. He's the Canadian Consul-General in Boston. He'll be an ambassador one of these days. What are you going to name your baby?"

"If it's a boy, we'll probably call him Tom Jr. My husband and his parents want that, but my mother is dead set against it. She thinks he should be named after my father."

"What name do you want?"

"Thomas Jr. is okay with me."

"Well, don't let your parents dictate to you what to name your baby. What name have you picked out for a girl?"

"Marietta."

"Oh! That's a lovely name!" Lucy went back to her meal and polished it off.

"Are you in one of the courses?" Betty asked.

"No," Kathy replied. "Tom is working on a construction project near here. They're living in portables, and he wanted me near him, but not way out in the woods in fairly primitive conditions, so I'm just here as a temporary resident for three weeks. This is my second week."

"Are you in a single room?"

"No. I have a roommate. She's a wonderful woman. She's had eight kids, and every time I tell her about some incident, or express some concern about my pregnancy, she hoots with laughter and says, 'Oh, my dear, how well I remember that!' She's been a really good influence for me. She said that for the first three pregnancies, she was always worrying about something. After that, she said, nothing fazed her."

Betty laughed. "I see I stopped too soon. I had three, and each pregnancy seemed to have a new set of problems."

"Are any of your kids here with you?"

"Oh no. They've all been kicked out of the nest and are busy producing grandchildren; four so far."

"Really! You don't look old enough to have four grandchildren," Kathy exclaimed, looking at Betty's curly blonde hair, creamy complexion and sparkling blue eyes.

I muttered in an aside to Douglas, who was sitting beside me, "I feel left out when women start talking about babies."

He smiled. "I do too. Now when men start talking about their babies it's another story."

"I feel left out there also."

"Are you sorry?"

"No."

"I didn't think you were."

No, I wasn't, even when surrounded by talk of babies. I wasn't cut out for the maternal role, and the thought of spending my days doing housework sent shivers down my spine. For all his shortcomings, my ex-husband at least had not expected it of me. He had anticipated that when he married me, he'd have a cheap secretary. He'd been wrong. All my life I've avoided any sort of secretarial role. I also disappeared when groups were asking for volunteers to make coffee, serve lunches, or do the dishes. My job is flying airplanes, and I'm damned good at it!

My musings about being left out of family discussions would be temporary, I knew. As soon as I got back to my sky chariots, I'd forget all about it.

As the crowd thinned out in the room, I caught sight of Colin Broadstreet sitting alone at a table on the opposite side of the room. He was eyeing our table and when we made eye contact his gaze shifted away. But not before I had seen the predatory expression on his face. Kathy saw my concentration and turned to look in the direction of my steady stare. She saw Broadstreet and gave an involuntary shudder.

"He gives me the willies," she said. "He's not in either of the courses, which means that when my roommate is, I have to find someone else to be with. I've been doing some volunteer sewing, curtains and things. That keeps me out of harm's way."

"Why don't you sit in on our course? I'm sure they won't mind. We have a lot of fun. Bishop Michael gives us an analysis of scripture in the morning sessions. He's very interesting. Then the Archbishop teaches us how to give a sermon in the evening sessions. Starting tomorrow, some of the people in the class are going to try their hands at sermons."

"I might do that. Are you going to give one?"

"I'm on at the Friday morning service. I don't know what made me volunteer. I've never done anything like that."

"Good. I'll be sure and be there on Friday."

That evening, Gordon Saunders came wheeling jauntily up to the building housing the classrooms, kicked the stand of his mountain bike into place, removed his helmet and shook his hair. Whistling softly, he strode into the meeting room and dropped into his chair.

"You look happy," I remarked. "How's the casino situation? Did you give your friend a license?"

"We gave a license to Demmy Scropos. The other outfit is all washed up. The building inspector finally got around to looking at the mobile home, and pronounced it structurally unsound. Margolin's wife and that fellow, Gilley, who seems to be a flunky, both made a big fuss, but I think it was mainly for show. Gilley was throwing his weight around until Diana Lovelace arrived on the scene, then he sort of slunk away like a dog being told to go to its doghouse. But I doubt if Diana has the know-how to keep the business running. At least that's what we took into consideration when we decided on the license."

"I'd hate to be trying to open a business in this town if you guys wanted to give it to one of your friends."

"Ah, come on Robin. We aren't that bad! You have to admit that Demmy had by far the better set-up."

"I'm always amazed that anyone wants to go into politics. I couldn't stand it."

"It's not so bad. I get a kick out of it."

Gordon could have it, I thought. Politics stood even lower than motherhood in the list of careers I'd be willing to take on.

"Has Demmy opened his casino?"

"Yes. I went to his opening this evening before I came here. He has the slot machines and some other stuff set up in the side of the building that will eventually be the offices. Starting tomorrow, he'll have the rest of the building remodelled into the gambling floor; then when that's finished, he'll have the offices done. They expect to be finished by fall."

"It must be hard to run a business in a place that's being built at the same time."

"Yeah. He didn't plan it that way. He was going to remodel that store as soon as we decided to allow casinos, and open it in the fall. But then Margolin arrived on the scene, and Demmy found out what he was up to. Demmy's done a lot of scrambling, but you can bet he'll be all right in the long run."

"You like him, don't you?"

"He's a great guy. You ought to eat at his place sometime."

"I'll tell Douglas and Betty. Maybe we will."

"Are those the people you always sit with at meals?"

"Yes. Douglas is my priest. Betty is his wife."

"They must be in the other course."

"Douglas is. Betty's along for the R and R."

At that point Archbishop John arrived, and soon we were totally immersed in the subject matter of our course, casinos and even murders forgotten.

At breakfast Wednesday morning, Kathy came to our table again. She beamed at us, looking much more relaxed. Colin Broadstreet sat morosely on the opposite side of the room.

"What are you looking so pleased about?" I asked.

She glanced across the room toward Broadstreet, then gave a secretive smile. "Tom came into town last night," she said, satisfaction oozing from her voice.

"Oh, oh!"

"We were in the lounge after dinner. Colin was trying to cozy up to me when Tom walked into the room. He took one look, marched across the room and took a fistful of Colin's shirt. Tom isn't big, but he has broad shoulders and lots of muscle, and in any altercation between him and Colin, it was no mystery who would come out on top. Colin just sort of wilted. Tom shook him a bit, and told him to stay away from me. Colin was so anxious to cooperate he almost peed his pants. I shouldn't laugh, but it really was funny."

I shared her glee. "Well, that's probably the last of our friend Colin!"

CHAPTER 14

At the Wednesday morning service, Gordon, an obviously polished speaker, gave an excellent sermon designed for the Reign of Christ, which is the last Sunday before Advent and falls in late November. Rather than using the gospel reading for the day, or even one of the other readings, Gordon built his sermon around the Collect. This collective prayer is said at the beginning of the service and summarizes the emphasis for the day. "Almighty and everlasting God, whose will it is to restore all things in your well-beloved Son, our Lord and King, grant that the peoples of the earth, now divided and enslaved by sin, may be freed and brought together under his gentle and loving rule; who lives and reigns with you and the Holy Spirit, one God, now and forever."

Gordon had gotten his blond hair cut and was dressed, for a change, in neatly pressed khaki shorts that came to the top of his knees, a dark green "March for Jesus" T-shirt, neatly tucked in, and brown moccasins. He delivered his sermon from memory.

The people, sitting in the warm morning sun, on a luxuriant green lawn, in one of the most beautiful parts of the country named by the United Nations as the best place on earth in which to live, were carried out of their pleasant lethargy to view the world's troubles, then imbued with the knowledge that they had a responsibility to help change the world — through prayer, through participation, through education, and (this remark directed to Wilson Noble) through evangelism of the unconverted in this land.

At the end of the sermon, I saw several people raise their hands from their laps, poised to clap; but looking around, they realized that one really doesn't applaud sermons, at least not in the Anglican Church, noted for being staid and elitist.

I groaned inwardly. I had to match that? How could I possibly give a sermon that anyone would listen to after such a compelling oration?

Bishop Michael had an answer for us; for all of us who were about to give our first sermons ever, two that evening, three the following night, and Lucy who was to perform the next morning, as well as myself.

He congratulated Gordon, then told the rest of us, "If every priest who has ever given a sermon were to think that he or she could not do so unless they could give a better one than everyone else, none of us who had heard Wilson Noble would ever again open our mouths. Don't be dismayed by hearing a sermon you think is really excellent. There are many ways to get your point across. Your style may be different, but you can be equally effective, and what you say equally inspiring."

That morning I had practiced mine for the first time. Since it was broad daylight by four thirty, even though the sun hadn't gotten down into the valley yet, I set out for the beach. It had been a warm night, and even at this hour I didn't need a jacket. The day was going to be a scorcher. I told Douglas the previous evening that I was going to go down to the beach early in the morning to practice aloud, and he, realizing that I didn't want an audience, said he would do his early morning walk elsewhere. No one, not a single one of the other early risers, was at the lakeshore. I walked along it looking for a solitary spot, and as I rounded a clump of trees, found myself staring at Margolin's doublewide.

The mobile home had been set on the old foundation of a house that had once graced the lakefront. Years of uncontrolled growth of vegetation had been cut back, and the driveway made into an access road. The remnants of another house were visible beyond. It was in the process of being dismantled.

The damage to the corner of one half of the doublewide had been repaired with some skill, but was still visible. The ground around it was littered with the debris of hasty construction, like a kitchen counter where vegetables are being prepared for a stew; bits and pieces cut off and not yet thrown in the garbage. A monster of a dumpster had been dropped off beside the house that was being ripped down, but no one had provided for the leftovers from the work on the doublewide. The whole place had a forlorn air about it, a feeling of destruction, not of creation. It might be quiet there, but it was not a place that felt right for my first attempts at composing a sermon.

I walked back along the beach, found a log to sit on, and pulled out my notes. After the first read-through, I knew that it had been a good idea to try it out loud. My text was too wordy, my sentences too complex. Things sound much different when spoken aloud than when read in silence. I pulled out my pen and began to edit. The paper became strewn with notes, asides, punctuation marks. It got almost to the point where I couldn't read anything at all, but gradually I worked out the kinks. I have not only a good visual memory, but also decent aural recall. I can remember how things sound, the nuances in the human voice. These traits are useful in instrument flying, where you have to visualize your position with relation to the terrain even when you can't see it, and where you often have to listen to a clearance when you're busy doing other things. Once I felt that I could call to mind the parts of my sermon I wanted to change, I folded my papers, stuffed them in my pocket, and made my way back along the beach to the old, unused road near the little creek. I knew I'd need another session by myself. I had once thought of going down into the canyon and using the little grotto as my practice pulpit, but now that idea gave me the shivers.

So after lunch I searched for another quiet place to work. The beach was out of the question. Everyone would be there. By noon the temperature had hit thirty-five. It would be up in the forties by late afternoon. The only place to be was in or on the water.

This then left me with more room around the grounds, and I found a spot in the shade, under trees at the top of the canyon. Not all of the wall of trees grew out of the chasm; some were rooted at the top of it. Though the sun had swung around to the south, there was still shade here.

I sat on the northeast-facing side of the largest tree I could find, on a carpet of pine needles, my back against the rough bark. The redness on the skin of my legs, from unaccustomed exposure to the searing sun, was beginning to turn to a tan that matched my face and arms. I had bought a floppy straw hat at the gift shop; also an Idylwyld T-shirt. If any of my flying buddies had seen me, they'd have laughed until they burst. I certainly didn't look like the professional aviator who could leap high mountains with the greatest of ease. More like a middle-aged matron of sedentary habits "taking the air."

I had re-written my sermon using short phrases, placing pauses in the text, underlining key words, and giving myself little cues as to how a passage should be stressed. I read it silently a couple of times, then, swivelling my head to ascertain that I was alone, opened my mouth to speak. But the voice I heard didn't come from my lips.

As clearly as if they had been standing beside me, I heard the voice of Constable Phillips and the bass tones of Sgt. Simchuk. The spot where I was sitting was slightly up the slope and around the gentle curve of the canyon from the Margolin house, and the south end of the overhanging deck, though I could not see it, must have been directly opposite.

"Dr. Dannenberg said he'd have his written report on your desk by tomorrow. He'll courier it up. But he gave me the highlights of it over the phone." I recognized the resonant speech of the tall young constable.

"Good. I hope he gave it to you in English."

"Yeah. Whenever he lapsed into medicaleze, I stopped him and made him say it in plain language. Let's see, I've got my notes here somewhere. Here they are."

I couldn't hear every word of what followed, as the person speaking must have turned his back toward me. But I could hear enough of it to fill in the blanks. This is the way you listen to aircraft radio. You listen for the key words, and knowing what goes with them, the whole conversation seems clear, when to a novice it is incomprehensible babble. Ever listen to a choir sing an unfamiliar song?

The two policemen must have felt secluded, on the back deck of the house, with no one in the neighbouring houses within range of their voices, and a dense wall of foliage opposite them. Diana Lovelace must be away, or they'd never have talked so freely about her husband's injuries. I felt vaguely guilty about eavesdropping, but not enough to overcome my intense curiosity.

"He sort of gave me the injuries from top to bottom, you might say. Oh, before that he describes the guy, and says he was wearing blue jeans with a plain black belt, a short-sleeved plaid shirt, jockey shorts, no undershirt, athletic socks and navy blue boat shoes. No watch. That was on the counter in the kitchen where he was working on the dishwasher."

"Yeah. I remember."

"The back of his skull was bashed in. The doctor didn't say it that way, but that's when I told him to please use the Queen's English. There was a lot of damage to the brain, which would have killed him before long, but didn't do it immediately."

"How could he tell that?" the sergeant asked.

"Because the other injuries all happened before the heart stopped pumping blood. They were the types of injuries where large blood vessels were torn, or there was a lot of damage to small ones so there was quite a bit of bleeding into the tissues."

"Okay. Go ahead."

"There were bruises and scratches to the face, and one wound had some bark from a tree in it."

"That figures."

"Let's see. He skipped the neck injuries for the time being, because he thought they occurred last. The left shoulder was dislocated, and the big bone in the upper arm was broken."

"The left arm?"

"Yes. It was a compound fracture, he said, which means that the bone came out through the skin. It wasn't that way when the body was found, so it popped back in, but it took some pine needles and bark in with it."

"So he probably broke his arm from hitting that small tree that was bent over. Could have dislocated the shoulder at the same time."

"Yes, or..." Phillips paused for effect. "Dr. Dannenberg found rough scratches across the palm of the left hand with a couple of brown wood slivers stuck in them."

Sgt. Simchuk's voice perked up. "So he did grab hold of something to keep from falling."

"It looks like it."

"That means he was conscious. He wasn't hit by that pipe and then heaved over the rail. Hendrickson says there's no blood on the pipe anyway. There would have been even if it was wiped off with a towel. By the way, that towel had been used to hold the pipe, he says."

"I've been trying to figure out how he'd land on his back just below the deck if he was thrown over."

"Yeah," Simchuk agreed. "How do you figure it?"

"I was thinking that if the person who heaved him over the rail had a hold around his knees or below and heaved hard enough, he'd flip him right over in a somersault. But that wouldn't work if Margolin grabbed hold of the post."

"Maybe not the post, but he might have caught hold of the top of the railing. In fact, that might be what flipped him onto his back. And it might account for the dislocated shoulder."

There was silence for a minute, and I could imagine the two policemen trying to visualize the contortions of the falling man.

"I don't know," Cst. Phillips said hesitantly.

"Well, go on. What other injuries did he have?"

"His ribs on the left side of his back, near the spine, were caved in, and his lung was punctured. There was quite a bit of bleeding into the chest because a fairly big vessel got torn. He had some bleeding from vessels in his belly, and his spleen was ruptured. The doctor said he'd have bled to death from those injuries, even without the bashed skull and broken neck.

"He said there were bruises and abrasions on his other arm, and bruises on the abdominal wall, the right hip, the right thigh, the backs of both knees, both shins (though that's not what the doc called them), and he had a broken ankle."

"And he was still alive after all that?"

"Yeah, but he wouldn't have been for long. He was apparently falling head down by the time he got to where that one tree had fallen against the other. His head went into the notch, but his body kept tumbling and fell around the standing tree. His weight, and the momentum of the fall caused his spinal column to dislocate. Let's see. There was a fracture of the second cervical vertebra, that's the second bone in the neck, and complete separation between the second and third cervical vertebrae. He says the spinal cord was severed, blood vessels were torn, and all the muscles stretched and some of them torn. That did him in."

"I would think so!"

There was a pause in the conversation, then I heard Simchuk reflect, "You know, those two guys certainly did meet messy ends. I checked on that story about his partner's death. That's what happened all right. Cpl. Nash, down in Exeter, said Margolin probably killed this guy, Conrad, but the Crown prosecutor doesn't think they can prove it. Margolin was out on bail on a criminal negligence causing death charge. His trial was set for September."

"Yeah? A lot of people are going to say that the two of them deserved it, but I don't think anyone deserves to die like that."

"Quick, anyway. At least he was unconscious through most of the fall. There's another thing people are going to say. If he did kill his partner, he died in the same way he would have from hanging, if we still executed murderers."

"I was thinking about those bruises on the back of the knees," Phillips remarked hesitantly.

"What about them? Funny place to get yourself bruised in a fall."

"That's just it! I was wondering if he was facing inward when he was grabbed. If someone tried to boost him over the rail, he might have tried to hang by his knees while he grabbed hold of something."

"That's a possibility. In that case his assailant had to be pretty big and strong."

"Or there were two of them."

"Hmm." Simchuk took some time to think that over.

I heard them move about the deck. Then Simchuk asked, "Did anyone hear anything yesterday morning?"

"No. We interviewed all the neighbours who were around. This house over here is empty. The people are off in the Yukon on a camping trip. The ones who live in that thing down there (I don't think you can really call it a house) don't get up before ten in the morning, and nothing disturbed their beauty sleep yesterday. They had the air conditioner on and everything shut up anyway. The couple across the street both go to work at eight. The wife saw Margolin walking home with a Tim Horton's bag as she was leaving for work. Hey, that reminds me. The doc said Margolin died from thirty to forty minutes after he ate the last of two jelly doughnuts."

"Hmmm! I'll have to talk to Mizzz Lovelace again. I think she said she'd just gotten up and put on the coffee when her hubby came back from the doughnut shop. They had coffee and doughnuts for breakfast, she got dressed and went shopping, and left him working on the dishwasher. That means that he couldn't have died before eight forty five, but we know that anyway, because that lady was down there in that grotto place until nine."

"Maybe. It could have taken her longer to get back to the top than she thought. She said she sat down on the bench at the switchback to get her breath. She might have been there longer than she realized."

"Let's say eight fifty five for her to leave. That still puts it at nine or after. I wonder whether she could have heard him crashing down the hillside from that bench." Simchuk pondered for a moment, then continued, "Let's see where this puts the later limit. If he was still munching on a doughnut as late as nine, then it could have been nine-forty when he was killed."

"No," said Phillips. "Dannenberg says his findings don't invalidate the coroner's. He agrees on the eight-thirty to nine-thirty slot, but says we can pin it down closer if we know when he ate."

"Okay, I'll see Ms. Lovelace again."

Their voices trailed off as they moved away, probably to go back into the house.

Evidence. Why did that word pop into my brain?

That was it! That was the lingering problem with my sermon. I said things I couldn't prove. So where would I get the proof? I had planned yesterday to spend the afternoon searching through the Bible commentaries for support for my position. But events had kept me from doing so, and at the end of the day, I was secretly glad. I wanted this to be my idea, not that of some eminent scholar. Now I questioned the wisdom of that decision. Time to do some research, to gather some evidence.

I rose from my seat under the tree, brushed pine needles off my derriere, and headed for the library.

CHAPTER 15

The library again was busy, with an air of studious quiet. A large fan swung slowly from side to side, but the place was still hot. I had noticed a few clouds developing in the west. The hot stillness carried a humid edge. Thunderstorms this evening, I thought.

It was not to the weighty commentaries lying on the table that I went, but to the shelves of popular books. On my way over, a phrase had popped into my mind, and I'd instantly remembered where it came from. I scanned the shelves. Surely it would be here. Yes, there it was. I pulled out a slender paperback, a book with more theological wisdom than half a dozen texts; C. S. Lewis' The Screwtape Letters. I had the vague memory that the passage I wanted was at the end of a chapter, so I leafed through the book, skimming over the last two pages of each chapter. It took me about fifteen minutes to find what I was looking for. I settled down to read and re-read it, to whittle and shape my argument and to re-write my sermon, now much stronger.

I had to face up to one drawback I could see in my sermon. It normally wouldn't have come up at all. But the events of this week, here at Idylwyld, might intrude into my audience's interpretation of what I had to say.

One of the three temptations presented to Christ by Satan was to throw himself off the pinnacle of the temple, with the expectation that since he was loved by God, he would be caught before he crashed to his death. Would my fellow worshipers at the morning Eucharist connect that with what had happened next door?

No! I decided.

These were people who knew the story. The temptation for Christ was one of proving that he was the Son of God. No one would think that God should have caught Harris Margolin!

That settled in my mind, I went back to my sermon. I had to write it out by hand. I used lined paper out of a notebook, double spaced my writing, inserted emphasis and pauses, and listened to it in my head. In the morning, I'd go down to the lake again to whip it into final shape. I began to be excited about giving this sermon, to look forward to Friday.

As I left the library, I heard the voice of Sam Gilley coming from the office. I stopped, then edged over toward the door to find out what he was up to this time. He was talking to Evelyn McNaughton, trying with a tone of fake sincerity, to imply that Harcon Holdings had no responsibility for the fiasco with the tree.

"It's the responsibility of the trucking company," he asserted.

Dr. McNaughton wasn't buying it.

"We will deal with the trucking company, but since they were acting as your agent, you share the responsibility." Her voice, quiet but firm, sounded like an elementary school teacher explaining to a problem child that he could be held accountable for his actions.

Gilley beat a retreat. Dr. McNaughton was way out of his league.

"I'll have Diana Lovelace come over and talk to you."

"Very good. That would be preferable. We will still want to know who you are insured with."

Gilley bolted out the door, running smack into me. Confused and embarrassed, he blurted apologies.

"It's okay, Sam. No harm done." I made my voice sound soothing.

Sam Gilley paused and eyed me quizzically. I could see remembrance dawn.

"Oh yeah! You're the lady from the airport in Exeter, aren't you?"

I replied that I was indeed. Very few people have trouble remembering who I am. They don't often meet a woman who is five feet ten, with flaming red hair, who runs a flying school. I am a memorable person, which often is an asset, but occasionally a disadvantage. Today's recognition, I decided, I could use on the asset side of the ledger.

"I'm sorry to hear about the mishap. Your company has certainly had its troubles."

Was I sorry? Well... yes. I remembered the policeman's comment that no one deserved to die like that. Margolin's death let me off the hook, with respect to the slander suit, but I would not have wished anyone to become a casualty in such a gruesome way.

Gilley failed to share my charitable feelings.

"Serves the old goat right!" he grumbled. His voice suddenly lost its belligerence and became curious. "What are you doing up here?"

"I'm here to take a course."

"Small world, isn't it?"

"I was thinking the same thing when I heard about Mr. Margolin's death. What will happen to the company now?"

Gilley shrugged. "Dunno. Furthermore, I don't care." Grievance crept back into his voice.

"I take it that the possibility of setting up a casino is gone."

"Maybe. But Diana is going to try to get the issue back before the town council. She claims we didn't get a fair shake. If they won't listen to her, she'll go to court. Those bums on the council have it in for us. They wanted their pal to get the bid, and we didn't have a chance."

He may have been right, but I didn't say so.

"Where does this leave you? You thought you'd be out of a job when Conrad died. How about now?"

Again Gilley shrugged. "I suppose Diana will keep me around because she'll need a man to do things."

"She'll take over the business then?"

"Yeah. I don't think she has any intention of quitting."

"Does she know enough about it to do so?"

"Ha!" Gilley's brief, humourless laugh was almost a bark. "If you ask me, the outfit would have folded right after Alec was killed if it wasn't for her. Old Harris, he didn't have enough brains to come in out of the rain."

"I saw your property down on the beach yesterday morning. It's a prime location. Could you do something else with it?"

"Yeah, I think so. Diana's got some feelers out. She might get a developer interested in putting in some sort of resort there. There's not much waterfront property left, so someone would probably be interested."

"So you haven't really lost. You just have to change your focus."

"I guess so."

"I heard that Ms. Lovelace said her husband bought that property to build a house for them."

Gilley gave another of his explosive barks. "That's a bunch of crap. He knew all along what he was going to use it for."

"Did she know?"

"How the hell would I know? He'd have had to build her a house somewhere, though. That place they're in now is a crummy dump."

"I take it they hadn't been here long. I got the impression last spring that all of you were from Georgetown."

"Not Georgetown; Castleton. We just came down here to be on the spot to put this casino thing over. Harris thought it might be a nice place to live anyway, so they sold their house in Castleton. Got a good price for it, too."

"It's a long ways from an airport, though." I was on a fishing expedition. I knew that Margolin's plane was still impounded as evidence and that his license had been lifted. I wondered if he was flying illegally. He seemed the type who might. But Gilley failed to rise to the bait.

"I don't know what his plans were along that line." He lowered his voice and leaned close to my ear. "Just between you and me and the gatepost, I think Harris was afraid he'd go to jail and didn't want the fair Diana to be in Castleton where she knows lots of guys. I think he was just whistling in the dark, though. If they'd put him in the slammer, she'd have moved back to the city like that!" He snapped his fingers for emphasis.

I laughed as if to show my appreciation. As long as Gilley was in the mood for spilling confidences, I'd make the most of it.

"What sort of a deal was it they were trying to put over in Exeter?"

"Oh, that! They were trying to buy up three houses in a row in an area that could be zoned commercial. They'd got hold of one a couple of years ago and had it rented out, and were working on the second, but they didn't want to press it or the owner would get a whiff of what was in the wind and raise the price. Anyway, the house in the middle belonged to some old fart who insisted on living in it until the day he died. He was aiming at living to be a hundred. All his children were dead and his grandkids were scattered all over, but they hired him a live-in nurse so he could stay in the house. We thought he'd never kick the bucket, but all of a sudden last spring he up and died. The grandkids couldn't wait to unload the dump, so we went after it. We went after the other house, too. Someone got onto what we were doing and tried to beat us to the punch. But we thought we'd got the other house sewed up, and just needed this one the old guy had lived in.

"Remember we were trying to beat some other guys to Georgetown?"

I nodded. "The other plane that took off into the storm?"

"Yeah. That was the other outfit that was trying to beat us out. They'd also topped our bid for the house on the end of the row, but we should be able to hang onto it. We might have to go to court to do so.

"The heirs of the old man, some of them lived in Georgetown. We were trying to beat that other outfit to them and get that house. Then we'd have all the available commercial property along that street."

"Did you manage?"

"Hell, yes. Alec got on the phone to the fair Diana, and she went over there in person and turned on the feminine charm. She got the sale."

Feminine charm was not anything I associated with Diana Lovelace. I suspected that money had probably been a deciding factor. It was another vision, however, that stealthily crept into my mind. A vision of two houses from a bygone era, both rented to welfare recipients, with high turnover in tenancy, flanking another house with an old man rocking away in an equally elderly chair on the front porch. I hadn't seen the old man this summer.

The three houses stood on the far side of the street across from the west end of St. Matthew's Church. The fourth structure on the block was a small commercial building housing a real estate agency and a travel bureau.

"Where in town are these three houses?" I asked tentatively, not knowing whether I wanted to hear the answer.

"In the four hundred block of Maple Street," Gilley replied.

Oh, no! I thought. Not right across from the church!

"What did you plan to do with that land?"

"Build a casino. What else?"

I launched myself on a frantic search for Douglas, though why my mission should be considered urgent, I didn't know. Nothing was going to happen in the next few days, let alone the next hour or two. I finally found someone who had seen him leave with the bishop and archbishop. They would be away all afternoon. I was left in the sultry heat with nothing to do until suppertime, so I took my swimsuit and towel and headed for the beach.

The water was too cold, the beach was too hot, the grassy area under the trees was too humid, and the mosquitoes were too numerous. I went back to my room and tried to nap. In fifteen minutes, I lay in a damp hollow on the sheet, sweat pouring off my body. I made my way to the library and sat in front of the fan.

I didn't see Douglas until supper, and he was still engaged in earnest conversation with the two bishops. I caught his attention as he left the dining room, and asked to speak to him after the evening session was over.

"Is something wrong?" he asked, sensing my urgency.

"In a way. Nothing personal. It can wait."

"Come up to our room after your session," he invited.

Gordon arrived for once in a car, a small Chevy Cavalier. His face was twisted with worry.

"What's the matter?" I inquired, alarmed by his expression.

"I've been with the police. They think Margolin was murdered."

I nodded, but didn't tell him this was not news to me. Gordon ran a hand through his thick blond hair, twisted his mouth into a grimace of pained disbelief and groaned, "The cops think I pushed him off the porch."

CHAPTER 16

"Oh, no!" I exclaimed.

"They've had me in there for the last two hours, questioning me. I didn't even have time for supper. They think someone was visiting him, he went out on that deck in back, and his visitor gave him a heave over the edge."

"But why you?"

"Because I'm opposed to casinos in the first place, and to him getting a license for one in the second place. They're quizzing all the members of the council, except one who's away. She was opposed to casinos also, and I think our mayor chose this period of time to deal with the issue because that would mean he had only one opponent present. The police also think we were trying to weight things in Demmy Scropos' favour."

"They're right, aren't they?"

Gordon twisted his face into a wry grin. "Yes, I suppose we were."

"I doubt that they really think you did it. They're probably questioning all kinds of people."

"They are. They were out at Demmy's place, but he was busy trying to get his operation set up. He was running around all over town and on the phone. Lots of people can say he was somewhere else. They've even talked to the man Margolin bought that lakeside property from. It seems he's been badmouthing Margolin because he thinks he got gypped."

"Well then..."

"But, you see, everyone else has an alibi. I don't."

I thought back to the previous morning. Gordon had come in late, somewhat out of breath. He had seemed compelled to explain his tardiness to me.

"I thought you said you were with the other council members waiting to give Mr. Scropos his license."

"I was, but I got there late. I had some personal affairs to attend to. The others were all at the Town Hall by nine, when it opens. They hung around there about ten minutes, until someone suggested they go to the coffee shop. When I got there, the receptionist told me I'd just missed the others and I'd find them at the coffee shop. It must have been about a quarter after nine. I pedaled on down there. I must have gotten there before nine-twenty. The others were all present. We stayed until about a quarter to ten, when we got word of what happened with the doublewide. Then we left, so no one could catch us all together, in case Margolin did get his place set up. I came over here to the class."

"So, do they think you did it before nine-fifteen?"

"Yes. They put it at about nine straight up."

"What were you doing before nine-fifteen? Would anyone have seen you?"

"No." He blushed a deep red. "I'll tell you something I didn't tell the police. I was talking to my kids. My wife and I are separated. She moved back to Calgary, so I don't see them very often. We have a regular time that I'm allowed to call them. My wife monitors the calls. We can't say anything private. This morning, my daughters who are twelve and nine, were left alone for about half an hour. My wife told them to stay in the house and not open the door to anyone, so Emily, the oldest, got the bright idea of calling me. I had the first good, chummy chat with my kids that I've had for a couple of years.

"But I can't give them as my alibi. Imagine the police going to those two little girls and asking them if they can give their dad an alibi because he is suspected of murder. Also imagine what my wife would make of that!"

"I see. But it's all going to come out when your wife gets the phone bill."

"But that won't be for several weeks and by that time, it will all be over — one way or another. My wife will be mad, but she won't have the kind of ammunition she would have now. I just hope I can convince them that I didn't do it before my wife catches on."

"I'm sure you can. I can't peg you as a murderer."

He grinned. "Thanks. I needed that."

I couldn't imagine him as a murderer. Not the Gordon Saunders who had given that marvellous sermon this morning. He hadn't merely been spouting some pretty words. He'd meant it. Also the questions he asked in class indicated that he was a serious scholar of Christianity. And yesterday morning, he'd come in late, with an air of little-boy delight in the way things were going. No normal human being would be as relaxed and at peace with the world if he'd committed a murder only an hour before. Gordon showed no indication that he was an amoral sociopath, the only kind of person who could have acted so at ease under the circumstances.

He couldn't have done anything like that! My fierce defence of him in my mind made me suddenly realize that I'd fallen for this man. I looked forward to seeing him at the beginning of each class, and thoroughly enjoyed our chats at the coffee break. He had a kind of physical attraction that was hard to define. He was level-headed, had a lot of common sense, was intelligent, and exuded a sort of joy in life. His previous wife must have been crazy to let him go. She sounded bitter and unforgiving, perfectly capable of using her children as pawns. That is, if Gordon was telling the truth. Was he perhaps one of those very convincing liars? No, I didn't think so. I couldn't believe that.

"At least they didn't arrest you," I pointed out.

"No. But they told me not to leave town."

The two students who gave sermons that evening were good speakers, but couldn't compare with Gordon, nor with the woman who had delivered the homily on Tuesday morning. One rather pompous man sounded like a political candidate whipping up enthusiasm for his party. He knew how to project his voice, he used humour well, he was a master of the pregnant pause. But he was too intent on relating some of his personal experiences, and the way he worked them in seemed contrived. There was no smooth transition from one theme to another, as he stretched to fit his material into the chosen subject.

A grey-haired woman of about sixty, obviously used to talking in front of people, was a contrast to the man; her speech quiet, dignified, pleasant to listen to. She presented her arguments in logical order. But it seemed to me that she had missed the point of the passage of scripture. She interpreted the parable of the lost coin as an indication that if you prayed hard enough, God would help you find what was lost. However, even I, as ignorant of scripture as I am, knew that this parable is one of a set of three, the other two being the parables of the lost sheep and the prodigal son. In all three, the point is that something that had been lost has now been found. The person who has suffered the loss is God; the object lost is a human soul. When the soul is found or restored to the fold, it means that a person who has turned away from God has now repented and returned to the Lord. Therefore, the Lord rejoices and throws a party.

We cheerfully picked the sermons to pieces, but it was done in a way that, oddly enough, didn't give offence. There was plenty of praise as well, and the criticism was indeed constructive.

At least, I thought, I might not match Gordon, but I could do better than these two!

Betty and Douglas had their window wide open, as was the door to the corridor. Even at nine o'clock, the air was hot and still.

"We're going to take some folding chairs out on the lawn where it's cooler," Betty said. "Come join us. Michael and Gerry are going to be there."

"Perhaps Robin has something she wants to say in private." Douglas raised his eyebrows in query.

"It concerns you both, and the Bishop as well, actually."

"Okay. Let's grab some cold drinks from the fridge. We stocked up this afternoon."

Betty pulled a six-pack of soft drinks out of the refrigerator in the communal kitchenette, and we trooped out to the lawn. We found chairs and carried them to an open area of level lawn. The Staines joined us. The others looked the way I felt — drained of energy by the humid heat.

Clouds began to blot out the remnants of twilight, and the stars overhead, causing darkness to descend earlier than usual. To the west, the black billows were periodically lit up from within by sheets of lightning. Thunder rumbled in the distance.

We engaged in lethargic conversation as we sipped our drinks straight out of the can. Bishop Michael remarked, "I glanced at the thermometer on the way out. It's still thirty degrees. They say that temperatures in the single digits are cold, teens are cool, twenties warm, thirties hot, and forties Hell."

"Then," said Betty, "if it cools off one more degree, it will be merely warm."

"Ha, not likely," Michael opined. "Not with this humidity."

Finally Douglas turned toward me in the gloom and asked, "What's troubling you Robin?"

"It's about this man who was killed, Margolin, and the others in his business," I started to explain.

Douglas interpreted to the Bishop and his wife, "Robin knew the man. He was a pilot, and last spring she prevented him from taking off with his business partners into some bad weather. Instead of being grateful, he sued her for slander. We were talking about the impending trial on the way up here."

"Slander!" Gerry exclaimed. "What on earth for?"

"You may well ask!" I responded bitterly. I told them about the events of that day last spring.

"They were in a race to get hold of some property. One of the owners lived in Georgetown. Each group was trying to get there first. At that time, Margolin lived in Castleton, which is between here and Georgetown.

Margolin's partner called Margolin's wife, who was also a partner in the business, and sent her to Georgetown to visit the property owner in person and clinch the deal. It worked. They got the owner's signature."

I took a swig of my soft drink and surveyed the advancing clouds. It wouldn't be long before we'd have to run for cover, I thought.

"This afternoon, one of those men was over here talking to Evelyn McNaughton about damage to the tree. I'd met him in Exeter two days after the storm. Margolin was getting ready to fly up to Georgetown, or maybe to Castleton — I don't know for sure. He ran his plane into his partner, killing him."

I heard Gerry gasp.

"The third man was this one, Sam Gilley, who was down here today. I had talked to him after the — uh, accident." I glanced at Douglas. He was waiting for me to commit myself about the cause of the supposed accident. I decided not to.

"Gilley had told me quite a bit about the business last spring, and he told me more today. He told me something that causes me quite a bit of concern."

In the faint glow of an outdoor light, I saw Michael nod.

"Their business was real estate speculation," I continued. "They bought up property in places where they had a good expectation that the value would soon go up. I think they had feelers out all over the place to sense what was in the wind. Then they'd get themselves in a position to take advantage of it."

"I understand that is what was going on here with this casino issue," Douglas remarked.

"Exactly. Anyway, I asked Gilley this afternoon, out of curiosity, what it was they were buying in Exeter. He told me that they were trying to buy up a row of three old houses on land that was ripe to be zoned commercial. The way he described the houses made me wonder if they were those dilapidated houses across Maple Street from the church. I was right. They were."

"Where the old man sits in his rocking chair? He always waves to me. Come to think of it, though, I haven't seen him this summer."

"He died last spring."

"I'm sorry to hear that."

"That's the house they were rushing up to Georgetown to get the signature on. I think that they probably don't have everything sewed up yet, but Gilley sounds very confident. So I asked him what they wanted the houses for. It's not the actual houses they want, it's the land. They want to build a casino."

I heard Betty gasp. "Not right across the street from the church!"

"Right across the street from the church."

"They can't build a casino in Exeter," Douglas stated, but his voice held concern. "The city government won't allow it."

"The current city government won't. But as Gilley so aptly pointed out to me, they won't be in power forever."

"Surely the citizens won't stand for a casino," Betty pleaded.

"Don't be so sure. I've talked to Gordon Saunders quite a lot this week. He's on the village council here in Mallard Beach. He and one other are the only councillors who are opposed to casinos. The others are out for tax revenue in any form they can get it. Mallard Beach isn't so different from any other place, Exeter included. I know that Victoria Bainbridge isn't going to run for mayor again. She says three terms are enough. She has run a rock-solid city government, balancing business needs with the necessity of maintaining Exeter's culture and beauty. But there isn't anyone to take her place."

"Someone will come along. We are a very stable city."

"That may be a disadvantage, actually. We're used to good government. Nothing has happened to rock the boat. We've probably become too complacent, expecting things to go along on an even keel forever. The opposition is probably licking its chops. The city could be a pushover for some high-powered group pledging 'reform' even where none is needed."

Douglas leaned forward, resting his elbows on his knees. "You're probably right. I think we should look into this. I take it that the land isn't zoned commercial yet."

"Not yet. They have to put up notices and inform the neighbours."

"Well then, we have to find out what sort of zoning they need in order to do this, and try to block it. I presume we will have the assistance of the Diocese, since it owns the church," Douglas inquired, directing his remark to the Bishop.

"You will. Find out what you can as soon as you get back, and let me know. Then we'll formulate a plan of action."

"Robin," Douglas said, turning toward me, "you seem to have an absolute genius for landing yourself in the middle of the action."

As if to give this remark veracity, the sky opened up with a blinding flash of lightning, followed immediately by a tremendous clap of thunder, which rolled away across the mountains. As abruptly as the searing light had illuminated the earth, the grounds of Idylwyld were plunged into total blackness.

But not before we had seen starkly etched against the brilliant background, several crouching figures, garbed in dark clothes, scurry like startled rabbits from a mound in the upper lawn, across the open space, then disappear behind the lodge.

CHAPTER 17

"What on earth was that?" Betty asked, startled.

"They came from that mound," Douglas asserted, rising. He turned to Michael. "What is it, do you know?"

Michael also was on his feet. "I think it's an old root cellar. It's been locked up ever since I've been coming here. Let's go take a look."

Gerry produced a flashlight, and the five of us trekked across the lawn in the inky darkness. Behind us in the lodge, we could hear people calling out to one another, looking for candles, finding their flashlights.

The mound loomed ahead. Gerry's light found a rickety wooden door with a hasp, to which was fastened a sturdy padlock. "It is locked," she stated firmly.

"Yes, but..." Douglas took hold of the hasp and gave a slight tug. The screws holding it pulled easily out of worn holes in the decaying wood of the door frame. The door swung outward on creaky hinges, no more solidly set in the wood than the hasp had been.

A musty smell wafted forth from the cavernous interior of the old root cellar, but along with it two other odours.

"I haven't been in the church for all these years without being able to recognize that!" Michael exclaimed. "Candle wax. Someone has just put out a candle." He took the torch from Gerry, stepped gingerly down the rickety steps inside the door, and played the light around the interior. We followed him, carefully trying each step before putting our weight on it.

In the centre of the space stood a small table, an old coffee table by the look of it. In a semi-circle around the near side were low stools that might have been rescued from some junkyard. On the far side, dug into the earthen floor, was a fire ring. Smouldering embers had been nearly extinguished by water from a pitcher, which appeared to be from the kitchen. Michael turned the beam of light upward, and we could see lingering remnants of smoke up in the rafters. The smell of wood smoke was still discernible.

On the table stood a candle, the last wisps of smoke dying away. Under it was a black cloth. There was nothing else in the room.

"I wonder what they were doing?" Betty ventured.

"Some sort of ceremony," Michael mused. "I don't like it."

"Not black magic, I hope," Gerry said, alarm in her voice.

"Something like that."

"Who do you suppose it was?"

Michael responded grimly, "The youth workers, I suspect. What do you think, Douglas?"

"I imagine you're right. They certainly seemed agile in the way they moved. I can't imagine the course participants doing this."

"They could have been outsiders," Gerry suggested tentatively.

Her husband sighed. "I suppose so. But they did dash off in the direction of the youth quarters. If they'd been outsiders, you would think they would take off up the hill."

We stood in silence as Michael shone the light carefully around the perimeter of the space. "I guess I'll have to go speak to them, but not tonight in the dark."

We could tell by the blackness outside that the electricity was still off.

Betty stirred in the background. "I wonder why they had the fire?"

"Hmm. I don't know."

"You don't think they could have been sacrificing anything, do you?"

Gerry gasped. "Not an animal sacrifice!"

"No!" I exclaimed. Everyone turned toward me, expectantly. But I had seen something when Michael was playing the flashlight around the room — a small, closely placed pair of dull red spots, reflecting the light. I reached out and took the torch from him, and directed the beam along one of the low rafters. A throaty sound like "Mrrph" emanated from overhead and Paprika, the fat orange cat, came waddling along the rafter toward me. I put out my hand and she bumped it with her head and began to drool. A nervous laugh flickered around the small group of people.

"If they had brought her in here to sacrifice her, she'd be scared out of her mind, and would have run past us when we opened the door. Look at her. She's perfectly calm. She probably followed the kids in here without them knowing."

"Then it's a good thing we saw what we did. Otherwise she'd have been shut in without anyone knowing where to look for her." This obviously bothered Betty a good deal.

"I expect we'd better tell Evelyn," Douglas suggested, always the practical one.

"Yes," Michael answered. "I'll go down to her cottage." The Director lived in a cottage on the lower edge of the grounds.

Gerry dithered, "Do we have to call the police?"

"Good heavens, no!" Betty exclaimed.

"I shouldn't think so," the Bishop said calmly. "If it was the youth workers, it's not even trespass, and certainly nothing criminal."

"In fact," Douglas counselled, "I think we should be careful not to say anything to them. If they hear about the possibility of some sort of sacrifice, someone might get the idea that the death next door was a part of the ritual."

"Oh, surely not!" Bishop Michael exclaimed.

"You'd be surprised. We had an experience of that, didn't we Robin?"

I nodded in assent, remembering all too clearly an incident from two years before. The man who'd made the claim was a nutty old codger, but he'd created a sensation nonetheless.

"Idylwyld doesn't need that sort of publicity," Douglas stated firmly. "So let's all keep mum about this, and let Michael handle it."

"Absolutely!" Betty expressed the feeling of all of us.

We carefully closed the shaky old door, and made a dash for our lodges, our way lighted by flashes of lightning in the clouds overhead. It was pouring rain. My room still felt like a steam bath. I undressed in the dark and dropped into bed, pulling only the sheet over me. In the middle of the night, I awoke feeling chilled. Rain driven in through the window screen made a puddle on the floor. I shut the window, pulled a blanket over me and nestled back into the bed.

I slept soundly, not wakening until almost seven. Too late to go down to the beach and practice my sermon. I looked out at the dripping trees, and decided that wouldn't have been a good idea anyway. The rain had stopped, but lumpy grey clouds obscured the mountaintops, and wisps of fog drifted across the lake. The sky looked brighter in the west, giving promise of better weather.

I met the Forsythes and the Staines on their way to breakfast. I fell in step with them. The power had come on during the night, and the kitchen was in full operation. We sat together, eating poached eggs on toast, porridge and fruit. At another table, Lucy showed nervousness about the sermon she was to give, and several other course participants were teasing her to get her mind off it. Kathy was with them. Colin Broadstreet sat morosely at a table by himself. Obviously he hadn't been able to pick up any other unattached woman. It didn't seem to have been a successful week for him.

Because of the lack of privacy, we said nothing about the events of the night before, but I was sitting facing the room, and about half way through breakfast I saw Todd, the handsome young worker, enter. He glanced toward our table, hesitated, then picked up a sweet roll, poured himself a glass of apple juice, and sat at a table near the door. He perched on the edge of his chair, ran a hand jerkily down the side of his face, and took a bite of his roll, probably not even tasting it.

Aha! I thought. One of our fleeing conspirators, no doubt.

Betty began to load dishes onto one of the trays. This seemed to be Todd's cue. He rose hastily, skirted another table, and made his way to ours. Distress showing on his face in the form of an anguished frown, he addressed the Bishop.

"May I speak to you a minute, Sir?"

"Certainly, Todd. In private, or is this good enough?"

"Oh, this is fine. You all know about it." Seeing the wonder on our faces, he explained, "We came back, you see. We just ran far enough to get under shelter of the porch at Spruce Lodge. We saw you go over there, so we snuck back. We heard what you said."

He stopped, gulped, and dropped his gaze to the floor.

"We're sorry about Paprika. We didn't know she was there. We weren't doing anything awful like sacrificing any animals. And if Paprika had gone missing, we'd have gone over there and looked while everyone was in their seminars. Paprika kind of follows me around."

"I'm glad to get that cleared up," Bishop Michael said calmly. "Just what were you doing?"

"Well, it's like this. A bunch of us thought we'd like to see if we could get in touch with something in the spiritual world, like. We thought that if we sat around a candle in the dark and kind of meditated, maybe something would come to us."

Michael sighed. "What about the fire?"

"Well, see, we didn't have much luck just with the candle, so we thought we'd try a fire. But we couldn't get it to go. It was all smoky and Sandy started to cough. We thought we'd be heard, or that the smoke would show up, or someone would smell it. There's a vent sort of thing in the ceiling, and the smoke sort of went up there."

That explained the relative lack of smoke by the time we had gotten there. I'd wondered about that.

Todd went on, "We could hear the thunder, and we sort of thought we should get out before it started to rain, so we made sure the fire and the candle were out and closed the door so it wouldn't look disturbed, and started to run across the lawn. I guess you saw us because of the lightning."

"How many of you were there?"

"Five last night. There've been others. We've been doing this for a couple of weeks."

Michael shifted uncomfortably in his chair. I could see he didn't want to ask the next question. "Sit down, Todd," he invited. The youth perched on the edge of a chair, like a wild animal ready to sprint for cover if the danger it perceived came closer.

"Why have you been trying to get in touch with the spirit world?"

"Not the spirit world! I didn't mean that. I mean… Well, it's hard to explain." He rested his head in his hands. "I mean, we wanted to have some real contact with God. We never have. We want to know that God really exists."

"Most people go to church for that reason," Michael said gently. "Others find God in their homes, or at work, or in nature."

"But we haven't." He lifted his head. There were tears in his eyes. "Sandy had a boyfriend who died of a drug overdose. Everyone told her to trust in God, but she can't find Him. Rick is gay. I guess you know that. And a guy he knows has AIDS. Everyone tells him that it is God punishing his friend. He comes from a real religious family, and they sent him off here to get him away from his friend. Nothing like that has happened to me, but I've just been going to church all my life and I can't say I've ever met Jesus, or had God answer my prayers, or anything. So before we give up on religion, we wanted to see if we could somehow, like, get in touch."

"And the programs we have here for the youth staff don't help you do that?"

Todd shook his head miserably.

"Then I have to apologize to you," Michael said gently.

Todd jerked his head up and stared at the Bishop, his mouth dropping open. "But...but..."

I had the impression that for a youth to have one of the highest officials of the church apologize to him was so preposterous in his way of thinking, he seemed unable to take it in. He had come to apologize to the Bishop, not the other way around. People like the Bishop had power. They could tell others what to do. The church is a hierarchy. The Bishop's power in his Diocese is absolute. He had caught them doing something that was wrong in the eyes of the church. Why wasn't he punishing them, kicking them out or something like that? What was this man saying?

"In the first place," Michael explained, "you have probably met Jesus and have had your prayers answered without realizing it. Not everyone has a 'Road to Damascus' experience. Do you know what I'm talking about?"

Todd nodded. "St. Paul."

"The realization of God working in your life may be very mundane. You may not even recognize it at the time, but if you think back over the events and changes in your life, you may be able to detect where it has occurred. Also, I wonder if you have really, seriously prayed."

"I think so."

"Private prayer is something we should all do, but we also need group prayer. I know of many groups who have faced a difficult challenge, decided to ask for the Lord's guidance, and surrounded themselves and their efforts with prayer, asking others also to pray for them, and for the success of their efforts. These groups often have amazing success. God doesn't send them a fax saying, "Well done!" but they know they have had God's help in accomplishing their task.

"Some individuals have sought God by emptying themselves of worldly distractions and opening themselves to God. They often don't realize the success they have had until later."

The youth nodded but said nothing.

"What would you like me to do for you?" the Bishop asked.

"I didn't come here to ask for anything. I came to say we were sorry. The others sort of elected me to go to you."

"And you have done your duty. But I see that we haven't done what we intended to do in bringing you here for the summer. You need something you aren't getting. I'd like to know what it is."

"Well…" Todd hesitated. He gulped hard. "We don't think much of the morning services. They don't do anything for us."

"In what way?"

"They don't seem, like, relevant. They're not like the real world."

"How could they be more real?"

"Well, there's all that scripture reading, about guys who lived thousands of years ago. There's nothing about guys who have to live with AIDS, or kids whose dads beat them up, or stuff like that. It's all about a bunch of old relics."

"What about the sermons? We try to relate the scriptures to modern life."

"Well, yeah. But it doesn't make up for all the other stuff."

"Would you like more input into the form of the morning services?"

"Yeah, that would be great! But..." Todd frowned. "That never got us anywhere before. We've always been told that our ideas are too wild."

Michael smiled. "I think perhaps what you should do is write your own psalms."

"What?"

"You might try it. Anyway, it appears that I need to have a talk with all the youth staff. Let's see. When can we do it? I have the morning conference, and you all have duties in the afternoon and evening. I wonder. I think I'll ask Dr. McNaughton if she will let the kitchen and dining room staff off during the late afternoon. Perhaps some of the adults can volunteer to help. How about four o'clock?"

"The guys at the beach don't finish till four."

"Would four-thirty be better?"

Todd nodded.

"Very well. Tell all the others, not just the ones in your little group, but all the youth staff, that there will be a meeting in your quarters at four-thirty. I'll fix it with the Director. We'll see what we can work out."

"Thank you, Sir." Todd jumped to his feet and scurried off.

We sat for a moment in silence, then Gerry said tentatively, "I hope he was right about the cat."

"Yes," I said. "I'm sure he was. Our first day here, we saw him talking to that cat. He obviously liked it, and I'd say he loved and understood cats, just by the way he spoke."

Douglas and Betty nodded their assent.

Michael heaved himself to his feet. "I'd better go find Evelyn again."

CHAPTER 18

Since those five fleeing figures had been illuminated by the flash of lightning, the subjects of murder and of casinos opening across the street from my church had not even crossed my mind. They had seemed to be issues of overwhelming importance, but when contrasted with the monumental problem concerning alienation of youth from the modern church, they suddenly became trivial. I was impressed, awed even, by the Bishop's approach to their plight. He might not solve the problem for all the youth in the world, but undoubtedly he would do something for this dozen seekers of God.

Whatever he planned to do, he must have gotten a big boost from Lucy, whose sermon was "right on" when it came to relevance in the modern world. But it wasn't the sermons the kids objected to, I recalled. The problem was deeper than that.

In class, we critiqued Lucy's sermon, praising her for it. She glowed with vitality, the shock of her gruesome discovery temporarily forgotten. At the coffee break, I sought her out and congratulated her.

"Wait until tomorrow," she said modestly. "You are going to leave us all in the dust."

"I doubt it," I replied.

"Oh, but you are. I can feel it. There's something special about you."

I can't say that I'd ever noticed it, whatever it was. But I couldn't dismiss Lucy as some sort of a crock. There was something special about *her*.

We took our coffee outside and found lawn chairs. The sun was trying to peep out, the air beginning to warm.

"I called my son last night. He was astonished that I was giving a sermon. He wished me luck, and would you believe, he asked for a copy!"

"What is this magnificent moniker you gave your boy, anyway?"

"Charles Frederick Edward Merriman. But to me, he's Charlie."

"I think I would like Charlie. I like his mother. And if he had become a jazz drummer, he could have called himself Charlie Merrie."

Her peal of laughter rang across the spacious lawns. "By the way," she asked, "is Carruthers your married name, or did you take your maiden name back?"

"It's my husband's name."

"Why did you keep it?"

"Because my licenses were in that name, and because my maiden name was Smith. I didn't think Smith Aviation would cut it."

"Let's see, you could have called yourself the Flying Smith. No, the Flightsmith! But you could still have used Red Robin."

"I hadn't thought that one up yet."

Colin Broadstreet hadn't given up. He waylaid me after lunch, asking me what I had planned for the afternoon. I pretended I had to do more work on my sermon. Actually, I had nothing planned, other than a short canoe outing with Betty.

"Then let's go out to dinner. There's a pub with a big screen TV up the road a ways. We can borrow someone's car…"

"Whose?"

"Oh, I'll find someone. The people I came with, maybe."

"No thanks."

"Why not?" He sounded annoyed.

"I have other plans."

I brushed past him and left the dining room. Outside, I bumped into Gordon Saunders.

"Hey, I've been looking for you," he exclaimed buoyantly.

"Well, here I am!" I responded, grinning at him. He seemed to bring out the merriment in me. Except for last night, when he had just come from the police, he radiated cheerfulness.

"I hear you knew this guy, Margolin."

"Yes. Where did you hear that?"

"Oh, word gets around."

"Gossip seems to travel almost as fast in a small town as it does in a church."

He threw back his head and roared with laughter. "Not quite. Nothing beats a church. Unless it's the government trying to keep the lid on a secret document."

"I understand that most government leaks are contrived."

"I expect so. We don't go in for that in our small domain."

"But you do keep your eyes and ears open to find out what's going on, and who's doing what."

"Oh, sure." His eyes widened with innocent wonder. I couldn't help laughing.

He lowered his voice. "I heard that you told the police Margolin was responsible for an accident where his partner was killed."

"Yes."

"How did you know about it?"

"I missed by about half a minute seeing it happen."

His eyes and his mouth opened wide in astonishment.

"Margolin murdered his partner."

"Robin!"

Well, at least I was one up on the Mallard Bay gossip network. He hadn't heard that one yet.

"How? I heard it was a plane crash."

"No. Not a plane crash. Margolin ran his plane into Conrad, his partner. Killed him with the prop."

"And you almost saw it?"

"I saw the aftermath. I wish I hadn't."

"Look, Robin. I'd like to hear more about this. How about going to dinner tonight? I'll take you to the Hilltop Steakhouse, Demmy Scropos' place. Do you like steak?"

"I love it! After the meals here, I could eat an entire prime, grade triple A steer."

"Good! It's a date. I'll pick you up about five-thirty. They open at six."

I turned back toward the dining room to tell my friends I wouldn't be there for supper, and found Colin standing a couple of yards behind me, his glowering face the colour of a ripe plum.

That's tough buddy, I thought. I'm not going to apologize for picking another dinner partner.

The Hilltop Steakhouse was aptly named. It stood about a city block off the highway, but visible to passing cars. Perched on the top of a small knoll, it had a commanding view of the valley. Not your neighbourhood cafe, it did not serve breakfast or lunch, but catered to the affluent retirees who had flocked to the lakeshore from the cities, where they had been used to a choice of fine restaurants. Gordon told me that it would be packed later in the evening, but he had been able to get a reservation for six o'clock.

I had not brought anything other than casual clothes, but Gordon assured me that dressing up was not necessary. Even the city folk caught on quickly to the laid-back country ways. They came in slacks and golf shirts. The waiters would be wearing dinner jackets, but you'd be hard pressed to find a necktie or a pair of high heels among the diners. He himself arrived to pick me up wearing light tan slacks and a short-sleeved shirt in a jungle print. I had donned my most neatly pressed slacks, light green in colour, and a blouse of a muted green and peach plaid. I wore a pair of white moccasins, rather than my runners.

We parked beside the restaurant just as the doors were being opened, and walked into a room of quiet luxury. Tinted glass filtered the light of the sun, now shining out of a brilliant blue sky. Mini-blinds had been closed over the west-facing windows and customers were being seated at the east end of the room. The entire dining area had been made into a number of small private nooks by artful arrangement of screens, potted plants and pillars. Soft music of a semi-classical nature, and indirect lighting added to the elegance of the setting.

The man greeting the early arrivals looked just as I expected a Greek to look. I assumed that he was the proprietor. His shiny black hair lay in neat waves, not a strand out of place. His small moustache was trimmed to perfection. Sharp black eyes took in the guests, and flicked around the room to see that all was in readiness. He stood about five feet ten or eleven, with a slim waist and broad shoulders. His finely chiselled features, firm mouth, and deeply tanned skin gave him an air of authority, of someone to be reckoned with. Contrasting him with what I remembered of Harris Margolin, I decided that the latter had never had a chance in the showdown between the two.

Would he have had a chance in a physical contest? The Greek was dressed in a perfectly fitting tuxedo, but muscles rippled beneath the cloth. His neck, thick and muscular, was not the result of the mountain climbing I had heard that he did. I suspected that Demmy Scropos had a weight bench in his basement, used with regularity.

"Robin, I'd like you to meet Demmy Scropos. Demmy, this is Robin Carruthers."

Scropos bowed, his smile turning to one of genuine warmth. "I am very pleased to meet you. I have heard about you from Gordon."

I could feel myself blushing. What had he heard about me from Gordon? I returned the compliment, and Scropos led us to a table for two beside the window, facing northward, overlooking the lake. The land shelved down to the lakeshore, each fairly level patch being occupied by neat new houses. I was happy to see that they'd built the houses without knocking down all the trees, and though the area was newly built up, it was green and shady.

Scropos handed each of us a large menu, doing so with a slight flourish. The menu was burgundy coloured with gold lettering that said, "Hilltop Steakhouse, Mallard Beach, British Columbia," and at the bottom, "Demetrios Scropos, Proprietor."

"Beware Greeks bearing menus," Gordon quipped. Scropos chuckled. They were obviously good friends, not merely casual acquaintances.

"Would you like a drink to begin?"

"What about a good wine of your choosing?" Gordon looked across at me with raised eyebrows.

"Whatever you like," I murmured.

He turned to the restaurateur. "Demmy, I'll let you recommend one. I think we are both going to have steaks, so probably a red wine."

"We have an excellent Pinot Noir, a local wine which has just won a prize in an international competition. You know, British Columbia wines are making a name for themselves these days."

"That would be fine."

Scropos himself returned with the wine, removed the cork, and poured a dark red splash into Gordon's glass. Gordon swirled it and sniffed, smiling happily. He tasted and pronounced it excellent. These preliminaries successfully accomplished, Scropos filled our glasses and departed, saying, "I'll send George, my son, over to take care of you personally." He stopped on the other side of the room and spoke to a lean young man, an immature copy of himself. George appeared at our table.

"Are you ready to order, or would you like more time?"

To me Gordon said, "They do a superlative T-bone steak here."

"That would be wonderful." I hadn't had a T-bone for months, and Idylwyld's food all week had been monotonously semi-vegetarian. I had begun to think I could never look another salad in the face.

We started with lentil soup, followed by a small Greek salad. The steaks came on sizzling platters. "The plate is very hot," George warned us as, holding each with a towel, he set them before us. On the steak was a delicate sauce of tiny onions and a blend of herbs I could not identify. The baked potatoes came with a tray full of condiments. Several vegetables were decoratively arrayed on the plate. The tender, juicy steak was not the same as the ones you can buy in the stores. I commented to Gordon, "Have you noticed that all the things that add taste to food are things we are told not to eat? Fat, sugar, salt."

"It's not just food that people treat that way," Gordon opined. "Everything people enjoy is on some religion's hit list?"

"Funny you should say that," I remarked. "It's part of my sermon for tomorrow."

"Oh! That's right! Tomorrow's your big day. How's it coming along?"

"Okay, I think."

We had small bowls of strawberries in cream for desert, then as George brought us coffee, Gordon leaned back, sighed and said, "Now for the lowdown. Come on, Robin. Give!"

"What do you want to know?"

"All about how you came to know Harris Margolin, and why you think he killed his partner."

I went through the entire story again, in more detail than I had given the police, since they could get the information from Cpl. Nash if they wanted it. To Gordon, I described the weather that had preceded the storm, the reactions of the three men from Harcon Holdings to the weather and to each other, my seeing them again two days later, and the events leading up to Alec Conrad's death. I explained why the circumstances as I had seen them when I returned from the flight with Lance Brock had convinced me that Margolin had deliberately run into Conrad. I had not gone into this detail with anyone else, but Gordon had that effect on me. He listened with rapt attention, occasionally asking a question.

Finally, he remarked, "What a bunch of wicked people. The townsfolk here have never liked the Margolins. It looks as if they have good reason."

We discussed Margolin's death, dragging out the various alibis and examining them.

"I hope you think mine is truthful," Gordon said with the air of a little boy asking for a cookie.

I laughed. "I can't imagine you in the role of murderer, whether or not you have an alibi."

He grinned happily. "Thanks," he said.

My eyes strayed to a neighbouring table, where Demmy Scropos stood talking to an elderly couple, his broad-shouldered back toward us.

"Just how good is Demmy's alibi?"

"He was running around town getting everything in order to set up his casino. Would you like to go there after dinner? We've plenty of time before the evening session starts."

"No thanks. Casinos don't interest me in the least. But to get back to Demmy, all this running around doesn't really give him an alibi. It may actually prevent him from being able to give a coherent account of where he was at the relevant time. People will just remember that he was in and out several times, and get mixed up on exactly when those times were. I'm sure the police will try to pin his movements down a lot better, but it might not be possible."

Gordon stared at Demmy's back, frowning. "I can't imagine him committing murder."

"I hope you're right."

But I wondered whether a man so dedicated to encouraging people who could not afford it to squander their grocery money, in the futile hope of instant riches, would be totally incapable of other anti-social acts. I'm afraid I had a less sanguine view of Demetrios Scropos' character than Gordon had.

CHAPTER 19

At the evening session of the course, two more students, a man and a woman, gave quite good sermons. The two bishops commented favourably on the quality of the effort by course participants. Since most of these people were going back to small parishes where they only had a priest in attendance every two to four weeks, they were going to be able to use their newfound knowledge. It would seem that the church was in good hands.

Lucy, Gordon and I, along with a few other students, whiled away the lingering minutes of twilight in lawn chairs under the cottonwood trees. Gradually the ranks thinned, Lucy being the last to say goodnight. Gordon saw me to the unlighted side door of Pine Lodge. We paused for a few last words before I entered my quarters. Suddenly, he took me in his arms and kissed me. Not a brotherly sort of kiss; a passionate one that spoke of years without an intimate female companion.

He's married, my brain told me. Don't get involved.

But my brain was not ruling my heart that night, and I too had been without any sort of tender caress for years. I gave in completely, returning his kiss with passion. After a while we came up for air. Gordon gave an embarrassed little laugh.

"I shouldn't have done that," he murmured.

"Why not. No harm done," I replied, trying to keep my voice light.

"I hope I'll see you again after you leave this session."

"You might. It's a small world." What I didn't say to him, which perhaps I ought to have done, was that I had no intention of becoming involved with a married man. After he got his divorce from his testy wife, we'd see. Not until then.

He said goodnight, and I slipped through the side door into the dimly lit hallway of Pine Lodge.

I glanced through my sermon again, but couldn't see any changes that needed to be made. I'd get up early in the morning, go down to the beach, and try it out loud one more time. I undressed, showered and turned down the bed. Somewhere, a door closed and a little puff of air blew down the corridor. My door had not been quite latched, and now it swung inward a few inches, opening a crack only a foot from the head of my bed in the narrow single room.

The last person in had shut off the hallway lights. Outside my door the place was in total blackness. I closed the door thoughtfully, listening to the latch click into place. I remembered the lady who had insisted on a lock on her door; this door. I had thought her silly, but now I wasn't so sure. I had a queasy feeling about this unlocked door, one that would open right at the head of my bed. I formed a mental picture of Colin Broadstreet's angry face. Would he actually try to come into a woman's room? I wouldn't put it past him. Perhaps she hadn't been so foolish after all.

Typically one hears of wedging a chair under the doorknob. I looked at the flimsy little chair at the desk and shook my head. My cat could probably dislodge that if he wanted through the door badly enough.

Once when I had gone somewhere on an airliner, I hadn't trusted the zipper on my bag to the ministrations of airline baggage handlers. I had secured it with a heavy elastic strap with a hook on each end that we normally used to tie down cargo in our planes. When I unpacked, I always stowed the strap in a side pocket of the bag. Might I have done that when I unpacked after returning home? I got the bag out of the closet and rummaged in its pockets. The strap was there.

I looped the strap over the doorknob and around a post of the bedstead, hooking the two ends together. I tried the door. In pushing the door open, the bed scraped across the floor far enough that a person on the outside could have gotten a hand through the crack. But my weight would be on the bed. I sat down on it and tried again. The strap held, and the door would not clear the frame. So, with this makeshift lock, I crawled into bed and turned out the light.

I didn't fall asleep for a long time. I lay there listening to the night noises. Nothing stirred.

Eventually I must have slept. I awakened with a start as I heard the click of the latch on the door. In the dim light of an exterior floodlight seeping through the slats of the blinds, I could see the door open slightly, the elastic strap expand just a little. The bed did not move. I could hear heavy breathing beyond the crack in the door, and a muffled grunt as the person there met unexpected opposition.

Colin? Probably.

The tip of a stubby finger tried to work its way through the narrow opening, searching to find whatever held the door shut. I watched with fascination, hardly daring to move. Then, as the man (it was obviously not a woman's finger) got his index finger through the opening between the door and the jamb, I quietly sat up. I waited until the finger had worked its way in far enough not to be easily removed, then flung my shoulder against the door, putting all my weight behind it.

The man screamed, a blood-curdling howl like a wounded dog. I removed my weight from the door, the finger was pulled out, and heavy steps stumbled down the corridor. I removed the strap, flung the door open, and stuck my head out into the hallway, not bothering to put a robe over my pyjamas. He was gone around the corner. Lights came on in other rooms. A man poked his head out of a room beside mine and called out, "What's going on?" Two women across from me cried out in unison, "Robin, are you all right?"

"I'm all right," I replied. "I think someone stumbled over something in the corridor. No one is here now, so I guess he's okay."

Doors closed, lights went out, and the lodge returned to its midnight stillness.

What was it that Lucy had said? Something about the presence of evil. Sam Gilley and Colin Broadstreet had been the men present at that time. I'd thought nothing of it then. Later when I'd recognized Gilley, I assumed he was the one she was talking about. Now I wasn't sure. Maybe it was Colin who had given her the shivers. No, she'd once referred to him as "harmless." Assuming that my nocturnal visitor was Colin, Lucy had for once been wrong. But I'd fixed him, I thought. He wouldn't come back, I was sure of that.

It must have been Colin. Anyway, in the morning I'd know. There was blood on the door jamb. I'd marked my assailant all right.

I slept until about six, waking with a start. I dressed hurriedly, picked up the notes for my sermon, and made my way down to the beach. No one was there. Way up the beach I could see a man's figure walking slowly toward me. It would take him a while to get down this far. I had plenty of time.

I went through my sermon aloud, but I had gone over it so often, it was now becoming boring. I'd even memorized the quote from Lewis. Enough is enough, I told myself. Leave it until the morning service. Nothing I do now is going to improve it.

I recognized the strolling figure as Douglas and waited for him. He saw the sheaf of papers in my hand and asked, "How's it coming? Nervous?"

"Yes, I'm nervous, but I think I've done all I can on it. I don't know why I volunteered to give a sermon in front of an archbishop, a bishop and you."

"None of us will bite. Don't let us worry you. You'll be fine."

"If I don't, promise you won't tell anyone back home."

He laughed. "Okay. I won't. Don't worry."

We walked back toward the switchback trail, and started toiling up it. When we paused for a rest about half way up it, I said, "I want to tell you what happened last night. I don't know whether I should report it or let it go. I'd like your advice."

Douglas nodded and waited.

"Remember that man who's been trying to make advances to Kathy?"

"You mean Colin, don't you? I thought Kathy's husband straightened him out."

"He did, but since then, Colin has been making a play for me."

"Yes, I noticed that, but I figured you could handle him. What happened?"

I told him about Colin's anger when I accepted a dinner date with Gordon just after I had turned Colin down; about my fears because of the unlocked door, and my makeshift barricade; about the man who had tried to get in during the night. I heard Douglas' startled intake of breath.

"Are you sure it was Colin?"

"I don't know yet, but it will be easy to find out. He has at least one smashed finger. It will show. If Colin has a bandage or an obvious injury, then he's the one."

"And you're worried about spending another night under the same roof?"

"Oh, no! I don't think he'll bother me again. But this place is so sure of the safety of guests and their property in unlocked rooms. I don't know whether to give them the bad news or not. It will probably never happen again."

We started up the trail again, Douglas deep in thought. When we reached the top, he stopped.

"Let me tell Michael about it in private. I'll see what he thinks. He is, of course, the ultimate authority here."

"Poor Michael! He's certainly had his problems here this session."

"He's very good at handling things in a quiet and diplomatic way. He will probably want to hear it from you personally."

"Okay. In between the police, I'll fit him in," I laughed. At least it was something to keep my mind off my sermon.

We went in to breakfast. Douglas saw Bishop Michael coming and waylaid him outside the dining room. I sat with my usual companions, Lucy and Kathy, and with the two women who had the room across from me. I took a chair near the wall, facing the room so I could watch for Colin, or for that matter, any other man with an injured finger. The other women asked me about my sermon. I laid the written notes on the table beside my plate.

I thought that Colin was going to miss breakfast, but eventually he came in. His right hand was thrust into his trouser pocket as he went to the coffee machine and ran coffee into a cup. He set it down, and still using his left hand, spooned sugar into his cup, and poured in some milk. Still with his left hand, he picked up a spoon and carried his coffee to a table on the opposite side of the room, sitting alone. It had been him all right!

Our group was breaking up. We piled our dishes onto our trays, and I offered to carry them to the far end of the room, where I placed various items in labelled tubs, scraped the leavings into the garbage, and stacked the trays. Lucy and Kathy were ready to leave, but the other two women were still sipping coffee and engaging in vigorous conversation when I left with the trays. I left my notes on the table, expecting someone to be there when I returned. But the women had left.

The notes were gone!

Gone also was Colin Broadstreet.

"Has anyone seen my notes?" I raised my voice and called out to the assembled diners. Most of them shook their heads, but one couple signalled to me to come over.

"A man went over to that table over there," one of them said, "and picked up some papers. He said you had forgotten them, and he would take them to you."

"Oh! Thanks. Who was he, do you know?"

"I don't know his name. He's sort of a big fellow, with sandy hair and a moustache."

Colin.

I sped out of the room and made a beeline to Pine Lodge and Colin's room. He wasn't there.

Trash cans! That's where he would throw my notes. I started going through all the waste receptacles in Pine Lodge, then headed back to the dining room. I met the Forsythes and the Staines. Michael indicated that he wanted to talk to me in private.

"First I have to find the notes for my sermon. Colin stole them."

"Stole them!" Betty exclaimed. "Are you sure?"

"Yes, I'm sure," I responded grimly. "Someone saw him take them from the table in the dining room, while I was getting rid of the dirty dishes. Colin's not in his room. I'm looking in trash cans."

I turned to the bishop. "Colin is the person who tried to get into my room last night. I know Douglas has told you about it. This morning, he's keeping his right hand in his pocket, and doing everything left-handed." I didn't care whether the others knew or not. I was angry enough to chew roofing nails.

"He did what?" Betty cried in consternation. "Robin! What's going on?"

"I'll tell you later," Douglas quieted her. "Right now, let's see if we can find Robin's notes."

206

"You folks help her," Michael commanded. "I'm going to look for Colin Broadstreet."

Fifteen frustrating minutes later we assembled again. We had found nothing. No notes. No Colin.

Bishop Michael turned to me and said in a gentle voice, "Robin, you don't have to give the sermon this morning. Douglas is celebrating. I'm sure he can do a bit of a homily off the cuff."

"I'll be glad to," Douglas assured me.

"You don't need to." Still seething with anger, I wasn't about to be deprived of my moment in the spotlight. "I can give it from memory. I'll be there!"

"Are you sure?" the bishop asked, but I could tell from his smile, and the tone of his voice, that he already knew the answer.

I nodded curtly. "I'm sure!"

CHAPTER 20

We gathered at the outdoor chapel, set up on the lawn, under a warm, cloudless sky, a faint zephyr playing in the trees overhead. A bird was calling from a tree nearby, and one of the women from across the hall was sweeping the forest with her binoculars.

"I'm determined to get a glimpse of him before I leave," she exclaimed.

"Is he something special?" I asked.

"Yes. He's called a preacher bird. He's out here every morning. I think it is so appropriate."

Too bad the preacher bird couldn't tell us who pushed Harris Margolin off his deck, I thought. He must have had a bird's-eye view.

As usual, Bishop Michael reminded us that the sermon would not be on the gospel reading for the day, but on another one. He gave the text and reminded us that this was about the temptations of Jesus. Douglas, in the Idylwyld uniform of shorts and T-shirt, a green stole draped around his neck, began the service.

The youth workers were all there. Most of the people I recognized from the courses were sitting in relaxed groups about the lawn. Kathy had plopped herself down on one side of me, Lucy on the other. Lucy gave my arm a reassuring squeeze.

Colin was nowhere to be seen.

The readings over, it was time for my performance. I rose and walked to the mike, surveying my audience, and taking a deep breath. Only then did I see Colin, over at the edge of the woods, furtively concealing himself behind the shrubs. Don't pay him any attention, I told myself, and tried to put him out of my mind.

I bade the standing crowd be seated, took another deep breath, and began.

"The gospel tells us that after his baptism in the River Jordan, by John, Jesus was led into the wilderness where he fasted for forty days. During this time, he was tempted by Satan. There were three temptations:

"Satan said, 'You must be hungry by now. You can perform miracles, so turn one of these stones into a loaf of bread.'

"He took Jesus to the top of a high mountain, and showed him all the kingdoms of the world, and said, 'I'll make you master over all of this if you will fall down and worship me.'

"Satan set Jesus on the pinnacle of the temple and said, 'Go on. Prove that you are the son of God. Throw yourself off, and if he cares that much about you, he'll catch you, won't he?'" I surveyed the group, looking for a reaction, a connection with the events next door. No one stirred.

"These accounts are usually referred to as stories of temptation, though they have also been deemed to be accounts of God testing Jesus. So what are we to make of them?"

My audience was sitting quietly, relaxed, giving me their polite attention. I hadn't said anything yet that excited them.

"Jesus resisted all three temptations. Is the Gospel writer saying, 'Resist all forms of temptation?' Some people take it that way. In fact, the followers of a number of churches take this literally.

"But is this what Jesus is telling us? I don't think so. What we know of Jesus' life certainly does not bear this out. Jesus probably walked many miles barefoot, wore a simple tunic, and ate many meals consisting of bread and fish. But he also enjoyed a party!

"There are numerous mentions of his sharing a banquet or feast with others. There are references to being decked out like a bridegroom, always very positive stories. Take the parable of the prodigal son. What does the father do when his son, who he thought was lost, comes home again? He attires him in the finest clothing, and throws a party. When a woman anointed Jesus with an expensive ointment, he apparently found pleasure in the experience. Jesus did not resist the temptation to enjoy life."

A few of my listeners were smiling, remembering the well-loved tales from the Bible.

"Jesus is said to be the one person who led a perfect life in the eyes of God. Not all God's chosen people were this successful in resisting temptation. Take King David, for example. Here was a man who was chosen by God to be a leader of God's people. Did he succumb to temptation? Did he ever!"

A tiny ripple of laughter went through the crowd.

"He saw a beautiful woman, the wife of an officer in his army, and seduced her, probably using his authority to get his way. When she told him she was pregnant, he was in a pickle. This was a serious crime in those days. So he tried to cover it up. When that failed, he had the woman's husband killed, and married her himself.

"Well! That certainly didn't go over very well with God!"

Laughter again.

"God sent word through his prophet, Nathan, that he was angry and disappointed. David, realizing the magnitude of his sin, repented and humbled himself before God. He was forgiven and thereafter led a righteous life.

"It's just as well he did. His descendants played major roles in the history of the Israelites, and Jesus could trace his ancestry back to David. Furthermore, what would we have done without the marvellous Psalms of David, like the one that begins, 'To you O Lord, I lift up my soul: my God, I put my trust in you.'

"These lines, I think, convey the message we should hear in the story of the temptation of Jesus in the wilderness. Trust. Trust in God. Isn't that what the story is about?"

They were sitting up now, leaning forward and hanging on my words. I'd struck a resonant chord. Good. I'm going to be able to put this across, I thought.

"By trust, I do not mean the trust Satan is talking about when he dares Jesus to throw himself off the pinnacle of the temple. Rather the trust Jesus is talking about when he answers, 'Do not put the Lord your God to the test.'

"When he is tempted to turn a stone into bread, Jesus quotes, 'One does not live by bread alone, but by every word that comes from the mouth of God.' Jesus is putting his trust in God to feed him the spiritual food he needs.

"When Satan offers Jesus all the kingdoms of the world, Jesus replies, 'Worship the Lord your God and serve only Him.' Satan's is an empty promise; the Kingdom of God awaits those who put their trust in the Lord.

"Jesus replies to Satan's dare to throw himself off the pinnacle, 'Do not put the Lord your God to the test.'

"Why not?

"Doesn't God have enough time to go running around catching people who throw themselves off pinnacles?" I looked out over the assembled crowd, again wondering how they were taking it. Again, I saw no reaction. I began to relax. "Of course He'd have the time, but that's not the point.

"The point is that if you say you trust someone, but require that they prove they deserve your trust, that's no trust at all."

They were listening intently now. The youth workers had moved forward, and had seated themselves among the course participants. They weren't there because they had to be. They were interested. I resisted my own temptation to look for Colin. I went on.

"We put God to the test all the time, don't we? God, cure me of this illness and I'll promise to go to church every Sunday. God, get me out of this financial mess and I'll give $1000 to the church. God, where were you? I go to church regularly, give my hard-earned money, pray every day, and now this happens. I don't deserve this. I expected you to help me. You failed me!

"There are other examples. Many relate to the age-old question; why do terrible things happen to faithful people?"

I was well in stride now, not hampered at all by the lack of notes, feeling the words flow effortlessly forth.

"I think our perspective is too narrow. Let's back off and look at the broader picture. God's concern is for our well being throughout our total life, of which the portion lived here on earth is but a fleeting moment, often likened to the blinking of an eye.

"We have been put on this earth for a purpose. That purpose seems to have something to do with learning to live the kind of life God intends for us. One of the things we must learn is that we can, indeed, put our trust in Him.

"If God picked us up every time we fell, protected us from disease and other calamities, sheltered us from want, we'd never grow or learn. We'd be like helpless babies all our lives.

"In order that our character will develop and we will learn how to stand on our own two legs, God has gradually withdrawn his visible support. He has given us free will. He has not abandoned us completely, but as C. S. Lewis has put it, His felt presence in any but the faintest and most mitigated degree would completely over-ride the human will. Just as a parent wants an infant to learn to walk, and takes away the hand that supports the child, God wants us to learn, on our own, to walk in His Holy Ways, and must withdraw His support."

There was absolute silence in the rustic chapel. Even the preacher bird had stopped. I'd gotten their attention all right.

"His book, The Screwtape Letters , was written as a series of letters from a senior devil to a junior one, instructing the novice on how to secure a human soul for Satan. Lewis gives us a veritable catalogue of temptations, but also has Screwtape explain to the novice devil how God works. The senior devil is usually sarcastic or insinuating, but when he tries to explain God's actions, he becomes at first incredulous, then frustrated.

"Screwtape, the senior devil, says, 'Our cause (the devil's that is) is never more in danger than when a human, no longer desiring, but still intending, to do (God's) will, looks round upon a universe from which every trace of Him seems to have vanished, and asks why he has been forsaken, and still obeys."

I paused to let these memorable lines sink in..

"That has a familiar ring, doesn't it? It's interesting that Jesus' ministry on earth started and ended in similar fashion, with a test of his trust in God.

"Knowing of his impending death, Jesus asks God if he really has to go through with it. But he adds, 'Not my will, but Your will be done.' He has put himself completely in God's hands. He trusts that his death is not the end, that God's Kingdom awaits him.

"And we know, because of the resurrection, that Jesus' faith was justified.

"Can we trust God to the same extent? Can we keep going when we feel forsaken? Can we do it when we pray for bread and all we see are stones; when we see others worship Satan in the form of money or power, and seem to succeed; when every day, people fall and die?

"Let's go back to the metaphor of the blinking eye. Suppose we are out in the desert (as Jesus was) and a large grain of sand gets in our eye. As we blink, the sand rakes down the sensitive cornea with a sharp stab of pain. We have a choice. We can keep our eyes tight shut, put our hands over them, fall on our knees and cry; or we can accept the second fleeting instant of pain, open our eyes, and behold the desert sunset.

"In our lives, when we are beset by trouble or racked with pain, we can shut ourselves off from God, turn inward,

214

and wail about our fate; or we can endure the pain and trust, turning toward Jesus, looking beyond into the eternal Kingdom in the glorious company of God."

I let my voice drop and bowed my head. "Almighty and loving God, we humbly ask you to watch over us as we take stumbling steps on our journey in faith, seeking to learn to trust you at all times and in all things. We ask this in the name of Jesus Christ, our Saviour. Amen."

I turned away from the mike to return to my seat, but was stopped in my tracks.

Applause! The congregation was applauding my sermon! Applauding long and loud. Even Douglas and the bishops joined in. I couldn't believe it! Not for a sermon! Not in the Anglican Church!

I stumbled to my seat, not even feeling the ground I was walking on, and Lucy threw her arms around me, giving me a great hug. She whispered in my ear, "I told you you'd leave us in the dust!"

CHAPTER 21

My classmates flocked around, congratulating me, before the morning session of the class began. In the class session, they critiqued my sermon, giving it a very good grade. The two bishops also expressed their enthusiasm, Michael reminding the class that my notes had disappeared and that I had given it from memory. I was on top of the world.

At the mid-morning coffee break, I found Todd, the youth worker waiting outside, asking to talk to me.

"I wanted to let you know how much your sermon meant to me," he said earnestly. "You know, I never thought of God acting like that, letting us do our own thing, so we could learn from our experiences. I think I've been, like, insensitive. No, I mean greedy. I mean, I expected God to do whatever I asked for. Now I see that He can't. I'm kind of ashamed, like."

"You needn't be," I assured him. "That's a hard lesson to learn. Lots of people never do. It took me about forty five years to get it through my head."

"And here I was thinking of giving up on the church 'cause I didn't think God ever answered my prayers."

"You're not alone. Lots of people think that way."

He scratched his head. "I guess I've got a lot to learn."

I gestured toward the library. "Do you ever go in there and read?"

He shook his head.

"Try it. I got a lot of my sermon material out of a book called The Screwtape Letters by C. S. Lewis. It's in the library. Also, you questioned whether God ever answers prayers."

"Yeah."

"Well, it wasn't exactly a prayer, but I think God noticed that I had a need and put the idea for my sermon into my mind. That's not the first time it's happened to me. I'm never aware of what God has done at the time, but I realize it later."

"Thanks. I just wanted to let you know how your sermon changed the way I look at things."

"I'm glad." I wrapped my arm around his shoulders and gave a big squeeze. "Tell it to the others."

"Oh, they got the point too! It's all we've been talking about all morning."

The euphoria of the morning was, however, not destined to last. Shortly before the class wrapped up, two men with determined scowls on their faces came into the room and stood just inside the door. As soon as Bishop Michael had finished, one of these men stepped forward, and told us in a loud voice that we were not to leave the room.

"We will be taking your statements of where you were, what you were doing, and who you were with between eight-thirty and nine-thirty on Tuesday morning. We understand that some of you are leaving today, and the rest tomorrow. We'll want your home addresses and phone numbers as well."

We groaned. It certainly burst my bubble of euphoria. I wondered if we would miss lunch.

The man went on, "There are a few of you who we want to interview in more depth. As I call your name, please come over to this side of the room."

He glanced down at a list and read out: "Lucille Merriman, Gordon Saunders, Robin Carruthers, Douglas Forsythe…"

"He's not in this group," I said.

"That's okay. They'll get him in the other. Betty Forsythe, Michael Staines, Evelyn McNaughton."

I leaned over toward Lucy. "At least they've let the Archbishop go."

"Yes. I wonder what they want with Michael?"

"I wonder just who they are. They don't look like police."

It wasn't long before we found out. The other man explained to us that they were from the crown prosecutor's office. What they expected to get from us that the police hadn't, I had no idea.

They led the chosen few to the library, then called us out one at a time, leaving the others to cool their heels. We complained that it was lunchtime, but our pleas fell on deaf ears. The two men left to go back to the meeting room, to get the statements from the remainder of the students. A uniformed policeman took up a position outside the door. Soon, the people from the other course, and those not in a course at all joined us. Dr. McNaughton announced that lunch would be delayed, and none of us would miss it.

"Unless they arrest us," I said in an aside to Lucy, who giggled. Gordon sat down beside me, looking worried. Lucy was called first.

I had never seen Lucy look angry, but when she returned, her face was an unhealthy shade of red, she was biting her lower lip, and she seemed ready to explode. I didn't get a chance to talk to her. Not only was she asked to leave as soon as she had picked up her books and papers, but I was the next one called.

I entered a small office and found myself facing another man I had not seen before, as well as a secretary who appeared to take everything down. All desire for cooperation vanished as soon as the man opened his mouth.

"Okay, you're a member of this cult thing. You've been prowling around, and I'd like to know just what you think you're getting out of it."

I had a tight feeling in the pit of my stomach. Had anyone said anything about the kids and their foray into spiritualism? If not, would someone spill the beans? Not me. I determined to button my lips.

"What cult?"

"You know what I mean. This place!"

"This is not a cult. This is a conference centre."

"Same thing."

"It is not the same thing."

"Any place a bunch of people get together to do religious stuff is a cult as far as I'm concerned."

I could feel the muscles in the back of my neck tighten. "Then you are sadly misinformed. You should find out what you're talking about before you spout a bunch of nonsense."

"Don't talk back to me."

"I'll talk however I please. You are the one who needs some lessons in courtesy."

"Look, I can take you in if I want to. You'd better cooperate."

"I don't think you can. You have no reason to charge me with anything. And I'll cooperate as long as you act decent and quit insulting me."

"Okay, lady, let's quit wasting time. Where were you Tuesday morning?"

"I was at the morning service…"

"What kind of service?"

"A regular Anglican Church service. The Anglican Church is one of the largest and most respected churches in the world. It is not associated with any cults."

The man grimaced but said nothing.

"After the service, I was walking around the grounds with The Reverend Douglas and Betty Forsythe. Reverend Forsythe is the priest of my congregation in Exeter. We were together until the courses started. Then we went to our respective classes. I was in the presence of other members of my class all the time I was not with the Forsythes. Also, we met Lucy Merriman at the top of the trail down into the canyon. That was about ten after nine. We were standing near there watching the affair of the mobile home that got stuck under the tree. There were a lot of other people watching also."

"Did you go down into the canyon?"

"No."

"Did you see anyone else go down there or come up?"

"No. But what difference would that make? He wasn't killed down there."

"I'll ask the questions," the interrogator snarled.

I said nothing. Who did this creep think he was, anyway?

"You went around to the dead man's house after his body was found. Why."

"I explained that to the police at the time."

"I want to hear it from you."

"I wasn't sure, but I thought the dead man might be someone I knew, and if so, I knew something about him that I thought the police would be interested in. It turned out that I was right."

"If you never saw the dead man, how did you know it was this person?"

"I didn't, but from what people said, and because I recognized Sam Gilley, I thought it might be Margolin."

"What was it that you knew about him?"

"That he had killed his partner."

"How come you knew about that when nobody else did?"

"The police in Exeter did because I told them."

"You saw him do it?"

"Almost. I saw the circumstances before and after. You can ask Cpl. Nash or Sgt. Jameson in Exeter about it."

"How well did you know this Margolin?"

"Not well. I only met him once." I braced myself for the inevitable questions about Margolin's lawsuit, but they never came. In fact, I had the distinct impression from my interview and what the others told me of theirs, that this man had only a sketchy idea of what the police had gathered. I wondered why he had not gotten all the information he could before tackling us.

Eventually Gordon answered that question. This crown prosecutor had a bee in his bonnet about religion. He thought that Sgt. Simchuk was being altogether too cordial to the hundred and fifty or so church members gathered at

Idylwyld. He could not be shaken in his determination to picture us as a cult, and had a twisted idea of what we did.

He asked, "You drink blood at all your services, don't you?"

"What?"

"Well, you do. I've heard that said many a time."

"Each time we have communion, we have a small sip of wine. Symbolically it represents the blood of Christ." As I gave this answer, a tight feeling gripped my stomach. I remembered something that had happened one Sunday in church. I would have to be very careful what I said to this man.

It had been an ordinary Sunday in late summer, not any special celebration. I had gone to the altar rail as usual, knelt down and waited for my turn to receive communion. It was quiet, with soft organ music playing in the background, the rustle of clothing as parishioners came to the rail, the soft words of the priest and communion assistants.

I knelt, my head down, gaze lowered. I crossed myself then held out my cupped hands, one under the other, to receive the wafer. As I did so, I rested my arms on the rail, and between my arms, below my cupped hands, I saw a drop of blood.

I have heard that the way to know that you have become proficient in another language comes when you can hear something said, process the information and form a reply all in that language, without translating into the one you are familiar with. There seemed to be a similarity with my experience at that moment. It was then that I realized I understood the significance of the sacrament of communion, when the words, "The blood of Christ, shed for you" took on its intended meaning.

In my logical mind, I knew that what I saw was a drop of wine. I know what blood looks like. It does not look like wine, even red wine. But at that moment, my mind would not process the logical explanation that this was a drop of wine, spilled when someone else had received communion at that spot. I saw it as a drop of blood.

I waited tensely for my inquisitor to continue on this line of questioning, but he didn't. He went on with more mundane questions and I gradually felt myself relax. Not completely, though. I still worried that these people would hear about the antics of the youth workers.

Later, I said to Bishop Michael that I hoped that they wouldn't question the youth staff. They did, he told me, then seeing my expression of consternation, grinned and said, "Don't underestimate those kids. They won't give anything away. I understand that they gave a unanimous performance of total ignorance. Their stock answer was, 'We don't know anything that goes on around here.'"

I laughed. "Good for them." Then another thought crossed my mind. "Why did you tell them to write their own psalms?"

"Think about the psalms. Many of them are by someone who is railing at God for letting him down. The psalmist bares his soul, and tells God everything that is troubling him. But having done that, he realizes that God has indeed come to his aid, and he becomes reconciled to God. These kids are going to write down their feelings in the form of psalms, some of which we will probably use in the morning services."

"I see."

"We'll let them help plan other parts of the services also, but they'll have to stick to the regular outline of the liturgy. They do have their own youth service one night a week. Our liturgical officer goes over it in advance to see that it is appropriate, but since it is not a Eucharist, we give them lots of leeway.

"By the way, they were impressed by your sermon."

I blushed, and Bishop Michael's face broke into a broad smile. He said, "I've been quite pleased with the results of this course."

"We've been quite pleased by the course!"

On Saturday morning, we prepared to leave, amid bustle and commotion. A few had left Friday night, but now the grounds were emptying of all but a few who would stay for the next week. As Douglas, Betty and I were loading up the Jeep Cherokee, we spotted the people whom Colin Broadstreet had come with. They were pulling out of the parking lot. Colin was not with them.

"Where's Colin?" I asked as they stopped beside us.

"He took the bus yesterday morning. I don't think he was having much fun here. Also he hurt his hand some way, and wanted to get it looked at."

Gordon wheeled down the drive on his bike, sliding to a stop beside the Jeep. I felt a brief surge of excitement.

"Good! I'm glad I caught you. I got hung up at the Town Hall, and was afraid I'd miss you." He pushed his bike over into the shade of a tree. I followed him. Then he reached out and took both my hands in his. "I'm going to miss you."

What should I say? I liked Gordon, liked him a lot. But he was married, his wife was on the lookout for anything she could use against him, and he had young children who could easily be hurt.

I replied carefully, "I've enjoyed it here. You've been a big help and fun to be with. Let's leave it like that."

"But don't be a stranger. Call me every once in a while. I hope you don't mind if I call you."

"I don't mind, but let's just be friends. I don't want to upset your divorce proceedings."

He let go of my hands. "I see what you mean. I guess I shouldn't have kissed you. I'm sorry."

"I'm not."

"Oh!" He smiled happily. "Well, here's to the future!" He gave me a discreet peck on the cheek.

The future, as far as I was concerned, would have to be unencumbered by crotchety wives.

As we were driving out, Lucy spotted us and flagged us down. "Did you hear? They've arrested that man, Sam Gilley, for pushing his boss off the deck into the canyon. They say he went over to the house when Bill and the truck driver were getting the mobile home out from under the tree. He probably had a quarrel with his boss, and heaved him over into the canyon."

As the others talked in excited tones, I sat there frowning. I pictured Gilley sitting in his car making phone calls, then driving off in a big rush, and later coming down the entrance road to the office. He hadn't gone straight around. In fact, he wouldn't have needed to leave the property and return to go straight to the office; he could have driven around the stalled truck and on down the little side road. But had he been gone long enough to drive to the house, get in a fight with Margolin, and drive back? I didn't think so. I couldn't remember exactly where I had been, or what I was doing, when Gilley reappeared, but my feeling was that not enough time had elapsed.

Gilley had said he'd driven around to the house, rung the bell and knocked, but no one had answered and there was no car in the driveway. My instinctive feeling was that there had been barely enough of a time lapse for that to have happened. A quarrel would have taken some time to develop, especially if Margolin had let him in and they had gone out to the deck.

No. There was something wrong somewhere!

Lucy spied my serious visage and asked, "What's wrong?"

"I think they've arrested the wrong man."

CHAPTER 22

Back in Exeter, I called the school, but didn't go over to the airport. I wanted to take the rest of the day off to relax, after the hectic pace of the week.

On Sunday, I went to church as usual, but in the afternoon the itch to be around airplanes overcame me, so I changed and went to the airport. The school hummed with activity, but nothing needed my immediate attention. I hung around for a while, then went home, changed again, this time into shorts, and took a cold drink into the back yard, under the shade of a walnut tree. Life was pretty good, I thought. I'd really enjoyed the course, my business was thriving, and I'd met a very nice man, but had avoided any serious entanglement with him. Furthermore, I knew that I had done something that had made a very positive impression on at least one youth.

I've always enjoyed teaching teenagers to fly; seeing them develop, not only in physical skill and coordination, but also in maturity and judgment. But nothing had compared with the satisfaction of seeing the change in Todd as a result of the bishop's actions, aided by my sermon. Was this what God's grace was all about?

I sprawled languidly in my lawn chair, sipping my cold drink. I felt like a fat cat; like Cloud Nine, who was lounging on the grass beside my chair, sniffing the air to detect any bird that might venture by.

Still, my mind constantly returned to the events of the past week. My worries about the lawsuit had disappeared, though I'd never have wished them to end in such a tragic way. I vowed to put that particular chapter of my life firmly into the past, and not dwell on it. If I thought the police had arrested the wrong man, I figured that in their further investigation, they'd find the real culprit. Anyway, I could be wrong.

Who else could have done it? I refused to even consider Gordon. Demmy Scropos? He had been running around town, and might have had time to go to Margolin's house? But was his motive strong enough? Would he kill to keep Margolin from setting up before he could? I had only met him once, but he was a good friend of Gordon's, and I thought Gordon would see through the type of personality that would kill so unthinkingly.

George, Demmy's son? He could have the same motive, as I presumed that he stood to take over his father's business one of these days. Where was he between eight-thirty and nine-thirty on the morning Margolin was killed?

Other town councillors? I didn't know any of them; their personalities, their possible motives. Besides, they had a collective alibi. Apparently there were other people in town who didn't like Margolin. For what reason? The only one I knew about was the man who felt that Harcon Holdings had gypped him when they bought the lakeside lot.

What about Diana Lovelace? She supposedly had gone off shopping to Castleton, forty kilometres away, and had later gone to have her hair done, but was anyone sure when she left home? What would her motive be? Was she aware that Margolin had killed Conrad on purpose, not accidentally? If so, and if she wanted to punish him for it, wouldn't she have done so earlier? They obviously had their marital spats, but so do a lot of other couples, and it rarely leads to murder. Besides, the police figured that she wouldn't have the physical strength to overpower her husband; to throw him over the railing. I had to agree with them.

What about someone at Idylwyld? We were certainly the crown prosecutor's choice! But who among us, other than Gordon and myself, had any connection with Margolin? What about Dr. Evelyn McNaughton? Might she have had a run-in with her neighbour? She lived on the Idylwyld property. Might Margolin have had some nefarious plans that would not be to Idylwyld's advantage? No, I couldn't believe that a person in her position could have resorted to murder. Besides, the same argument about size and strength, that caused the police to dismiss Diana Lovelace, also applied to her.

Oh, well. It wasn't my problem. Forget it!

I knew that Douglas and Bishop Michael had huddled long into the night on Friday, and had mapped out a strategy to deal with the threat of a casino being built across from the church. Douglas had asked if I would have time to help out, but I'd pleaded that I would be far too busy when I got back. But I'd felt the same fillip of emotion that I had the last time I'd seen Gordon. I was back in Douglas' good graces.

I learned later that Douglas and the church's two wardens had gone to city hall, first to mayor Victoria Bainbridge, then to the city planners, then to the council. As long as Vickie and her crew were in power, there would be no casinos in Exeter, but everyone realized that we couldn't expect this state of affairs to last forever. Procedures were put in place to zone the area in question as multi-family residential, in other words, for an apartment house. Harcon Holdings fought this all the way, but lost, and in the long run, the other outfit that had been trying to buy the property got hold of it. I don't know all the details. There were all kinds of shenanigans going on. All I know is that one day a sign, with an architect's drawing of a new apartment house went up on one of the lots. At the church, we all breathed a little easier.

For me it was back to business as usual. There were flight tests and progress checks to perform, maintenance to work into the airplane schedules, bills to pay. On hot summer days, I get up early, the cool of the morning being the best time of day. One morning, I was in my office by six thirty, tackling a backlog of paperwork that had accumulated while we spent all the time during the good weather flying like crazy. I was busy writing out cheques for the inevitable bills, and reviewing students' progress.

Terry McGregor had a student at seven, and he popped his head into my office as he went out with the student. He had a welcoming remark and a happy smile for me. Tall and good-looking, with his dark hair carefully coifed, I continued to wonder why no pretty girl had yet sunk her hooks into him. Terry's original plan had been to work his way up through the ranks; to become an airline pilot. Like many others, he had become a flight instructor as a way to build up the hours needed to qualify for an airline pilot's license.

I didn't usually hire these young pilots with airline ambitions. I wanted professional instructors, ones who really enjoyed teaching others to fly. I've had some good ones, of all types and both sexes. Terry had taken all his flight training at Red Robin, was one of the best pilots we'd ever turned out, and had shown a genuine interest in teaching. With some reservations, I'd taken him on as an instructor. I soon realized I'd made the right choice. He turned out to be as good an instructor as he was a pilot. He also had the knack of conveying his enthusiasm for flying to anyone he talked to. If I'd hired a sound truck with a PA system to tour the town, broadcasting messages about the school, I couldn't have gotten better publicity.

He had done a good job as temporary boss while I was away. He got on well with the other employees, as he did with his students. Everything had gotten done; there were no loose ends to tie up when I returned.

So, in my expansive mood, I started to contemplate what I could do to hang onto him.

In the midst of this reverie, I was hardly aware of the increasing bustle about the place as the morning's work began. I was awakened from my dreaming when Joyce popped her head in the door of my office.

"There's a man here to see you."

"Okay. I'll be out in a sec."

Gayla, the afternoon dispatcher, had left a message for me, that while I was away the previous day on a long flight that would last well into the evening, a man had come in saying he wanted to see me, but not about learning to fly. Gayla told him I'd be back in the morning and he said he'd come then. It didn't seem urgent.

He was wearing the same clothes he'd been wearing last spring. No overcoat tossed across a chair this time, but the same red tie, loose at his neck, the top button of his rumpled white shirt undone. He carried the jacket of his shiny blue suit across his arm as he strode purposefully across the room toward me.

"Robin Carruthers?" the bailiff asked.

"That's me."

He shoved the papers into my hand. As he departed, I had the strange feeling that one of us had missed our cue. This scene should have been taking place several months ago.

I shuffled back into my office, and flopped into the chair. I ripped open the envelope, and removed the official looking document inside.

Diana Lovelace Margolin was suing me for destroying her business.

I had a hard time digesting the material. What was I supposed to have done? It seemed that Mizzz Lovelace, as I still thought of her, was claiming that since I had refused to allow her husband to fly to Georgetown that stormy day last spring, all of Harcon Holdings' chances of obtaining property they were after in Exeter had been ruined.

That's a bunch of bullshit! I thought. How does she think she can get away with this? It's ridiculous.

But as I read the information over again, doubt crept into my mind. Could she really make it stick? She was asking for a million dollars. That would ruin me. I saw my life's work crashing in a heap around me. I didn't think my insurance company would be any happier about this lawsuit than they had about the one for slander.

I reached for the phone to call Wilf Meredith.

One thing was better this time. Wilf would be available when the case came to trial. A former student at Red Robin, and the husband of Ginny, my accountant, Wilf still rented planes from me on a regular basis. Ginny and their two small children were his enthusiastic passengers.

He was a competent pilot, one who planned his flights carefully; who didn't take unnecessary risks. He knew aviation, and had no patience with Mortimer Thurlow, who was again handling the case for the plaintiff.

"What's with these people," he snarled. "They should know they can't win. Mort probably just took the case because he doesn't like you. He'd be really delighted to put you out of business."

"Is he as bad a lawyer as he is a pilot?"

"No. He's a helluva good one. He's the bombastic type — booming voice and all kinds of theatrics. One thing that bugs him though is sarcasm. He hates being made fun of."

"Even if he is an incompetent pilot, he must know aviation law, and realize he hasn't a leg to stand on."

"You'd think so," Wilf mused. "Which means one of two things. Either he's so anxious to get at you, in which case he'll collect a big fee ahead of time, or he has something up his sleeve. I can find out."

"How?"

"If he's collected a fat fee up front, he knows he may lose the case, but wants to jerk your chain. But if he's taken the case on a contingency basis, then he feels confident that he can win it. Robin, I think you had better tell me everything you know, suspect, or even vaguely think about this case."

So I spent hours with Wilf, dredging up every minute detail, including my reservations about the woman from Transport Canada who had been assigned to testify on my behalf in the slander suit. Wilf assured me that he would get the most impressive witnesses. By the time we finished, I felt a lot better.

The evening of the day I'd gotten the summons, or whatever it was, I hadn't felt so good. Who could I talk to? No one in Exeter. Not even Douglas, who was busy with the casino issue anyway. I pulled the phone toward me, extracted a card from my purse, and dialled Gordon Saunders in Mallard Beach.

He sounded both surprised and pleased to hear from me. Making small talk, I asked, "How are things over there?"

I heard him chuckle. "Well, anyone who thought that things would quiet down when the police made an arrest was way off base."

"Oh? Do others think they arrested the wrong man?"

"It's not that. Nobody could care less. Everyone thinks it's their own tough luck that one of the employees bumped off the boss. Nobody liked Margolin, and nobody knows Gilley. No, it's not the murder, it's what Diana Lovelace is up to."

My ears pricked up. "And what is she up to?"

"She's suing everyone in sight."

"Really? Who is she suing, and for what reason?"

"Let's see. She's suing the trucking company…"

"That's understandable."

"…and the guy who sold them the land down by the lake."

"Him? I though he was suing her."

"He is, so she tossed a counter-suit at him."

"Anyone else?"

"Demmy Scropos, for using underhanded tactics in getting his bid accepted."

"And does she have a case?" My voice must have sounded sarcastic.

"Come on, Robin! That's just normal business practice."

"Okay. Are there more?"

"The town council, for supposedly rigging the bidding process. That's all so far."

"No, it's not," I told him. "She's also suing me."

"What! What on earth for?"

I explained about the episode of the cancelled flight.

"But Robin! That's ridiculous!"

"I know it. But tell it to Mizzz Lovelace."

"Robin, I'm sorry. It must be miserable for you. When did you find out?"

"This morning. Her husband's suit went by the wayside, since he was no longer alive to pursue it, and I thought I could put that whole business behind me. Then the same bailiff came around this morning and shoved some more papers into my hand. The whole thing is outrageous. She can't win. I wonder why she's throwing all these lawsuits around? She must like supporting lawyers."

"That's interesting, you know. Maybe she's just a belligerent type of person."

"Having met her, I can believe that."

"But it still doesn't make sense to throw your money around on a bunch of frivolous lawsuits."

I wondered whether the ones against Scropos and the Mallard Beach Village Council were as frivolous as Gordon seemed to think, but decided not to comment on it. We talked a while longer, with Gordon reassuring me, and offering a willing ear whenever I needed to talk about my problems. I felt the tension in my body ease as I talked to him.

If I don't look out, I told myself, I'll find I'm involved with this man even though I've vowed not to be.

I expected things to drag on for a long time. I'd heard about congestion in the courts, resulting in long waits for cases to come to trial. I was surprised at the dispatch with which this one was scheduled. Someone told me that was because Thurlow had pull with the clerk who did the scheduling, since his cases seemed always to be scheduled quickly, but I took that with a grain of salt. I asked Wilf.

"No, I don't think so," he replied. "Besides, I haven't noticed any such trend. I think the reason for the rapid scheduling is that this fellow Sam Gilley is a witness for the plaintiff, and if he's convicted of murder before this case comes up, it will make his testimony seem unreliable. And they can't put off his trial indefinitely. The guy has a right to a trial within a reasonable time."

"I'm surprised that Diana Lovelace is willing to use him as a witness, if she thinks he killed her husband."

"She hasn't any choice. He's her star witness to what happened. Besides, from what I hear, she may think he did her a favour."

"But in that case," I objected, "she can't think that what I did caused the company's troubles."

"Of course she can! In the first place, it led to Conrad's death, and he was the brains of the outfit."

"But, that's ridiculous," I protested. "Margolin would have killed him anyway, as soon as Conrad tried to crowd him out."

"If Margolin killed him."

"Of course he did! You can't deny that."

Wilf could and did, ripping my story to shreds. I was furious. Then Wilf grinned mischievously and admitted, "He probably did. But there's no way to prove it now. Furthermore, I want to remind you, don't say anything to anyone about it. We want you to appear detached from these people, with only the interest in saving them from a disastrous situation. It wasn't only when Margolin was suing you for slander that you need to keep mum about accusing him of murder. You can slander the dead as well as the living."

"Okay. I'll keep my mouth shut."

"Have you told anyone else?"

"The police, for one."

"We don't have to worry about them. But you've told someone else."

I admitted that I'd expressed my belief that Margolin had murdered Conrad to Douglas and to Bishop Michael. I hadn't the nerve to tell my own lawyer that I'd done it in the presence of their wives. Wilf frowned, and questioned me about the reliability of the two clergymen. I knew that Wilf was a non-believer, with a somewhat scoffing attitude to anything religious. I assured him that top-ranking Anglican clergy could be counted on to keep a confidence. I didn't tell him I had equal confidence in their wives.

As the preliminaries to the lawsuit took their inevitable course, my confidence and my mood underwent wild swings from certainty to severe self-doubt. If I didn't call Gordon every few days, he called me. I felt very comfortable talking to him. If I had not had Gordon to talk to, I might have gone to Douglas with my misgivings. But it was Gordon who gave me the bit of advice I really needed.

"Remember, Robin, when you are hurting, you need the help of the rest of the flock. We can't expect to handle all our problems alone. We're like sheep. We need to be with the flock. Go to your prayer group if you have one, or your bible study group. Ask them to pray for you. It helps, you know."

"I guess I should."

"Robin. Think back to the sermon you gave. Remember what you said?"

"Yes."

"Well then, practice what you preach!"

I took his advice. I told my bible study group, and they immediately rallied round with counsel and prayer. I had never before been personally prayed for. It was comforting, even though I had my doubts about whether God would listen. God probably had more important things to deal with. I was really surprised when Sue Ambler laid her hand on my head while she prayed for me. I can't say that I felt anything special happen as a result of the laying on of hands. Yet the thought that these people cared to the extent they obviously did, brought a lump to my throat.

CHAPTER 23

I had never been inside the new Law Court building, an imposing structure with neat landscaping surrounding it, in the downtown area, not far from the church. Inside, there were spacious corridors with comfortable chairs, in groups, where people involved in court cases waited. The courtroom itself was a model of both comfort and efficiency.

These lawyers do all right for themselves, I thought.

Wilf met me outside the courtroom. He wore dark grey and black striped trousers, shiny black shoes, a black vest, and that funny little winged collar with the long white tails. Over his arm he carried a voluminous black robe. At least in Canada they don't wear wigs. But he did have one new hirsute decoration. He had grown a small, neatly trimmed moustache. I did a double take when I saw him, and commented on it. He grinned like a little boy, and fingered the fringe.

"Actually, I wanted to grow a beard; one of those small ones. But Ginny objected. She said she'd rather not kiss a hedgehog. So we compromised on the moustache."

We could hear Mortimer Thurlow from way down the corridor as he greeted other lawyers. His progress toward the courtroom resembled the docking of an ocean liner; a great deal of fuss over a very large object. Large he was. Tall, big-framed, and moderately fat. The floor seemed to shake under his feet as he strode imperiously along. Wilf's face showed a secretive smile. He seemed to be waiting for something.

Thurlow stopped where we were sitting, his huge frame blocking the light. "Well, well! You've managed to grow some facial hair. Before long, you'll be old enough to shave," he boomed.

He turned and walked into the courtroom.

Startled, I exclaimed, "Of all the nerve!"

"Calm down, Robin." Wilf didn't look the least bit upset. "Mort always has to get in his little dig. He can't do it in court, so he catches you beforehand. This one wasn't bad. I've heard a lot worse from him."

At five minutes to ten, we went into the courtroom. After leaving me in a soft, comfortable spectator's seat, Wilf went to his table, spreading out the documents he would need. He greeted the clerk, a middle-aged lady with a perpetual smile. Throughout the trial, I was to find her efficient, friendly to everyone, a comforting influence in a stressful, foreign world. She sat at a long desk below the judge's bench, facing the courtroom, a computer screen on her left, a telephone on her right.

Below her desk, facing the judge, were the two tables used by the lawyers, the plaintiff on the right as one faced the judge, the defence on the left. Between them was a lectern. Wilf stood here when questioning a witness, while Thurlow used another lectern beside the jury box. The witness stand was to the far left, the witness facing in toward the room, at right angles to the other desks. The jury box was along the opposite wall, with the jury facing the witnesses.

As the trial progressed, the action centred around the witness stand, to the left as one faced the bench. There was a gap between the ends of the judge's and clerk's desks and the jury box, whereas the witness stand was directly below the end of the bench. The jury seemed separated from the action. The exception to this was when Thurlow conducted a long examination of a witness, at which time he used the lectern on the outside of the jury box. This allowed him to lean his heavy frame on the lectern, while directing his booming voice directly across the jurors. And since jurors couldn't look at him and the witness at the same time, perhaps this was a defence against showing any emotion he might want to hide, or a way to distract the jurors' attention from the witness.

There were eight jurors, five women and three men. Wilf had rejected only one of the jurors whose names were called. This had been a tall, thin young woman with long, lank blonde hair pulled into a ponytail. She had a pale, hawkish face, frowned constantly and fidgeted. Wilf told me later that he knew her to be a professional agitator; a woman who was paid to be a demonstrator for one protest or another. She was an organizer for these demonstrations. She might not be at all interested in the subject of the demonstration, and if there were protesters on both sides of an issue, she would sign on with the side that would pay her most.

Wilf reasoned that if she were on the jury, she would probably look for the side she thought she could get something out of.

"But jurors can't be bribed, can they?" I protested.

"Oh no! Not that. But she might go to the winning side afterward and say, 'Look, I swung the jury your way. What are you going to do for me?' And if she were looking for something like that, she would recognize very soon that it wouldn't be Red Robin Flying School where any profit to her lay.

"Furthermore," Wilf went on, "I saw her when she came into the building. I watched her interacting with other people. She's a bully. She would make life miserable for any jury panel she was on. I said to myself at the time, that if she were chosen for our jury, I'd boot her off."

"So you did. Good for you."

Of the three men, one was a retired building contractor, someone who worked with his hands, but had managerial tasks as well. A good person, I thought. Another was an older retired businessman, with a thick mane of white hair cascading from a leonine head. The third was young, with long blond hair and a scraggly beard, clad in jeans and denim jacket. He always seemed to be one page behind everyone else, but looked a pleasant sort, a half smile on his lips most of the time.

I had pegged one of the women to be a retired professional of some sort. She turned out to be the former curriculum director of the local university college, a lady with a Ph.D. Another woman had the appearance of being little more than a lump of flesh occupying a seat. She did not take notes, or appear to use the large, black-covered binder containing copies of all the documents in the case. The other three women were all of a type; youngish workers at low-paying jobs, average intelligence.

I asked Wilf what he thought of the jury. He seemed satisfied. I said I'd like to have seen more of the professional, educated types. I liked the look of the two older men and the retired professor of education.

"Don't worry," he assured me. "Intelligence and common sense don't always go together. I read something by a famous trial lawyer in the States, who felt that blue collar workers were more apt to be impressed by technical proofs, while professional people could be swayed by emotional appeals."

"So, if your case is based on fact, you want a jury of horny-handed sons of the soil, and if you don't have a leg to stand on, and you're going to have to rely on tear-jerking emotion, you want some university educated jurors."

"Something like that."

"It doesn't say much for education, does it?"

Wilf grinned. "Just remember, Robin, that is a generalization. It doesn't apply to thee and me."

"Come to think of it," I remarked, "it can be that way with flight training, too. The average students are often more willing to accept things at face value, while the really intelligent ones are always looking for ways to question what they're taught. The guys who should be able to ace the written tests, often don't do as well as they should, because they can't bring themselves to consider that a simple question requires a simple answer. They're always looking for the catch. Not you though." I remembered Wilf as being both intelligent and sensible. He'd gotten a perfect score on the written exam for the private pilot license.

At ten the clerk ascertained that everyone was present. She then lifted the phone and talked quietly into it. From snatches that came to me, I gathered that she was calling the jury room and the judge's chamber. The clerk then rose and made her way to a door at the left rear and soon returned, followed by the judge.

"Order in the court," the clerk said in an ordinary tone of voice. Everyone inside the bar rose to their feet, facing the judge's bench. As he took his seat, they all made a small bow in his direction, resumed their seats, and the trial began. I was surprised at how little pomp was involved. The atmosphere was formal, but not pompous, contrasting with the courtroom scenes one sees in TV dramas. I remembered Lew Stern once saying, "We're really a boring bunch of people." On that day, however, I thought that Mortimer Thurlow appeared anything but boring. I wondered how much he would be allowed to get away with. Not much, if I'd read Wilf's comments accurately.

The first suit against me, Margolin's slander suit, had been assigned to a woman judge. I expressed my disappointment when I heard that she would not be presiding over this case. Wilf reassured me. "This man is a former Armed Forces officer. Not a pilot, but he will understand things like the responsibility of the pilot-in-command. He will also understand technical stuff about weather and flight planning. I think he's a good one for this case. He'll give simple, understandable instructions to the jury. He's one of the best at that."

The lawyers took care of a few matters of procedure. The judge, a thin, grey-haired man seemed very decisive, getting straight to the point, and chastising Thurlow at one point for unnecessary rhetoric. These questions settled, the judge nodded to a deputy sheriff standing beside the clerk's station. "Bring in the jury."

The deputy opened a door beyond the jury box, knocked on another door and was admitted. A minute or so later, he returned, the jury filing in behind him and taking seats in the jury box in pre-determined order. There were twelve chairs, six to a row. The jurors were directed to the middle seats, leaving one empty seat at each end of the row, there being only eight jurors in a civil trial.

The deputy sheriff, a young man, wore a flak jacket over his uniform; also a fearsome-looking revolver. He had a small radio attached to the jacket near his left shoulder, and an earpiece in one ear. During the proceedings, he sat silently, surveying the room, occasionally making a written note of something; I had no idea what.

I was fascinated by the smooth, coordinated working of the courtroom. Surely this was a place where justice would be done. The thought was reassuring, but it was soon followed by a persistent feeling of doubt. If I lost this case, my life's work could go down the drain.

Thurlow called Diana Lovelace, the plaintiff, as his first witness, and the remainder of the morning was occupied with her account of the effect on Harcon Holdings of my supposedly refusing to allow her husband to fly his plane on March 8 of that year. She was obviously well prepared, and had practiced her testimony. It sounded like a script. As Thurlow told the judge, he preferred to have her give her testimony in narrative fashion. Occasionally when she stated something that was obviously hearsay, Wilf would rise to object, but usually before he got his objection in, the judge cut Diana off and admonished her in a kindly voice. She occasionally scowled at this, but went back to her recitation.

The jury followed along as Diana talked about financial statements. The young man on the jury, however, seemed lost, unable to find the place in the folder of material. Without even looking toward the jury box, Wilf had noted this. He rose.

"My Lord, I would like to ask my learned friend to advise the jury members as to where they can find each document as the witness comes to it."

"Yes, I noticed the jurors flipping pages. Mr. Thurlow, would you abide by your friend's request?"

Mortimer Thurlow didn't seem to consider Wilf his friend at that point, but I was to learn that this was the fashion in which the lawyers addressed each other. Civility must be maintained — at least by appearance. He responded gruffly, "Tab B." The retired lady professor leaned over and showed the youth where to find the page.

At lunch I asked Wilf why he had asked, when only one juror was having a problem.

"Because the witness was getting into a rhythm and I wanted to break it up." He had succeeded. After the interruption, Diana had trouble getting back into her narrative. She forgot where she was, left things out, and had to be prompted by frequent questions from Thurlow.

The gist of her testimony was that as a result of Margolin and Conrad not being able to fly to Georgetown, they lost the chance to snap up the property on Maple Street in Exeter that they were very anxious to acquire. Consequently, Harcon Holding's profits for the next few months were substantially reduced. I had to sit through this stuff without a chance to counter the obvious errors and inconsistencies in her testimony; such as the facts that I hadn't prevented them from going, and that the two partners had died shortly after that event. Wilf calmly took it all in, and at lunch reassured me that all would be well. Thurlow had managed to prolong his questioning of the plaintiff until the noon break, so that the jury went off to lunch with Diana's complaints firmly implanted in their minds, but Wilf would have his chance at her in the afternoon.

Wilf tore right into her. "Mrs. Margolin…"

That got a scowl from her. Thurlow had addressed her as Ms. Lovelace.

"…isn't it a fact that the reason your profits diminished in the second and third quarters of the year was that one of the two partners, Mr. Conrad, was killed on March 10 and the other, Mr. Margolin, on July 18?"

Diana didn't answer immediately, as if she didn't know how best to answer the question. She shifted her weight from one foot to the other, and fidgeted with her hands.

"There were three partners. I was a partner, too."

"I beg your pardon. But you haven't answered my question."

I'd seen the jurors' heads jerk up when Wilf asked it. Even the judge showed a trace of surprise at the mention of the deaths.

Diana paused before she answered. You could feel the sudden tension in the courtroom.

"They both died, yes."

"Mr. Conrad was killed two days after the event you were describing, when your husband ran into him with his plane."

"He walked into the propeller."

"He was dead."

"Yes."

"And your husband, Harris Margolin, was killed in a fall off the deck of your house on July 18."

Pause. Faintly, "Yes."

"And don't you think that these two events may have had an effect on the affairs of the company?"

Thurlow was on his feet. "M'lord," he boomed, "I object."

"To what, Mr. Thurlow?"

"The manner in which these two men met their deaths has nothing to do with the matter at hand."

"But the timing of their deaths would seem to be pertinent."

I realized that Thurlow was trying to give his client time to get hold of herself. He continued, "You can imagine how traumatic these events have been to my client. I think my learned friend should treat her with more sensitivity."

Wilf bowed toward Thurlow, turned back to the witness, and in a subdued tone remarked, "I'm sure Mr. Conrad's tragic death must have been very upsetting to you."

Not half as much as Wilf's comments were, I'll bet!

Several members of the jury caught the implication of Wilf's commiserating with her on the death of her husband's partner, rather than her husband. Thurlow appeared ready to leap to his feet again, but thought better of it. I supposed he didn't want to hammer the point home.

The jurors had abandoned their slumped positions and quiet listening postures. They leaned forward. One made a vigorous note. They were listening like high school students to a lecture on sex. Even the lump-of-flesh one showed signs of being alive and awake.

"To get back to my question; don't you think that the deaths of two of the partners, who controlled three fourths of the company, might have had an effect on the profitability of the company?"

She sat there without answering. Finally the judge prompted, "Answer the question, please."

Diana Lovelace glared at me. "Maybe. But if she hadn't kept them from flying back on the eighth, Alec wouldn't have died."

Want to bet? I thought.

"But that is not my client's fault."

"Of course it is!"

"How do you figure that?"

"Well, if they'd flown to Georgetown on the eighth, they wouldn't have done so on the tenth." She said this in a tone that one might use to explain something simple and obvious to a five-year-old.

But Wilf was ready for her. "Then he might have been killed on the eighth instead of the tenth."

"M'Lord," Thurlow roared, rising to his feet so rapidly that the motion sent his chair wheeling off to the rear. "I object to this…"

The judge had already raised a hand as if to push away the objection. "I understand, Mr. Thurlow. We are getting into territory we previously agreed not to delve into. Mr. Meredith, I must remind you of this, and ask you to confine your questioning to appropriate areas."

"Yes, My Lord." Wilf made a small bow toward the judge. "However, the witness has virtually accused my client of causing Mr. Conrad's death."

"Please restrain yourself in your questioning."

"Yes, My Lord."

Thurlow retrieved his chair, a high-backed one on casters, and lowered his bulk into it, making as much of a production out of doing so as he thought he could get away with.

Wilf turned again to the witness. "Your husband was a pilot?"

"Yes."

"He was preparing to make a flight from Exeter to Georgetown on March 10 and was prevented from doing so by the fact that his passenger, Mr. Conrad, was killed by being struck by the propeller of the plane."

"Yes."

"At this time, where was Mrs. Carruthers?"

"How should I know?"

"Was she anywhere near the plane?"

Diana Lovelace shrugged. "I don't know."

"Did Mrs. Carruthers have any contact at all with Mr. Margolin or Mr. Conrad before they went out to the plane?"

"I don't know."

"Then how can you say that my client had anything to do with Mr. Conrad's death?"

Diana shifted in her chair, her eyes flitting around, as if looking for a means of escape. Thurlow came to her rescue. "M'Lord, haven't we had enough of this?"

"Yes, I think so," said the judge. "You've made your point, Mr. Meredith."

And he had. Admirably. The jurors' eyes glittered as if they had been invited to lunch with the Queen. They had probably expected something pretty dull when they had been chosen for jury duty in a civil case. They were finding that civil cases can have excitement in them; that depressing balance sheet and lost opportunities didn't happen in a vacuum, but were associated with human drama. As the saying goes, they hadn't seen anything yet!

CHAPTER 24

"On March 8, when Mr. Conrad and Mr. Margolin decided not to fly to Georgetown…"

"Objection," Thurlow boomed. "There is no evidence that they made any such decision."

"There's no evidence that they didn't make such a decision, and there is evidence that they didn't go. In fact, that's the point of the plaintiff's case," Wilf argued.

"Do you think you could rephrase the question, Mr. Meredith?"

"Yes, My Lord. Mrs. Margolin, did you receive a phone call from either of the other partners on March 8?"

"Yes."

"From which one?"

"From Alec… Alec Conrad."

"Why did he call you?"

"He wanted me to go to Georgetown to see these people, and get them to agree to sell us their property."

"The property being a lot on Maple Street in Exeter?"

"Yes."

"Did you do so?"

"Do what?"

"Go to Georgetown and make the sale."

"I went to Georgetown to see them, yes."

"And did you make the sale?"

"I got a provisional agreement from them. They backed out of it later."

"You are a partner in the business?"

"Yes. I told you so."

"Then you know the business?"

"Of course."

"You know how to deal with properties?"

Diana hesitated. She began to see the trap.

"Answer the question."

"Yes."

"So if you knew how to get the property sale for your company, what did it matter if the other partners couldn't get there?"

"Well, they usually did that."

"So you were a last resort?"

Thurlow rose. "M'Lord, does my learned friend have to lower himself to making these insults?"

The judge stroked his chin. "I think I'll allow the question."

"I know what I'm doing," Diana blurted out. "It just didn't work that time. Those other guys talked them into stalling. Then when she saw to it that we couldn't get proper zoning, they backed out and sold to those other guys."

"The 'other guys' managed to get all three lots that you were after?"

"Yeah! All because of her. " Diana gave me a venomous look.

"What did Mrs. Carruthers have to do with it?"

"She saw to it that we didn't get the zoning. Just because those holier-than-thou creeps don't want a casino."

"Mrs. Margolin, I must remind you to watch your language," the judge snapped. "You cannot call people names." Diana glared at him.

Wilf smiled at her discomfiture. "Actually, Mrs. Carruthers had nothing to do with that. The application was made by the Anglican Church."

"But she put them onto it."

"And how did my client know that you were after the property, and wanted to put a casino on it?"

"Why, I…" I could almost hear the clang as the trap sprang shut. She was fully aware that I knew because Sam Gilley, her employee told me so.

"How?" Wilf insisted.

"I… I don't know."

"No matter. We'll find out in due time. However, even if you had kept it a secret, eventually the information would have become public, and the church would have had its chance to object."

Wilf continued throughout the afternoon, ripping her story to shreds. Thurlow got one last kick at the can, trying to resurrect his witness, but Wilf got in the last question before we left for the day.

"Actually, Mrs. Margolin, isn't it true that your loss in business was due to the fact that Conrad was dead, and your husband was not nearly as astute as he, and isn't it also true that you have more business brains than your husband, and have been doing quite well since he died?"

She didn't know how to answer that and Wilf didn't need a response. He'd planted the idea in the jurors' minds.

The next morning, Thurlow started by calling Sam Gilley. Gilley had shaved his beard, and you could see why. His face was broken out with acne, and he was using a medication on it. He had also lost weight. He would not look directly at me, and seemed very tense when I came near him.

Thurlow set the stage for Gilley's testimony about the aborted flight. Then he asked, "Was it the defendant, Mrs. Carruthers, who prevented you from making the flight?"

"My Lord, I object." Wilf popped to his feet. "There is no evidence that they were prevented from making the flight."

"I think I will sustain that objection."

"When did you first see the defendant?"

"When we got there."

"What was she doing?"

"She was out by Harris' plane talking to him."

"What did she do then?"

"She came back into the building and talked to Alec."

"And what did Harris Margolin do?"

"He taxied his plane over."

"What did the defendant say to Alec Conrad?"

"She told us we shouldn't go."

"Shouldn't go on the flight?"

"Yeah. She'd told Harris that, but he…"

"Objection. This man doesn't know what took place between Mrs. Carruthers and Mr. Margolin."

"Mr. Gilley," the judge said, "you can't testify to a conversation you didn't hear. Please confine your answers to what you personally were a party to."

"Okay."

"So you were forced to stay…"

"Objection. There's no evidence of any force."

"Please rephrase your question, Mr. Thurlow. And try to avoid stating conclusions when none are warranted."

"Yes, M'Lord. The outcome of the defendant's conversation with Alec Conrad was that you didn't fly to Georgetown. Is that correct?"

"That's right."

"Whereas, until then, you'd had every intention of doing so."

"Yeah."

"So you went to a motel?"

"Yeah. That one on the airport."

"What was the weather like?"

Gilley shrugged. "It seemed okay to me."

"But the defendant told you that you would crash if you went flying?"

"Yeah. That's right."

"Was Harris Margolin upset?"

"You bet he was."

"And Mr. Conrad."

"I don't know. He was in another room, on the phone."

"Trying to keep his business operating?"

"I guess so."

"Do you know what Mr. Conrad's view was on the outcome of the business deal they were working on? Did he say anything to you?"

"When he was through phoning, he said he guessed that was the best they could do under the circumstances."

"He wasn't happy with the result though?"

Gilley shot a sideways glance at the judge. "I wouldn't know," he said.

"Your witness."

Wilf rose and moved to the lectern, his face only a few feet away from Gilley's. Gilley cringed. I wondered if he expected to be asked whether he had killed his boss.

"Now Mr. Gilley, when my client came back into the building from apparently talking to Mr. Margolin, did she not describe the approaching storm?"

"Yeah."

"And informed you that this storm was between you and your destination."

"Yeah, but I don't remember there being any storm."

"You don't? Do you realize that you are probably the only person in this province who didn't?"

"Well, I don't think Harris or Alec noticed either."

"That's amazing!"

"Well, we were busy."

"You must have been very busy. So there must have been a great deal that Margolin and Conrad could do with regard to their business."

"I don't know."

"To go back to the scene at Red Robin Flying School, who was it who made the decision not to fly to Georgetown?"

"Alec."

"Alec Conrad?"

"Yeah."

"Did Mrs. Carruthers do anything of a physical nature to prevent your going?"

"What do you mean?"

"Did she block the plane, or take away the keys, or anything like that?"

"No."

"Did she make any threats?"

"No. I guess not."

"And it was Alec Conrad's decision not to go?"

"Yeah. It was him. But I still don't know what all the fuss was about."

"Stick around. You'll find out."

The plaintiff then called several people with whom Harcon Holdings had business dealings, who testified to the decline in the company's business during the late spring and summer. Wilf showed little interest in these witnesses, letting them have their say. There was only one incident to relieve the tedium of this testimony. At one point, Thurlow referred to Wilf as "My learned friend," putting every ounce of sarcasm he could into his voice. He had planted himself between Wilf and the jury so that his huge frame and flowing robe blocked the jury's view of his seated opponent. But Wilf had anticipated the move. He rolled his chair back from the table so the jury could see him, giving them a big grin. They smiled back.

Diana Lovelace's accountant then took the stand. Thurlow led him through the monthly financial reports of Harcon Holdings, from the first of the year. There had been a decline in income in March, the accountant said, starting after the aborted flight on March 8. He droned on and on through one dry financial report after another, over the period of January through July. He painted a picture of doom and gloom.

I tried to follow, but not having the binder full of copies of the financial reports that the jurors did, I got hopelessly lost. I thought of the church finances. I'd found them much more complicated than those of my own business, but nowhere near as confusing as these. The terminology was incomprehensible, and the accountant was doing nothing to make it easy to understand. My concentration lapsed. I became drowsy. I nodded off.

For some reason, I imagined the room filling with smoke. I came to with a start and looked around in alarm. Nothing was happening except the droning testimony. There was no smoke in the climate-controlled room. I stifled a yawn.

During this testimony, Wilf remained inactive, leaning back in his chair, not following the details, though he of course had his own copy. He seemed bored, and looked as though he might fall asleep himself, his head occasionally lowering and being brought back up with a jerk.

Why was he not paying more attention? Why so inactive?

I became more and more nervous. It seemed to me that Thurlow was very effectively showing that the business had declined dramatically. The flood of paperwork seemed to impress the jury. Occasionally one or another would nod as the accountant made a point. Obviously, the business had been going on the rocks.

As the time for adjournment drew near, I could see both lawyers take surreptitious glances at the clock. Thurlow finished his direct examination with only minutes to spare, I presumed so that the jury would go home with the plaintiff's case firmly in mind.

The judge looked at the clock also and opened his mouth to speak. Wilf shot to his feet.

"My Lord, I have only one or two questions of this witness. It will take less than five minutes.

The judge hesitated, then nodded. "Go ahead, Mr. Meredith."

Wilf turned toward the accountant. "I notice that you only went through the financial reports of Harcon Holdings through July."

"That was when Ms. Lovelace asked me to prepare information for this case."

"Isn't it true that after that time, the company's financial affairs have taken a definite turn for the better?"

The accountant frowned and paused, as if searching his recollection. He put the fingers of his left hand over his mouth, a gesture that I thought meant that he was about to tell a lie. He removed his hand, shook his head and said, "I don't think so."

"And," Wilf went on, "isn't it true that the reason for the company's decline, which started in March, was that Alec Conrad, the brains of the outfit, was dead?"

He didn't wait for an answer, but turned, strode to his chair and sat down.

***

When court had adjourned, Wilf hurried over to where I was standing, just outside the rail (or is it a bar?) that separated the spectators from the participants. His black robe fluttered behind him and billowed out to the sides. I suppressed a giggle as I imagined him taking flight in his flowing robe.

As he reached me, his wife, Ginny, materialized at my side. Ginny Meredith is my accountant. Her husband asked her, "Is he lying?"

"Like crazy. Directly and indirectly."

"Indirectly?"

"In the language he used. When he wanted to be positive, as in the financial reports from January and February, he used upbeat words. Later, he talked about the same things in words that sounded down and out. Also, he skipped things he didn't want to talk about."

I wondered if Mortimer Thurlow had coached him to do that. Probably.

Ginny had in her hand a sheaf of papers. She saw my questioning glance and said, "Copies. I follow right along."

Wilf explained to me, "When I have to deal with accountants and their ilk, I have Ginny sit in. She can follow it better than I and takes notes. That leaves me free to do what I'm good at."

"What's your impression?" I asked Ginny.

"The company isn't as bad off as they're making out. Their problem has been one of waste. After Conrad's death, they didn't keep track of their expenditures, but just threw money around. You could see Conrad's frugality, then you could see Margolin's squandering."

"You said he was lying. What about?"

"About how well things are going now. I've asked other accountants and they think Diana Lovelace is getting things back on track. No wonder they didn't want the more recent financial statements shown."

I turned to Wilf. "Are you going to get a chance to bring that out?"

Wilf grinned. "I couldn't care less!"

"Why not?"

"I don't care if they go bankrupt. All I care about is showing that you weren't the cause of it."

Ginny, Wilf and I slid into a booth at Curly's and while waiting for the waitress to take our order, continued our discussion of the trial. Ginny handed me the financial report, which I glanced through.

"And I thought the accounts at the church were complicated! They seem a lot more so than the reports you give me for the school."

"Your business is pretty simple and I like to keep the accounts as simple as possible. My feeling is that excessively complex reports often hide problems."

"They sure create problems. Why do you say they hide them?"

"Because if something is not quite right, you make things as complicated as possible so it won't show. I'm always suspicious of a company that comes to me with a lot of convoluted bookkeeping. By the way, I ran into Lew Stern in the hallway of the courthouse."

"Oh! Do you know Lew?"

"All the lawyers and their wives know all the other lawyers and their wives. Do you know Lew?"

"He's a member of my church. I hope he isn't upset that I've asked Wilf to represent me."

It was Wilf who answered. "No. He's relieved. He told me he didn't really feel comfortable with an aviation case. From your expression, Ginny, I gather that he let drop some pearls of wisdom."

Ginny waited until the waitress had taken our order, lowered her voice and said, "Lew overheard Mort Thurlow talking to one of his partners in an empty courtroom early this morning. Mort's voice carries, and since Lew knew your case was on, he eavesdropped shamelessly."

"And…"

Ginny looked me in the eye. "He said he was going to mop the floor with you over some religious thing."

I stared at her. She went on, "Lew seemed to know what Mort was talking about. Do you?"

"Yes."

"Yes," Wilf said, "and I want to talk to you about that, Robin."

"About what?"

"It's about this quote from the Bible coming to your mind, and making you go warn those two guys not to try to make the trip. Did you tell anyone else about that?"

"Sure. I told several people. I didn't think it was any secret."

Well, Mort has evidently heard. I don't think you should say anything at all about that. He can't ask you questions on cross-examination on anything that wasn't brought out on direct. If he tries, I'll object. But if you spill the beans on direct, he'll do as he says, mop the floor with you."

CHAPTER 25

The next morning, Wilf started his defence. He called the controller from the tower, the one I had talked to, who brought the tapes of all the conversations, radio and telephone, including my two phone calls to him, and his call to Flight Service to inquire about the competitor's plane that had taken off before Margolin had gotten to the airport. The jury got to hear first-hand about that pilot's harrowing landing at Raymond Bay as he was caught in the leading edge of the storm, making his Cessna 210 almost uncontrollable. The controller had obtained the tape from Georgetown Flight Service. We heard the actual tapes of the Georgetown Flight Service Station's conversations with the pilot. I found that in listening to the tape, my fear reactions, which I had experienced only a few times while flying, kicked in and left me a wreck. Wilf said he felt the same way. Experienced pilots really don't like to listen to that kind of stuff. We know that we all have come too close to the line between being in control and not. We don't want to listen to anyone else going through it.

Wilf asked the controller what it was like to be in the tower during the storm. "Scary!" was his answer. He described hail flung horizontally by the wind, and visibility at the height of the hailstorm that was so poor, he could not see the flag pole right beside the tower. There was no flag to see anyway. It had been torn to rags and blown away. He said that the tower shook as the wind buffeted it. He also described seeing, as he drove home that evening, trees in the park along the lakeshore that had been blown down, and hail piled up like snowdrifts along fences and the sides of buildings. Occasionally a juror would nod as if recalling a similar instance when they themselves had experienced the storm.

There was little that Thurlow could object to or cross-examine the controller on. All straight, factual stuff. Wilf hadn't asked him for any opinions. The facts were dramatic enough.

Wilf then called the airport manager to ask about damage at the airport as a result of the storm. The manager detailed preparations they had taken when they knew a major storm was on its way. Fortunately, damage was, as he put it, "Light." This light damage included one wrecked plane, pitting and paint chipping of the surfaces of other planes from the hail, one building with broken windows, assorted other damage, and things blown away. The owner of one ragwing had to re-cover his plane as a result of hail punching holes in the fabric. The landscaping at the terminal needed to be replaced, as the hail stripped leaves off the rose bushes and pounded the newly flowering crocuses into the ground. The manager had circulated a memo to all airport tenants asking for a report on any damage they had incurred.

"Mr. Thurlow is one of the tenants?"

"Yes, he has a light twin at the airport."

"And did he report any damage?"

"Yes. He claimed hail damage to his plane."

There was not much that Thurlow dared challenge him on.

Wilf's next witness was the Flight Service Station specialist who had been on duty at Pine Hill. He testified to circulating a "Sigmet" over the radio and telephone to everyone who called. A Sigmet, he explained was a warning of severe weather of concern to pilots of all planes, regardless of size and type. He testified to Margolin's flight plan, filed by computer with a company in eastern United States; the flight plan having been passed on to Flight Service four hours after it was filed, causing them to search for the pilot, who had neither opened nor cancelled it. They had found him in the motel at the Exeter airport, and told him he should have cancelled the flight plan, even though he hadn't taken off. The specialist described Margolin as "uncooperative" and referred to previous encounters they'd had with him. When challenged by Thurlow on his testimony that Margolin had been uncooperative, the specialist offered to play the tape of the conversation. Thurlow did not ask him to do so, but Wilf did. I recognized Margolin's surly voice, though I had only heard it that one previous time.

When the specialist asked Margolin if he had received a weather briefing, Margolin told him he had gotten the Exeter and Georgetown weather through his computer and they were both VFR, which the specialist defined as "Visual Flight Rules." Margolin had not gotten any other weather information before starting out. Should he have? He should have gotten the weather for his whole route. If he'd gotten that weather report, might he have changed his mind about flying? He jolly well should have!

Wilf told the court that he would call a meteorologist to give evidence about the actual weather.

Thurlow lit into the Flight Service specialist, but could not make a dent. Not only was the fact of the storm firmly proven, but Margolin's preparation for the flight was glaringly inadequate. I began to think about smoke again, and wondered why.

One verbal exchange provided comic relief. Thurlow asked whether it was really necessary to get a detailed weather briefing at all times. "I mean, sometimes you can just look out the window and know everything is okay. I don't always go through all this rigmarole when I go flying."

"I know," said the specialist.

At least two jurors, the retired professor and the older businessman got the implication and smiled. So, I thought, did one of the young women.

Just to pound the point home, Wilf called a meteorologist from the weather station. He brought a ream of charts, rolled up and tucked under his arm. I could almost feel the jurors groan, but after a stand to hold the charts had been set up and the man qualified as an expert witness, we were to find that he was capable of conveying an excitement about weather phenomenon that had us all on the edge of our seats.

He had not only brought the regular weather charts, but also a pictorial display of the weather on that day last spring that showed the warring elements in the sky in vivid detail. I'd have to have him come to the school someday and do a weather presentation, I thought. Wilf had promised to get good witnesses, and he had certainly done so.

The weatherman showed the approach of the storm at critical times for our case, then described the devastation it had wrought as it passed through Exeter.

But Thurlow waved away the dramatic presentation, saying in a bored tone, "No questions."

So much for the facts. Now for the opinions!

I felt the muscles in my neck tighten. I'd felt relaxed and comfortable through the defence testimony so far, but now I was to hear how I rated with the aviation authorities. Would the old boy network kick in? Would the witness from the MOT give me faint praise saying I did pretty well for a woman? Thurlow would love that! Did the boys at the MOT know some of the things that had happened early on that weren't quite proper, when Dale, my ex-husband, was running the show? Or would the masculine fraternity protect him if it did know?

Could I be sure I wouldn't be thrown to the wolves?

I feel confident in my own realm, and can make decisions that involve flying without a qualm. Now I had to trust the expertise of someone else, when a blunder by that person could cost me my livelihood.

Wilf had gotten none other than the head of the federal office that oversees the licensing of pilots and operation of flight schools in our region, and which handles violations of regulations by people in the segment of the industry known as "general aviation." I knew Charles Tabor from way back when Dale and I had been running the business as Carruthers Aviation.

Wilf put him through his paces, seeking to qualify him as an expert witness. Tabor handled the interrogation with dignity and aplomb, perfectly relaxed. He had a craggy face, a deep tan, and sandy hair turning grey. His clear blue eyes sought out the jurors and when he answered Wilf's questions, he talked in a deep, resonant voice not to Wilf, but to them.

He detailed his career, first in the military, where he flew several large aircraft including the huge C130 Hercules, then as a pilot of fire bombers in Northern Alberta, British Columbia and the Yukon, then as the operator of a flying service in the rugged north country. He held just about every flight instructor authorization there was; was licensed, like myself, as a pilot examiner; and held a number of type ratings for large aircraft. He had logged around 30,000 hours, an impressive figure in anyone's book.

He then described his appointment to the MOT office, his duties there, and said that he had been the director of the office for the last three years.

Thurlow's cross-examination sought to belittle the office itself, and question its purpose. The thought he tried to implant in the jurors' minds was that this was one more example of bureaucratic interference with the lives of ordinary citizens, and a waste of taxpayers' money. Tabor countered every objection with well-prepared arguments.

I wondered if, when Wilf had his opportunity again, he would ask Tabor about the times Thurlow himself had been hauled up before them for some violation. Wilf didn't. He knew that these violations had been reported by me in my role as safety officer. He wanted to avoid any implication that I had an axe to grind, or that I was trigger-happy, always reporting people for things I didn't like.

Wilf then asked that Tabor be qualified as an expert witness.

"I will so qualify him," the judge replied.

That done, the questioning turned to the matter before the court.

"Mr. Tabor, do you know Robin Carruthers?"

"I've known her for about twenty five years."

"What is your opinion of her as a pilot?"

"Excellent."

"And as a flight instructor?"

"Top notch. Her students are all very well trained."

"Are you familiar with Red Robin Flying School?"

"I am."

"What is your opinion of the school?"

"Excellent."

"Are you familiar with the operation of the school?"

"Quite." He went on to detail the supervision his office exercised over schools such as Red Robin, and told of his experience with us in particular. The report was good.

"Has the school had any violations of the regulations throughout its history?"

"None."

"Has Robin Carruthers had any violations of the regulations since she has become a pilot?"

"None."

"Do you have any record of violations by any other pilots flying as students at the school, or licensed pilots renting planes from the school?"

"None."

Thank heavens he had never received a report about a couple of things Lance Brock had done!

"Are you familiar with my client's former job as safety officer at the Exeter Airport?"

"Oh yes. We cooperated fully with her in providing staff and materials for safety seminars."

"Did that stop when the city of Exeter discontinued her job?"

"No. She still calls on us to help with safety seminars she holds at Red Robin Flying School. They are just done on her own, not as a program of the airport."

"Mr. Tabor, would you define for the jury what is meant by 'pilot-in-command'?"

"The pilot-in-command is the licensed pilot responsible for the operation of the aircraft, whether or not that pilot is actually flying it."

"Can you give some examples of instances where the pilot-in-command would not be flying?"

"Flight instruction. The instructor is pilot-in-command even though the student is operating the controls. Also with large, multi-crewed aircraft such as airliners, when the co-pilot, the second-in-command, is flying."

"Can you make a general statement about the responsibility of the pilot-in-command?"

"The PIC is responsible for everything regarding the flight."

"Specifically, on a cross country flight such as Harris Margolin was planning on March 8, what would he be required to do?"

"He would have to determine whether he himself were fit and legal to make this flight. He would have to plan his route, his altitude, his time enroute, his fuel consumption, and his use of radio communication and navigation aids, and ascertain that the flight could be made within the limits of safety. He would be required to ascertain that the weather conditions for the entire route during the time of the flight would be suitable. And he would have to determine whether the aircraft was in proper condition to make the flight legally and safely."

"Are there times when a perfectly airworthy airplane would not meet the requirements of the flight?"

"Yes. For example, a light aircraft like Margolin's Cessna 182, is not suitable for flight into either severe turbulence or into any degree of icing — that is, conditions that cause ice accumulation on the aircraft surfaces in flight."

"Would Margolin's proposed flight on March 8, present any of these problems?"

"Yes. Severe turbulence, severe icing, limited visibility, inability to climb high enough to get above the weather, no possibility of flying under or through it, and the likelihood that hail would so severely damage the aircraft as to make it unairworthy."

"Was the weather on that day suitable for larger aircraft?"

"Not in the area of the storm. Nothing was flying in that storm."

"Except for Mr. Margolin's competitors."

"Not for long, they didn't. It just happens that when they crashed, there was an airstrip underneath them."

"Did they crash?"

"Yes, though it was not a serious one. The pilot forgot to put his landing gear down because he was too busy trying to stay right side up. They caught a wing, and skidded off into a ditch. Fortunately there were no injuries."

Thurlow made a big production out of rising to his feet. "Oh, M'Lord. Is all this really necessary?"

"I think so," the judge replied curtly. "It seems quite relevant to me." He nodded to Wilf. "Continue."

"If Mr. Margolin had gone on this flight, what would have been your official reaction to it?"

"To assign someone to investigate the accident, most likely."

Someone snickered and received a glare from the judge.

"If they had managed to get on the ground in one piece, what then?"

"We would have called Mr. Margolin to account for his actions, and quite possibly levied some sort of penalty."

"So, in trying to talk him out of making the flight, my client would have been doing him a favour."

"I would say so."

"And since he would not listen to her, do you feel that she was correct in going to his passengers to advise them of the danger?"

"Absolutely!"

"Your witness." Wilf bowed in Thurlow's direction and sat down.

Thurlow rose and ponderously walked to the lectern beside the jury box. Addressing the witness, but looking at the jurors, he boomed, "Do you think that slandering Mr. Margolin in front of his associates, and ruining his business, was doing him a favour?"

I expected a vigorous objection from Wilf, but he sat in his chair, his hands folded, and said nothing.

Tabor skewered Thurlow with a withering glare. "I am not aware that either of those things happened."

I could almost smell smoke.

"Well, tomorrow is your big day!" Wilf told me as we left the courtroom. "Don't get uptight about it. We've

272

got them on the run, so get a good night's sleep. And when you are cross-examined by Mort tomorrow, don't let him annoy you to the point where you lose your cool. He'll try. Stick to the truth. Answer questions with simple answers. If he asks ambiguous questions, or ones that insult you, I'll come to your aid. He hasn't been able to discredit any of our witnesses, so he might get rather mean. Just keep your head and don't let him bother you. By the way, he collected a sizable fee up front, so he doesn't think he has a good case. We've got him whipped.

"But…!" He paused for effect. "Keep off the subject of religion or God. Don't give him an opening."

I opened my mouth to object, but Wilf hurried on, "Trust me, Robin! I'm your lawyer!"

On my way home, I decided to stop at the church. No one else was there, but since I was one of several people on rotation to open up the church on Sunday morning and prepare it for the early service, I had keys. I let myself in, deciding not to turn on the lights. In the winter dusk, the glow of streetlights, traffic, and lights from the government building across the street on the north side, cast enough illumination through the large windows that ran the length of the nave.

I knelt at the altar rail, crossed myself, and prayed. I had never expected God to stop everything and come to my immediate and visible aid, so I didn't pray for a verdict in my favour. Instead, I asked for strength for the ordeal on the morrow, and hoped that in telling Margolin's passengers about the danger, I had done the right thing. Of that, God, as well as a court of law, would be my judge.

As I drove home, in a calm, reflective mood, it occurred to me why I kept dreaming of smoke. Diana Lovelace Margolin was spewing out a smoke screen. She had filed all those impossible lawsuits, not because she thought she could win them, but to obscure something else by occupying everyone's mind with other matters, and putting them on the defensive.

But why?

The answer to that didn't occur to me until late that night. I picked up the phone and called Gordon, sighing with relief when he answered it on the second ring. He didn't sound as if I'd awakened him from sleep. Good. I needed his advice, his calm helpfulness.

"Robin! It's wonderful to hear you. How's it going?"

"Nerve-wracking."

He laughed.

"But in other ways, it's going too well. She really hasn't a prayer of winning it, knock on wood. I keep wondering why she's doing it. Gordon, what's happening with her other lawsuits?"

"They're all still in the works. She tossed a few poison pills around before she left for Exeter."

"Don't you think there's something funny about all these lawsuits?"

"What's on your mind, Robin?"

"I have a theory."

"Are you going to tell me?"

"That's why I called. If it doesn't pass muster with you, I'm going to drop it." So I told him what I thought, and what I planned to do. He was silent for several seconds, then he said, "Robin, I think you have to do it."

I went to bed that night with two voices ringing in my ear. "Trust me! I'm your lawyer!" and over that, "Trust God! Practice what you preached!"

CHAPTER 26

Wilf asked me routine questions about my training and experience. I said I held a commercial pilot license, a first class flight instructor license, and was rated for single engine land, multi-engine land, and single engine seaplanes and was qualified to give instruction on all of those. (I didn't have a multi-engine seaplane rating, so couldn't act as pilot-in-command of the Canso water bomber as Charles Tabor had, during his years of fighting fires. I remembered my one flight as co-pilot on the Canso, where we scooped up huge loads of water from a mountain lake, then flew through smoke and turbulence to drop them on a fire that was just topping a ridge.) I also held an instrument rating, and was qualified to teach instrument flying. I was a pilot examiner, qualified to give flight tests for private or commercial licenses or instrument ratings, on any of the planes I was qualified to fly, which included a few complex aircraft, as well as the simple ones. I didn't have as many hours as Tabor, but had logged a lot anyway. I flew about 500 hours a year on a regular basis.

I described the dual operation of Carruthers Aviation, with my ex-husband, Dale, and my acquisition of the business when our marriage broke up. I had changed the name to Red Robin Flying School, and had run it under that name for twenty years.

I had been safety officer at the Exeter airport as long as the Airport Commission had mandated the position.

"Now let's go to March 8 when Margolin and his two passengers arrived at the school. Had you ever met any of them before?"

"No. They arrived on the morning of the seventh when I was out flying, made arrangements to park the 182 for several days, and got fuel. By the time I got back from the flight, they had gone into town."

Thurlow rose from his chair. "Objection. The defendant doesn't know where they were going."

"We'll allow that part to be struck out," Wilf said smoothly. "When did you first see Margolin?"

"On the afternoon of the eighth. He and two other men, who I now know to be Mr. Conrad and Mr. Gilley, came in the airport limo. The two passengers came into the office, while Margolin went over to the plane. They had luggage with them, so I assumed they planned to leave on a flight."

"Objection. We're not interested in the defendant's assumptions."

"It would seem to be a logical deduction," the judge countered with asperity.

"What did you do?" Wilf asked.

"I went out to Margolin's plane to talk to him."

"What did you talk about?"

"I advised him that the weather was not suitable for a flight in a light aircraft."

"What was his response?"

"He told me to mind my own business."

That got a laugh from several spectators and jurors.

"Did you explain why it was not wise to go flying?"

"I did."

"How did he react?"

"He was quite belligerent. I could see I was not going to persuade him to change his mind."

"Objection."

The judge held up his hand to stop Thurlow and said to me, "Please confine yourself to facts, Mrs. Carruthers." I nodded.

"What did Mr. Margolin do?"

"He started the plane and swung the tail around, so that I had to jump out of the way to avoid being hit. Then he ran it up so that I got the full blast of the slipstream."

"What did you do then?"

"I went back into the office, and spoke to Mr. Conrad and Mr. Gilley."

"What did you tell them?"

"The same thing I had told Margolin. That it wasn't safe to fly."

"What was their response?"

"Mr. Conrad said that some people they knew had taken off for the same destination, Georgetown, a short time before."

"So what did you do then?"

"I called the tower to inquire about that flight. I put the speakerphone on so that they could hear the answer."

"That was the second phone call from you that we heard on the tower tape?"

"Yes."

"What was Mr. Conrad's reaction to that?"

"He made the decision not to go."

"And was Mr. Margolin in the office at that time?"

"Yes. He'd taxied over, and come into the office. He told the others to get a move on, but Mr. Conrad said they weren't going. Margolin got mad at me..."

Like a jack-in-the-box, Thurlow popped to his feet. "M'Lord, the defendant keeps interjecting her opinions…"

Again the judge held up his hand to stem the flow of words. He turned to me, and in a kindly voice instructed me, "Mrs. Carruthers, I know we are used to talking differently in normal conversation, but you must remember that in testifying in court, you must avoid opinions and stick to facts."

"I'm sorry, My Lord."

Wilf changed the subject. "Now, had you been following the weather on that afternoon?"

"Yes, very closely. We get printed weather data, and also, I had been listening to the tower. We knew that a major storm was coming, but the thing that really alerted me to its severity was the extremely rapid drop in barometric pressure. So I was keeping a very close watch on the weather reports."

"Causing you at one time to call the tower and ask?"

"Yes."

"That was the first of your two phone conversations with the tower?"

"Yes."

"At what point did you decide to tell the passengers of the danger?"

"As I was walking back to the office."

"Did you hesitate about telling them?"

"By the time I'd gotten back to the office, I'd made up my mind to tell them."

"You had to make a decision as to whether to do so?"

"That's right."

"Was this a difficult decision?"

"In a way, yes."

"Why?"

"Because I knew…" I paused and shot a quick look at the judge. "Because of the possibility of the pilot being offended, and making trouble for me."

"As in fact, he did?"

"Yes."

"In what way?"

"He sued me for slander."

"Did you, in fact, say anything to his two passengers about his competence as a pilot?"

"No. I only advised them of the danger."

"Did you do anything to actively prevent them from flying?"

"No."

"Whose decision was it not to make the trip?"

"Mr. Conrad's."

"Did he appear to you to be upset or angry?"

"No. He seemed quite calm."

"Did he or Mr. Gilley say anything to the effect that they didn't trust Margolin as a pilot?"

"No."

"And did they not come out two days later to go on a flight with him?"

"Yes. They both came, but only Mr. Conrad was going on the flight."

"I object," Thurlow was on his feet again. "The defendant doesn't know any such thing."

I was getting sick and tired of being called "the defendant."

Wilf responded, "It is common knowledge, as a result of investigations by the police and the MOT that Conrad was going on the trip, and Gilley was to stay in Exeter."

"I will allow the answer."

"To get back to your decision to tell the passengers of the danger, was this done in anger over the way Mr. Margolin had treated you?"

"No. In fact, that made me rather leery of telling them."

"So what made you decide to do so?"

"The word of God."

Wilf's jaw dropped open, and he stood there for a long moment, speechless. That was definitely not the answer he had expected me to give. Nor was it what the jurors expected to hear. I saw their eyes widen in astonishment.

"I remembered the passage in the Bible where God tells the prophet, Ezekiel, that He is making him a sentinel for the people of Israel. If the sentinel warns the people of danger, and they fail to heed his warning, they will die, but he will not be at fault; but if he fails to warn them, and they die, he will be held accountable for their deaths."

Wilf had regained his composure. He asked, "Did you feel that as a result of your years of experience, and your role as a safety officer, that you would qualify as the 'sentinel' when it came to aviation safety?"

"Yes. I imagined how I would feel if these people were killed because I didn't warn them."

"Your witness," Wilf said, sitting down as if his legs would no longer hold him.

Thurlow didn't bother to go to the stand over by the jury box, but stood where he was, leaning toward me and giving me the full blast of his powerful voice. "Oh, so you're one of these holier-than-thou Christians, eh?"

"I'm a Christian, yes." I'd like to have added, I don't know whether I'm holier than thou, because I don't know how holy you are, but I squelched the desire to do so. I didn't bother to explain to him that Ezekiel lived several hundred years before the Christian era.

"Can you prove you're a Christian?"

Wilf, whom I knew to be an atheist, started to get up. But his eyes were on me and I gave him a firm look and a slight shake of my head. He subsided nervously into his chair. His case definitely wasn't going according to plan.

"I can't prove I'm a Christian. No one can. A Christian is defined as a person who has been baptized into the Christian Church, and who believes in God, and in the divinity of Christ. I can prove that I've been baptized…"

"I'm not asking for a dissertation on the Christian religion."

"You asked me a question. I'm answering it." I snapped. I turned toward the judge for support, and got it.

"Let the witness answer, Mr. Thurlow."

"As I was saying, I have been baptized. As to my beliefs, only God and I know what they are. I can say I'm a Christian because I go to church regularly, but you might say I do that for social standing. Or I can say I'm a Christian because I tithe, that is I give one tenth of my income to the church. But you might say I do that for the tax deduction. I might say that I take part in the services, but that might be out of pride; or that I do administrative work on a volunteer basis, but you might think that was for power. I go to bible study, but that could be for the social life. I attended a course at Idylwyld, but you might think that was just for recreation. I know that I do these things out of faith in God, but no, I can't prove it."

I didn't need to. I saw the answer on the jurors' faces. Thurlow changed the subject.

"So you told them not to fly with Margolin..."

"Objection." Wilf was back on firm ground. "She did not tell them any such thing."

"Sustained."

"You recommended that they not go on the flight because you thought God might get mad at you?"

"No. Because I felt I had a responsibility to warn them."

"Does God talk to you very often?"

"Never, that I know of. Not directly."

"But you take instruction from him?"

"Of course."

"Even though the instructions were given several thousand years ago? Were they flying airplanes then?" Thurlow's voice dripped with sarcasm.

"Advice of the kind I described is applicable to people in all eras, and in many situations."

"And what does God say about ruining other people's business."

Wilf was on his feet, but I got my answer in before he had a chance to object. I'd been looking for the opportunity and this was it. I rushed into speech. I knew I'd have to say it fast, and drown out Thurlow's objections. But I had the benefit of the PA system. I intended to use it to the fullest.

"I did not ruin their business. Mrs. Margolin was conspiring with Conrad to oust her husband, because he was a drain on the business, which went downhill after Conrad was killed because he was the brains of the outfit."

Thurlow was on his feet, shouting, but I hurried on.

"They were both home when they heard the commotion over across the canyon where their mobile home got stuck. Margolin set down the length of water pipe he was installing, and went out on the deck. But he was too short to see what was going on, so he climbed up on the railing of the deck to get a better view. His wife saw her chance to get rid of him, picked up the piece of pipe, holding it with a towel, and whacked him on the back of the knees, sending him tumbling into the canyon to his death."

This speech had to be made over the roar of Thurlow's objection, but I moved close to the two mikes and shifted into my preaching voice. I could be heard over Thurlow's squawking, and the last statement dropped into a deathly silence while he paused for breath.

No one moved. Thurlow recovered his wits first.

"That's outrageous. It's pure conjecture. And if that had really happened he would have screamed all the way down. No one heard him scream."

"One person did," I told him. "Most of us couldn't because of the noise at the site where the trailer was stuck, but there was a witness standing at the top of the trail down into the canyon, on the Idylwyld side, about fifty yards away. Just as the trailer was being backed out from under the tree, she heard him scream."

"M'Lord, this is the most outrageous nonsense," Thurlow shouted.

No one was paying any attention to him. They were watching instead as Diana Lovelace Margolin rose unsteadily to her feet, her clenched fist between her teeth to stifle a scream, her face the colour of a dirty sheet. Her knees gave way, and she toppled through the gap in the rail that separates the spectators from the rest of the courtroom, hitting the floor with a resounding thud.

The deputy sheriff ran to her aid.

"Please God," I prayed, "let me be right. Otherwise I'm in for one helluva suit for slander!"

About the Author

Anne Barton is a retired veterinarian and flight instructor. In her retirement, she has taken up writing mystery novels. She has also written one autobiographical book and numerous articles and short stories. Her short story won the Bloody Words Crime Writers' Conference contest in 2001 and is published in Bloody Words, The Anthology.

Born in Drumheller, Alberta, she grew up in Northern Idaho, returned to Canada, and now lives in the beautiful Okanagan Valley in British Columbia, where she is deeply involved with Habitat for Humanity and her Anglican Church work – that is, when she isn't riding horses or curling.